The Dairy Queen

The Dairy Queen

Allison Rushby

RED
DRESS
INK
™

THE DAIRY QUEEN

A Red Dress Ink novel

ISBN 0-373-89574-7

© 2006 by Allison Rushby.

www.RedDressInk.com

Printed in U.S.A.

ALLISON RUSHBY

Having failed at becoming a ballerina with pierced ears (her childhood dream), Allison Rushby instead began a writing career as a journalism student at the University of Queensland in Brisbane, Australia. Within a few months she had slunk sideways into studying Russian. By the end of her degree she had learned two very important things: that she wasn't going to be a journalist; and that there are hundreds of types of vodka and they're all pretty good.

A number of years spent freelancing for numerous wedding magazines ("Getting On With Your Draconian Mother-in-Law Made Simple!"; "A 400 Guest Reception for $2.95 Per Head!") almost sent her crazy. After much whining about how hard it would be, she began her first novel. That is, her husband (then boyfriend) told her to shut up, sit down and get typing.

These days Allison writes full-time, mostly with her cats, Vi and Flo, purring contentedly on her lap, and her baby girl, Ivy, playing quietly with educational toys on the floor (she wishes…). Oh, and she keeps up her education by sampling new kinds of vodka on a regular basis. You can visit her to discuss vodka flavors and poopie diapers at www.allisonrushby.com.

Also by Allison Rushby
and available from Red Dress Ink:

It's Not You It's Me
Hating Valentine's Day

ACKNOWLEDGMENTS

Thanks heaps to the weird and wonderful town of Mooball (in Northern New South Wales, Australia, if you ever feel like visiting!), for being the inspiration for the very fictional town of Moo; to Tash and Teen, for the crawly page ants (spare lessons at high school just wouldn't have been as interesting without the crawly page ants); to Dave, for the Wookie comment (and for saying "it's a mug's game" at the weirdest times and then laughing himself sick even years afterward); to Ivy, for putting up with me having to write the whole book rather than doing prenatal yoga, flotation sessions with piped-in dolphin music, fetal bonding weekends in Byron Bay and all that jazz; to the guinea pigs again; and to Sam B., who liked it the best.

'Are you having an affair?' Jean-Luc asks me, just as I've speared an overly large piece of (really excellent, I have to say) Asian barbecue duck, topped it with a smidge of (blanched to perfection) bok choy and popped it into my mouth.

Quack.

Fuck.

I start, but don't choke. Instead, I fix my eyes to my plate and chew slowly. Much, much more slowly than the rate at which I'd been wolfing down my food hungrily before. I chew and chew and chew, until the duck is liquefied in my mouth, swimming (ugh, sorry duck). I'm buying time— trying to work out just how much I should tell the man sitting opposite me, who looks very much like he wants a few answers and he wants them now, at our anniversary dinner.

Finally, I place my knife and fork down and raise my eyes. 'Um, yes. Yes, I am,' is all I manage to come up with.

We stare at each other while the restaurant continues living and breathing around us. Orders are taken, cutlery scrapes against plates, a glass is knocked over, laughter bounces off walls. After a good few minutes of staring, something clicks and my brain begins to whir into motion, piecing the last few weeks together—the absences, the missed phone calls. My breathing quickens as I think about what I'm going to ask.

'Are *you* having an affair?' I throw the words back at my husband.

He pauses, but holds my gaze firmly. 'Yes,' is all he manages to come up with as well.

Funnily enough, we don't stick around for dessert.

Grrrrrrr…

'Get that fucking hairy thing fucking off me. Right fucking now!'

I watch as Simon struggles down the steps, his left leg inside his trousers, the other leg dragging behind, his arse jiggling—the male form in all its red-underpanted glory. His belt dangles, clinking against the metal railings as he descends. As for me, I cross my arms and eye that belt hopefully—it is just *begging* to be tripped on. Who knows? It's late and we're both still half drunk. I could get lucky.

Grrrrrrr…

'I fucking mean it.' He stumbles on the last step, but misses the belt. Damn. 'If that dog so much as spits on me…' He looks up at me, one finger pointed, his face a lovely puckered pink.

If only the ladies at the Clinique Skin Supplies for Men counter could see him now.

Grrrrrrr…

'Fergus—park.' Within sweet biting distance of Simon, Fergus does what he's told and sits.

Simon eyes me evilly.

'Anything else?' I say, my head to one side.

'Oh, fuck you, Dicey. Just…fuck you.' On solid ground now, he loops his belt through his trousers and with a quick mean tug does the lot up. Then he grabs his briefcase from beside the dining table and makes for the door. It isn't until he has one hand on the doorknob that he remembers his pride. 'Stupid bitch,' he mutters. 'Loser.'

It's the third word that pierces my toughened skin. I pause for a moment before readjusting my facial muscles. 'Fergus,' I say, raising one eyebrow. 'Sic.'

With this, there's a very loud *grrrrrrr,* a grey lunge, and a swift opening and closing of the front door.

I stand quite still and wait.

Silence.

He's gone.

One hand still on the railing, I sink down shakily to sit on the steps. I'd been acting far, far braver than I'd actually felt back there. To tell the truth, Simon's yelling and screaming had surprised me. I'd never had a guy do that to me before, and it had made me grateful to have Fergus around.

Now, Fergus trots up the stairs to me with the spoils of war—a large piece of shirt material. He just manages to clutch it in his mouth, between his slobbery smile. I take it from him and reach over for a pat. He wants more, however, and moves in close to lean up against me, forcing me into the metal railing. I breathe as deep a breath in as I can with a seventy-five kilo Irish Wolfhound pressing against my lungs.

Grrrrrr. Fergus sits up suddenly.

I shake my head. 'It's OK, Fergs, he's gone.'

He glances over at me. *How would you know?* His eyebrows say, before he turns his attention back downstairs.

That dog is far too rude to me for his own good. 'Look,' I tell Fergus. 'He's stupid, but he's not that stupid.'

Fergus doesn't look back this time, but pads down the stairs and across the living room floor.

Grrrrrr.

Bang, bang, bang.

The noise at the window makes me jump at least halfway to the ceiling.

'I'm sending you a bill for this,' Simon yells in the darkness, holding his torn shirt up against the living room window.

Grrrrrr.

Bang, bang, bang. 'Well?'

I realise Simon expects me to say something. I get up, run down the stairs and make my way over to the window.

'Well?' he tries again, a hint of a smirk on his face.

'Brave with the glass between us, aren't you?' I snort. 'Fine. I'll buy you a new shirt. Just go home, Simon. Piss off.'

Raff-raff-raff-raff-raff.

With this, Simon stops. He looks down at Fergus for a moment, a strange expression on his face, then backs away into the darkness.

I hear his car start up and speed off down the street. Then I stare out the window into the blackness for quite some time.

Stupid bitch.

Loser.

'Loser.' I say the word out loud. Fergus thumps down on the floor at my feet. 'Loser.' I say it again for good measure.

He's right, I realise. I am a loser.

In the past few months, I have lost everything. My company, my husband and, now my…ugh, whatever Simon was. Bit on the side?

I guess there's nowhere else to go from here—this *is* rock bottom.

I turn around and take the few steps over to the couch. I sit down, slide my open fingers through my hair and finally rest my elbows on my knees, holding my head up. The tears start to slide out.

It's November, and pretty much the whole of this year has been a complete disaster. You know when life feels like a pit that you're scraping your nails down the side of, trying to stop from falling further? Well, I've hit the bottom of that pit. Like I said before, rock bottom. And something tells me Lassie isn't coming to save me. She's gone myopic in her old age and just can't see this far down the well.

The funny thing is how fast it's all happened. I can't remember the point where things turned, where things started to go bad. It was like everything was perfect, and then suddenly I was left with nothing. Only six months ago I had a snowdome of a life. A life that was shaken constantly by some divine hand, glittering and sparkly. I had my own multi-million dollar pyjama empire that I'd built from scratch. I had journalists queuing up to interview me. I had a husband who loved me and I loved him back. I had a dog that behaved himself. Well, OK, most of the time. I was happy. And then some clumsy oaf dropped the snowdome.

The stupid thing is that clumsy oaf was me, Dicey Dye. (No, Dicey's not my real name. I don't reveal my real name to *anyone*.)

Behind me, I hear Fergus haul himself up off the floor.

He comes over and leans up against the couch, sniffing my now wet knees.

He barks.

Raff-raff-raff-raff-raff.

And, with this, I can't help but smile a tiny smile, because it reminds me of Simon's expression at the window when Fergus barked at him. I glance up to see Fergus looking at me indignantly, aware that it's not usual for ladies to laugh at their knights in shining armour even if they are overly large, furry and grey.

'Well…' I grab his face between my two hands and give his cheeks a good rub. 'I have told you before—you sound like an asthmatic pensioner when you bark!'

After a good five minutes of forced positive thinking, I manage to stop feeling quite so sorry for myself. I head for the kitchen, where I give Fergus his mini Wagon Wheel fix, locate a packet of pistachios for myself, and go about finding my two favourite pistachio bowls—one for the nuts and one for the empties. I rip open the packet with my teeth and decant the nuts. That done, I open a bottle of white, grab a glass and head for the lounge.

Only pistachios can make me feel any better. I think it's something to do with the rhythm I get into as I eat them—reach for nut, pick up nut, open nut, put nut in mouth, chew, swallow, reach for nut, pick up nut, open nut, put nut in mouth, chew, swallow. It's very soothing.

I plump up the cushions on the couch, settle myself down with my bowls and my wine and get cracking—literally.

It was a dumb idea to bring Simon back to my place at

all. I realise that now. I'd only ever done it before when Fergus had been staying with Jean-Luc. I knew Fergus would jack up about it. About anyone who wasn't JL, that is. But I was semi-drunk, and miserable about my life in general, and I also thought that at the end of the day Fergus would behave like a gentleman.

Except, of course, he didn't.

Semi-drunk as I was after our dinner out, I still had the good sense to secrete Fergus in the back garden while Simon made his way upstairs on arrival. I knew it would save me trouble on several fronts. Simon didn't like Fergus, for a start. And then, of course, there was the fact that Fergus didn't like Simon and, given five minutes and the opportunity, wouldn't hesitate at ripping out and gobbling down the guy's spleen.

It started something like this:

1. After five minutes I feel guilty about leaving Fergus outside (sucker that I am), and sneak downstairs to let him back in, ordering him to stay downstairs.

2. Fergus hot-tails it upstairs as soon as I turn my back and hides out in the hallway.

3. He stays there until the voices from behind the partially closed door start to become slightly raised.

4. Whereupon he pushes open the door and sees a man in my bed. Fergus assumes the man in my bed is JL.

5. Fergus launches himself on the man in my bed, overjoyed.

6. The man in my bed decides he does not want to end his days being suffocated by a grey shag pile with legs.

7. It dawns on Fergus that the man in my bed is not JL but Simon.

8. Fergus freaks out.

The whole affair (in both terms of the word…), ended with Fergus on the floor, cowering, and Simon with a raised hand.

I've never seen Fergus cower before. I didn't like it.

'Don't even think about it,' I barked at Simon, on behalf of my dog.

There was a long pause before the hand went back down again. 'Well, it's nice to see where your fucking loyalties lie.' (Simon likes to say 'fuck' a lot. I think it makes him feel taller than he really is.)

'Well, you scared him! Look!' I pointed at Fergus's tail, slinking out the door. 'He was confused. He thought you were Jean-Luc.'

Simon rolled his eyes dramatically at this. 'Oh, I should have known. Jean-Luc. Tall, dark, handsome, and French to boot. Jean-Luc, whose farts probably smell like freshly baked croissants. Well, *oh-la-la*. I'm sick of hearing about Jean-Luc. Everyone loves fucking Jean-Luc…'

I waited until his store of knowledge on France, the French and JL (whom he'd only met once and was actually Swiss, not French) had depleted. Croissants and *oh-la-la*. That was it?

'Are you done?'

'Yes. And so are we,' he snarled as he picked his trousers up from the floor. 'I'm sick of you and I'm sick of that fucking dog.'

I glanced towards the door then, wondering where Fergus had got to. He was a few feet down the hallway—out of Simon's striking distance, but keeping an eye on things.

When I turned back I took a good hard look at the guy I'd practically left my husband for, wondering what I'd ever seen in him in the first place. I couldn't remember. I couldn't even remember why I'd hired him as my media advisor—because, come to think of it, he wasn't much chop at that either. Really, the only thing he had going for him was the fact that he was easy on the eye. Now I was sick of looking.

'Done, are we? Well, I'm glad to hear it,' I snorted.

'Yeah, sure.' He picked up his clothes and pushed past me as he left the room, making me stumble.

I followed him out, just catching sight of him giving Fergus a push for good measure. By the time he reached the top of the stairs Fergus had decided enough was enough and his few growls saw Simon exit the house with his pants only just buckled and half his shirt remaining behind as the dog's dinner.

Reach for nut, pick up nut, open nut, put nut in mouth, chew, swallow, reach for nut, pick up nut, open nut, put nut in mouth, chew, swallow…

My pistachio sounds bring me back to reality as I realise it's far too quiet in here. I swivel my head around to locate Fergus. 'Hey, how about Titch time?' I call out, and he galumphs over and lands on my feet.

Raff. He looks up hopefully when he's finished squirming his way into the most comfortable position for him and the least comfortable position for my toes.

'No. No more mini Wagon Wheels. You know you're not supposed to have any at all. You know I get lectures from the vet.'

Raff.

I ignore him, turn the TV and VCR on and press play. Today we've come in halfway through the ads.

Raff.

I roll my eyes at him. 'Sorry to waste your time, Your Highness. She's coming. It'll be on after this.' I press fast forward, until I see my sister standing in the bright morning sunshine. It's weird watching daytime TV at night, but I never miss her show. Not that I've been doing anything very exciting lately that would make me miss her seven-thirty a.m. slot. The truth is, I just haven't been able to drag my sorry butt out of bed early enough to catch it.

Fergus sits up as soon as he catches a glimpse of her. He loves Titch. (No, that's not her real name either. I'm sworn to secrecy on that one.)

'Hello, Sunshine!' my sister says, with her half arc wave, just as she does every weekday. 'And hello to you, Karen and Tony.'

The two anchors hello back, with their usual 'the men in white coats are coming' false cheer. There's a pause before Titch continues.

'Yes. Um, today we're at the orphaned ferrets' home in outer Melbourne. As you can see, there are several volunteers who've come out today to help with the ferret feeding…'

The camera moves around the large room Titch is standing in to show a few women sitting on couches and bottle-feeding ferrets wrapped up in towels.

'And aren't they, um, sweet? Apparently it's all a big myth that they bite, and also that they smell. I have to say that I didn't know much about ferrets before this morning, but I'm quickly becoming a big fan. Especially of these poor, um, homeless and, ah, um…motherless babies.'

I look down at Fergus, who looks up at me. Something's not right. Titch's face is a pasty white, and she looks like she's struggling to speak. I wonder if she's sick, or whether the show's having technical difficulties. It happens. Titch has done many a weather report flying by the seat of her capri pants.

'They're gorgeous,' Karen coos. 'And where will we find you tomorrow, Titch?'

There's another, longer pause from Titch at this, and something that looks like a shuddery cough. I can't tell for sure, because she's looking down at the ground, away from the camera. Something is definitely going on here, I think, leaning forward closer to the TV. There's another cough. Wait. Oh, my God, was that a sob?

'At the multiple birth association, Tony.'

'Ah, I guess we'll be seeing you with your hands full there, eh? No freebies now, do you hear? And careful you don't drink the water! So, tell us, Titch, how's the weather looking today?' The camera crosses back to Titch.

But there is no Titch.

Hang on. Yes, there is. The camera pans to show her running off into the distance.

Oh, shit.

'Well, looks like we're having a few technical difficulties, folks,' Tony says, as I scramble off the couch and lunge for the phone.

Raff.

'I don't know,' I tell Fergus. 'I'm going to call her.'

But as I dial the numbers my heart sinks, because I already know what's wrong with Titch. I know why she's run off. First the orphaned ferrets' home and then the multiple birth association. Combined with those two cracks about not taking any freebies and steering clear of the water. How could *Hello, Sunshine* be so cruel?

'Titch? Titch?' I say as the phone answers. But it's the answering machine that kicks in. I remember then that Andrew, her husband, has just started his month on shift at the remote mine where he works as a mechanical engineer. He won't be home for another three and a half weeks. But Titch…Titch is always at home and in bed by this time of night because of her early starts. And she hates the answering machine—she never turns it on. This is bad. Very bad.

Raff.

'I'm *trying*. Sit down and shut up.' I hang up the phone and quickly try another number—Titch's mobile.

'Hello?' The phone answers after a good six or seven rings.

'Titch! I just saw this morning's show on tape. What's going on? Where are you?'

There's silence for a moment. And then Titch starts bawling. I can tell by the way she gulps in between bursts that she's been crying all day.

'Titch?'

'They've made me take three weeks off…' she manages to get out, before she starts up again.

My eyes move around the room at double-quick time. 'Look. Don't go anywhere. I'm going to fly down to Melbourne right now. With Fergus. We're coming to get you.'

There's another silence. A gulp. And a blowing of a nose. 'That's nice of you, but there's no need. My cab's turning into your street right now.'

Outside, Fergus and I push and shove, vying for the prime spot on the driveway, waiting for the cab to pull in.

When it does, none of us worries about formalities. We skip the hellos and how are yous and get right down to basics. Titch flings the door open, forgetting about her goods and chattels, Fergus bounds straight for her, then leaps, pushing her against the car, and I run over and hug whichever bits are left sticking out. Meanwhile, the cabbie sticks his head out of the car, asks if that's a wolf I've got there, and when I say no, it's an Irish Wolfhound, nods and exits the car. Sane and quite unemotional, he arranges Titch's things on the grass and patiently waits for the three of us to compose ourselves. Eventually I recover enough to go over and give him the thirty-dollar fare from the airport.

'Good luck, sweetheart,' the cabbie says, before he gets back into the car and drives off.

The sad thing is, when I head back over to Titch and see her puffy, tear-and-mascara-streaked face in the harsh spotlight shining down on the front terrace, I can't help thinking the cabbie was on the right track. Titch is going to need all the luck she can get.

'Come on,' I say, picking up her things with one hand and guiding her by the waist with the other. 'Let's go inside.'

I sit Titch down on the couch, fetch her a glass of mineral water and then watch her drink it, saying nothing. I don't want to push her. I know my sister well enough to realise that it will all come out in good time.

'I need to see the tape,' she says quietly, Fergus's head now in her lap.

I don't argue, but switch the TV on with the remote, rewind the video and press 'play'. If she needs to see the tape, she needs to see the tape.

This time it starts at the right spot—Titch in Ferretville.

On the opposite couch, I want to cover my eyes with one hand and peep through, rather as if I'm watching a horror movie, but I can't because Titch isn't. I have to be brave for her, and she's sitting there on the other couch, eyes wide, mesmerised, unable to look away from the glow of the screen. And it's a different person that I see sitting across from me—different from the one I see on the TV screen every day, I mean.

Titch competed in a junior newsreader competition along with all her classmates at the age of ten. She won the competition and never looked back. It's strange, because she's the last person anyone would think would enjoy being in front of a camera, but somehow it brings her out of herself and lets her personality shine through.

Not today though, I think to myself as I switch the TV off again.

Titch shakes her head. 'It's worse than I thought, if that's possible.'

I swivel myself around to face her, bringing my legs up to cross them in front of me on the couch. 'So, what happened?' I say slowly.

There's a long pause before Titch speaks. 'I don't know. Nothing. Everything.'

Once more I keep quiet.

'It was just all too much at once.'

'The ferrets?' I ask.

Titch gives me a puzzled look.

'Sorry.' I grimace. *The ferrets?* What am I talking about? Shut up, Dicey!

Titch finishes her mineral water. When she's done, she traces the edge of the glass with one finger. 'You know the last course of IVF failed?' She doesn't look up.

I nod. 'Yes.' How could I forget? Titch was heartbroken— both that time and the time before.

'Well, um, I don't know if we can afford to do it again.'

I keep right on looking at her, waiting for more information. But after I've waited quite a while I begin to wonder if any more is actually coming. That's it? *I don't know if we can afford to do it again?* My forehead wrinkles as I look at my sister. I know she's lying. Well, maybe not *lying* as such, but not telling me the whole truth and nothing but the truth.

I watch her and wait, wait, wait for the rest of her answer, all the time contemplating whether she's really just worried about starting up a third IVF cycle. If that's what this is all about, I really don't blame her—the injections, the drugs, the time, the crossing the days off the calendar and, worst of all, the hope she's had and lost along with her one pregnancy. It's been hard on her. Really hard.

'Right. So, you can't afford it? Well I could…'

'Don't look at me like that, Dicey. Please. And don't offer me any money!' Titch still hasn't looked up from her glass. 'OK, so that was just an excuse. We can afford it. It's just, um, I don't know if I can do it again. Andrew's all set for it, but I don't know…'

She looks up now to meet my eyes, and that's when I know it for sure—she's worried, all right, but there's something else as well. Something bigger. Something that she's considering not even telling *me*. And Titch and I—we've always told each other *everything*.

'Titch…' I'm starting to get worried.

She pauses. Our eyes are still locked. 'Dicey, I…'

I edge forward on the couch, and with my movement Titch suddenly glances at her glass again. 'Like I said, I don't know if I can do it again.'

I stop edging, realising I've lost her. Shit. I suppress the urge to give the couch a good thump. Instead, I sit back and start quietly picking at a loose cushion thread, hoping she'll do her usual nervous rabbit trick and hop right back to what she was saying before I frightened her off.

As I wait, I remember what she'd said before, about the money. Well, at least Titch has admitted the story she was spinning there isn't true. I knew the minute the words came out of her mouth that it wasn't right—if Titch and Andrew wanted to go for another round of IVF they'd find the money. It was enormously expensive, but I thought that was why Andrew was working away from home—for the mountain-loads of extra cash the job was providing?

Whatever's going on here just doesn't make sense. And what Titch is holding back from me, I have no idea. I pick at the cushion a bit harder. Maybe it's something to do with

Andrew? Maybe Andrew doesn't want to go for a third try? No—no way, I think, shaking my head a touch. Andrew's what you might call original recipe Mr Clucky.

I sit and watch Titch stare at her glass, feeling more helpless than I think I've ever felt before. What should I do? Maybe she just needs a little talking around? I mean, the IVF really did do horrible things to her last time—including one unfortunate set of drugs that made her puff up like a balloon. But she's been through the process twice already, without the smallest of snivels, and I have no doubt she'd do it again. So, what else can be wrong? I have no idea.

Titch looks up then.

And bursts into tears.

Right on cue, Fergus lifts his head from Titch's lap and begins to howl.

I uncurl my legs, get up and go over to Titch's couch. She puts her head on my shoulder and lets the waterworks flow.

It takes a while for her to let it all out, so I pat her hair as I wait. When she lifts her head again, with a final sniff, my shoulder is soaked. She leans back against the cushions with a sigh and I decide it's officially Time. She needs to talk about this—whatever it is. Bottling things up inside is Titch's forte, and I'm guessing she's been storing this one for a while now. Like a dodgy bottle of homemade ginger beer, she'd popped this morning, on *Hello, Sunshine*.

'Titch, you've got to tell me what's going on.'

Titch looks down at the glass that's still in her hand and runs her finger around the rim a few more times for good measure. 'All this trying…lately I can't stop thinking that maybe it's fate. That maybe I'm wasting my time.'

I pause at this. Fatalism? From Titch? It's not her scene. Lately it's been my stomping ground—the reigning Mayor of Fatalism in the province of Inevitability, situated on planet Pessimism. In fact, this is such a strange thing for Titch to say I can hardly believe what I'm hearing. For years now this is all Titch has wanted. *Everything* has taken a back seat to starting a family. And Titch would be a fantastic mother. I've seen her with her friends' kids—she's a natural compared to my neutral. How can she be doubting it's going to happen now?

'Titch—' I start, but don't know what to say. Maybe it's just become less painful for her to think about it this way—that it's not meant to be. 'Maybe this time—the third time…' I start again.

Titch shrugs. 'You can't say that.'

'I know, but…' I stop, because I know she's right. I can't promise her that this time will be different. I wish I could, but I can't. Round and round her finger goes on top of the glass. Round and round. So many times I start to wonder if she'll wear the glass out. Round and round and round.

And still I can tell there's something else.

Something she's holding back.

Round and round and round and round and round.

After what seems like the five millionth dizzy turn round the glass, I decide that maybe we should just let this go for now. Titch is tired and stressed, and if she needs to talk, she'll talk tomorrow. It can wait. And, whatever it is, it'll be OK in the end. The thing is, it doesn't matter why Titch is here, or what she needs from me. We'll work that out in good time. All I care about is that she came and that she's here in one piece. It's so good to see her again, for real, in the flesh, I can hardly wipe the smile off my face.

'Hey,' I say with a grin, making her look up from her glass. 'I still hate you, you know.'

Titch smiles at this. And this smile reaches her eyes. 'Well, I hate you more.' She leans over to punch my arm.

I smile back at her and know, looking at her, that one day Titch will make a fantastic mother. As compared to ours. Ours was completely crap at the job. So crap Titch and I have only ever had pretend fights—like the one we're having now.

We're too precious to each other to have anything else.

I send Titch off for a shower and, when she's gone, stand in the middle of the living area and look around me. I know I should tidy up before my sister (aka Little Miss Neat-and-Tidy) nags me about the mess, but I can't be bothered.

Instead, I go and sit down at the kitchen table, push aside a pile of stuff and start flicking idly through an old magazine. Soon enough I hear Fergus start to snore, and this makes me realise how tired I am myself. But I'm way too wired from this evening's events to go to bed, and I know, once again, that I'll have to wait till I'm exhausted.

It's been happening a lot lately, this staying up until all hours. I've been going to bed at two a.m., three a.m. most nights. I used to be able to fall asleep the minute my head hit the pillow, but these days I can't go to bed unless I'm too tired to think. Without sheer exhaustion, my thoughts buzz in my ears—at first far away, but then closer and closer—like annoying mosquitoes in the night. What if? What if? What if? The noise fades in and out, soft, then piercingly loud, penetrating my skull. What if this was your one chance to be? To do?

Don't think about it.

I won't think about it.

I concentrate hard on sitting and flipping until Titch appears again. She starts down the steps in my dressing gown, rubbing her wet, shoulder-length black hair with a towel. She looks one hundred and ten per cent better.

Halfway down the stairs, she stops and looks around her with a shake of her head. 'I don't know how you can bear this beautiful house of yours looking like such a pigsty.'

I close my magazine with a shrug. 'It's not mine for much longer.'

Still rubbing, Titch makes her way down the final few steps. 'When do you have to move?'

'Four weeks from—' I check the time '—today.'

Titch's eyes keep flicking around the room. They come to rest on the coffee table near the TV. 'Dicey, is that what you had for dinner?' She's looking at my bowl of pistachio shells and the matching empty bottle of wine.

'Um,' I say slowly. 'No.'

I get the big sister look in return.

'Well, what did *you* have?' I counter.

She stops rubbing her hair for a second and frowns, thinking back. 'Oh,' she says, when it comes to her. 'A, um, I had a Kit Kat, actually. But one of the white ones, so it was probably better for me. You know—more dairy.'

I give her the look back and we both laugh.

My stomach grumbles at the mention of Kit Kats. Pistachios or no pistachios, I'm hungry. I push back my chair and get up from the table. 'Want me to make you something? A cheese *jaffle?* I could go for one.'

Titch nods as she starts combing through her tangled hair with her fingers. 'Sounds lovely.'

'There's probably a comb in that pile on the table,' I say as I start pottering around the kitchen, pulling out cheese I'll have to cut the mould off, bread that thankfully hasn't quite got to that stage yet, and the *jaffle*-maker. 'I think I saw one hanging around the pile on the left a while ago.'

'And there's probably a pot of gold at the end of the rainbow.' Titch starts picking through the mess. 'It doesn't mean we'll ever find it.'

'Ha-bloody-ha.'

She abandons her picking at the pile. 'Well, can you blame me for being scared? If I get too close the junk will suck me in and you'll never find me again.'

'I'm in stitches. You're killing me.' I place the now de-moulded cheese on top of two pieces of bread, add a touch of salt and pepper, the second two pieces of bread, and close the *jaffle*-maker with a snap.

'What are you up to here?' Titch is picking through the mess at the other end of the table now. The sewing machine end.

'I'm making something for you, actually. Or I was until you started in on the nagging routine.' I head over to the table.

'Really? For me?' Titch becomes more animated and starts picking a little harder. 'Oh, this fabric is gorgeous,' she says, lifting a sheer green piece with leaves embroidered on it to her face. 'And this is sweet.' She picks up another piece, brown this time, with cowboy printing.

'It's not quite finished,' I say, bending down to pick up the hatbox I store stuff in. I place it on the table and open it up.

'There are still a few last-minute touches. I've got to sew the label in and...' I hand a bag over to her.

'Oh, Dicey,' she says slowly, her eyes rising to meet mine. 'It's beautiful!'

She's right. It is beautiful. The minute I saw the fabric I knew that I had to keep this piece aside for Titch. With her black hair, porcelain complexion and rosy cheeks, anything pink always comes up a treat on Titch, and this fabric— white sparkly organza with huge blushing pink full-blown roses—was made for her. I'd accented the roses with tiny pink and clear crystal beads, added a few green crystal beads to the leaves and hand-sewn it into a little drawstring number with a matching piece of pink velvet ribbon.

I'd had such a great time making it, keeping my hands busy and my mind occupied, I spent almost twelve hours straight on it one day without even noticing. It was almost like the old days, when I started up my pyjama business. There never used to be enough hours in the day then, and I liked redis-covering that feeling. Not to mention keeping so busy meant I was able to stop my mind ticking over. I was also better able to ignore the fact that the answering machine was picking up calls every few minutes that I never listened to or returned.

'Dicey, I just love it!' Titch brings the bag closer to her now to examine the beading. 'I wish I could do things like this. You're so talented.' She shakes her head in wonderment and comes around to give me a hug.

This makes me laugh. Titch is always astounded by my ability to make things. Even as children, making toilet roll *objets d'art,* as demonstrated clearly on *Playschool,* mine would always be the one to 'turn out'—despite Titch's three-year age advantage. But Titch never recognises her own talents. Sure, I can make things with my hands, but Titch can stand in front of a camera and a) look good, and b) act natural. Something I'll never be able to do in a million years. I've offered to teach her to sew before, but she's probably right in thinking that it's never going to happen for her. She says sewing machines like to nip at her fingers, that they're natural-born enemies.

'Oh!' She looks up with a start from the bag and sniffs. 'The *jaffles,* um, smell ready.'

'You know, it's OK to say the *jaffles* are burning. You don't have to be polite,' I say, racing over and opening the *jaffle*-maker up.

Just in time. They're nice and brown, but not burnt. I flick the power off and slide a knife under both of them, scraping up the cheese that's melted over the sides as I go. I put one onto each plate, and then cut them in half before I head back over to the table with a plate in each hand.

'Here we go,' I say pulling a seat out. Titch sits down beside me. Both hungry, we eat without speaking.

It isn't until she's finished the first half of her *jaffle* that Titch pipes up. 'Dicey, I have to ask. Are *you* OK?'

I look up, surprised at her question. 'Me? Of course I'm OK. Don't be silly.'

'It's just that it seems awfully quiet here without JL around.'

I busy myself with my *jaffle,* but the piece I shove in my mouth I quickly swallow without chewing, and it becomes lodged in my throat. My eyes start to water.

Titch's gaze moves around the living and dining area slowly. She's looking, I know, at the dusty squares and rectangles where JL's things used to be, until one by one he picked up what he needed and ferried the items over to his new house. His new house where he keeps his new life.

'I'm fine—really,' I say, not looking up. I don't want to talk about JL. Since he moved out I've avoided talking about him, just like I've avoided looking at those dusty squares and rectangles.

'OK.' There's a long pause. 'So what have you been doing lately?'

'Making bags. Watching *Oprah.* Eating pistachios. Not much.' Even I can hear that my voice sounds too flippant. Too high. *I'm fine,* it says, *just fine! Don't worry about me! Everything's just dandy! Super-duper!* And that stupid piece of *jaffle* in my throat—it still won't go down. My eyes are about to brim over. I take a gulp of water. Another gulp.

Meanwhile, Titch waits—just like I waited for her before.

I put my glass down and look at the mess on the table. 'I've been trying to keep busy. But it's like the less I have to do, the less I seem able to do. Does that make sense?'

Titch looks at me, pauses, then nods. She gives me a small smile before she continues. 'Don't worry, you'll—' she begins, but the phone interrupts her.

We look at each other. It's two-seventeen a.m. Who could be calling now? That would be the obvious question. But the fact is, both of us already know who's going to be on the end of that phone line. Sally. That girl has some kind of a radar for trouble.

I take my time going over to pick up the phone.

'Dice, can you come and pick me up?' she slurs.

I knew it. I roll my eyes at Titch. 'Sal, it's past two a.m. Can't you catch a cab home?'

'No!' She says too loudly and I have to pull the phone away from my ear. 'No, I can't!' Her voice rises into a wail now. 'I'm in Accident and Emergency. Like ER, you know? Except it's nothing like ER. I've been gypped! There's no

George Clooney. There's someone that, at a push, could re-semble Doogie Howser. But there's no George Clooney. I've a mind to send a formal complaint to the...'

As Sally keeps talking, my eyes grow wider and wider. Oh, my God. She's not drunk, I realise. She's drugged.

We don't lose any time making our way to the hospital. Titch shoves one of JL's baseball caps over her wet hair and we both grab any clothes in sight. We're still pulling them on as we leave the house, just as Simon was doing only a few hours before. Fergus isn't happy about being left to defend the fort, but there's no way I can take him to a hospital. He howls from the other side of the thick wooden front door as the car takes off down the street.

We drive in silence for quite a while, intent on getting to our destination. 'Trust Sally to ring this evening. And in the middle of the night too,' I say, with a shake of my head, when the silence gets to be a bit too much.

Titch glances over at me. 'You mean it's a very timely accident she's had? That's a bit mean.'

'Is it? What other kind of accident would Sally have?

Heaven forbid someone else should be the centre of attention for five minutes.'

Titch exhales. 'She can have all the attention she wants as far as I'm concerned. She's welcome to it.'

'Yes. Well…' I decide to quit while I'm ahead. It's just that it's… She's… Ugh, so *annoying* sometimes. Sally always wants to be in the spotlight and always has, ever since Titch and I have known her—which is a long time—since high school. Since I was twelve years old.

Sally moved to our high school in the middle of my first year there. There was a lot of mystery surrounding her appearance. Mainly because her family had just come into a lot of money. A whole lot of money. They'd won the lotto—a big, first division, truckload-of-money prize. Yet the strange thing was Sally was moving not to a big fancy private school, but from the tiny high school one town over from ours—to another tiny high school. The rumour was she'd been kicked out. For what, we weren't sure (though we sure did speculate…).

On her first day at school we half expected her to arrive in a limo. But she arrived in an old family ute it looked like they'd had for years, dressed in the same uniform the rest of us wore (if a little stiffer and newer).

The other rumour was that her sister had just died. Well, to be fair, that wasn't so much a rumour, because we knew it was true—some of us had even been to the funeral. The thing was, Lisa Bliss—Sally's sister—had been kind of…famous around those parts. She'd always been in the local paper for something or other—fundraising, inter-school athletics, helping out at the animal shelter, donating kidneys. She was one of those golden children—the kind of child every parent wants, every grandparent wants to boast about and all of us want to be. What do they say? Only the good die young? In this case it seemed the saying was all too true.

Anyway, from her first day at school, for some reason or another, the kids at school circled Sally warily. Maybe because of the money. Maybe because of her sister. Maybe because, from that very first day, Sally had that radar for trouble I mentioned. If you hung around her for more than fifteen minutes you could pretty much guarantee that within the hour you'd be sitting on the hard chairs outside the principal's office.

So, that's where I spent a great deal of my high school career—sitting with Sally on the hard chairs outside the principal's office. Because, although she was trouble, and her radar would always get on my nerves, Sally and I hit it off right from the very start. We had something in common, Sally and I. We were different. It was something the other kids could always sniff out, rather like dogs can smell fear. Sally's point of difference was her sister. Mine was my mother. And though we never really talked about it—not till years later—it was always there. In the background. Following us like our shadows.

Titch and I arrive at the hospital counter, panting and frantic. 'Sally Bliss—Sally Bliss,' I repeat over and over to the nurse behind the computer that can tell us where she is and what's wrong with her. She looks at me, and then at the computer, blankly.

'Oh, yes. Bliss…Sally.' Another nurse comes over as she hears the name.

Titch and I turn to look at each other. There's an oh-too-familiar tone in the woman's voice.

'Hmm,' she continues. 'Sally Bliss.' She turns to the nurse

behind the computer and crosses her arms. 'You know—the *blonde* with the *shoe*.'

'Oh, *that* Sally Bliss,' she replies with a knowing nod.

How many Sally Bliss, or Bliss…Sally's, have they got in here, I wonder? It's a scary thought that there might be more than one Sally Bliss in this world, let alone this suburb. Still, at least Titch and I know that Sally's OK. If she was at death's door she'd be too sick to be up to no good. And by the sound of things she's definitely been up to no good.

With a shoe.

The nurses don't give us any more information about either Sally or her footwear. Instead, they tell us to sit and wait for the doctor. We go over to perch nervously on the bone-coloured plastic chairs that line up row after row. There's no one else in sight.

After what seems like an eternity, a doctor approaches us. 'You're here for Sally Bliss?' he asks.

We both nod. 'And her shoe,' I add for clarification.

'Ah, yes. The shoe.' He nods in the same knowing fashion as the nurse did before.

'What's happened?' I say. 'All I could get out of her on the phone was that she was here, and a lot of nonsense about George Clooney and Doogie Howser.'

'Mmm…' He pauses and inspects the ceiling. 'George Clooney. We've been hearing a lot about George Clooney tonight. And Doogie Howser, of course.'

Titch and I edge a bit further forward in our seats, waiting for news. The doctor continues to inspect the ceiling. 'Um?' I try, with a wave of my hand.

He looks down suddenly, focusing on us. 'Right—sorry. It's been a long night. Sally had a bit of an accident. It seems she tripped on a set of stairs and broke her ankle.'

Titch and I turn to look at each other in horror. 'Is she OK?' I glance back up at the doctor.

'Oh, she's fine now. She'll be in plaster for about six weeks.'

Titch and I look at each other—again in horror.

'She'll just need to take it easy.'

Take it easy? Is the guy kidding? Sally doesn't know the meaning of the term. And I'm guessing this is going to mean she won't be able to work at all. Sally's job as one of the city's top wedding photographers is kind of a feet-on job. Both feet. I'm afraid, very afraid, that she's not going to take this news well.

Maybe that's what the business with the shoe is all about…

'Can we see her?' Titch asks, bringing me back to reality.

'Sure, sure—come on through.' The doctor heads off across the lino floor. We follow him past several interesting-sounding noises behind curtains until he stops in front of Bay 12 and swishes open the swathed light blue material in front of us.

And there is Sally.

Dress askew, lipstick smudged across her cheek and fairy-floss dishevelled hair everywhere. She's half sitting up—plaster on one foot and shoe on the other.

'Not happy!' she huffs the moment she spots us.

I stand very, very still for a moment and fix my gaze at a spot just above her head, doing all I can not to laugh. Finally I give myself a pinch on the back of my leg and get it together.

'Sal…' I go over and wriggle onto the bed beside her. (I think about, but don't attempt, a hug—she doesn't look quite ready for one yet.) 'How are you feeling?' I pat her arm.

She rubs her mouth with the back of her hand, wiping

more lipstick across her face. 'Broke my ankle,' she says. 'And then they cut my shoe off. Brand-new! $875!'

Finally—the shoe…

'We've put her in a walking cast, so she can still get around.' The doctor leans forward. 'She's, er, had a few painkillers…' he whispers in my left ear.

I nod back conspiratorially. *No shit, Sherlock.* Does he think she's always like this?

'I heard that about the painkillers!' Sally shrieks at the doctor. 'Don't think I didn't!' She turns her head back to look at me when she's finished with him and her expression goes all gooey. 'I love you, Dice.'

'I know.' I pat her arm again. 'Now, why don't you tell us what happened, Sal? How did you hurt yourself?'

'All righty, girls.' Her face changes once more and she sits up suddenly, rolling her eyes wildly and dramatically at Titch and myself. Story time with Sally. 'I was making a fucking fantastic exit from the restaurant I was at with my date. I knew for a fact that *at least* four guys were watching my arse—that Pilates works, I'm telling you. Anyway, then, well—bang! The next thing I know, I roll out on my ankle and I end up here. Here! I mean, what have I got private insurance for? But, no. The ambos wouldn't take me to a private hospital, would they? Said it was too far and—'

'You were in a lot of pain, Sally,' the doctor interjects. 'In cases like this it's best to go to the closest hospital.'

'Well,' she says, still talking way too fast, and now gesturing maniacally as well. 'At least in a private hospital they might have understood how much these shoes *cost*. They might have *appreciated* a pair of Terry Bivianos when they saw them. And, I mean—I could catch something in here.

Look at this.' She points up at the wall beside her head and we all peer to see what she's looking at. 'Blood!'

The doctor, Titch and I peer harder, squinting. She's right. There's a small spattering of blood.

'And *not* mine! No, no, no. Not mine. It's probably some…prostitute's blood!' she splutters, and the three of us turn to look at the doctor.

'It's, er, *dry,* prostitute's blood…' he says, trailing off. He leans back then, and crosses his arms.

There's a pause. Sally cocks her head to one side and, still looking at him, half closes her eyes. 'You know,' she says, 'you do look a *bit* like George Clooney. When you get all hoity-toity like that, I mean.'

The doctor's eyes take on a frightened glaze. I get up off the bed fast, to stand in front of him and block Sally's line of vision. 'Ha-ha. Can we take her home now?' I ask, before she corners him into a date.

The doctor nods. Hard. 'Definitely. She has her crutches, and instructions written down for medication. She's all set to go. I'll just arrange for a wheelchair.' And with this excuse he's out of the cubicle like a speeding bullet.

Sally can be a bit of a man-eater at the best of times. But with lipstick all over her face and pumped full of pain medication? It's a whole other realm of terror.

After a while the doctor returns with another man who's pushing a wheelchair. 'This is Ben,' he says, standing behind him. 'He'll help Sally out to your car.'

Titch and I move so that the wardie can get in to help Sal out of bed. She flings her good leg out of the bed inelegantly, flashing whatever's underneath (I don't want to know) in a very un-Sharon Stone-like way.

'Um…' I turn quickly and grab Titch's arm (her face has

been set in a silent small 'o'-like shape for some time now) and pull her towards me, forming a human shield in front of the doctor. We're standing too close to him, really—less than an arm's length away—but there's no room for anyone to move back a step.

'Hey,' he says then, giving me a strange look. 'Aren't you Dicey Dye?'

'No,' I say quickly.

He smiles. 'Yes, you are! And that's your sister.' He moves his gaze to Titch. 'The one that's on TV. You do the weather on *Hello, Sunshine.*'

'Not anymore!' Sally pipes up from behind us.

'Sally!' I hiss, but can't turn around to give her an evil look. Who knows what her undies will be up to now?

The doctor's eyes narrow. 'Hey, are you two really sisters?'

'Yes!' we both say, a little too loudly.

He looks down at me and then up at Titch, standing a good head and a half above me. No doubt he's also taking in the colour of our skin and our oh-so-very-different body types. 'Really?'

'Well...half sisters,' I say sullenly.

'Yes. Half sisters.' Titch's tone matches mine.

'Oh, right. That explains it, then. Could have written a case study on it otherwise, couldn't I? Ha-ha. Well, anyway, it was fantastic to meet you. Wait till I tell my girlfriend. She loves your pyjamas. She's got about five hundred pairs.'

I try to smile. 'Great.'

'No, really. She does! She loves those original black and white ones the best. The proper cow ones. She's got the whole deal—the slippers and the mask, and even the dressing gown with the tail. Pity about that whole media thing.

That got a bit nasty, didn't it? Maybe she should have bought some extra pairs to put away. Could be a collector's item in a few years couldn't they?'

It's at this point that I glance at Titch's face. The small 'o' has disappeared to be replaced by a furious glare. I stare at her in surprise. Anger—it's not something I often see in my sister.

'Hey!' Sally pipes up then, with remarkable timing, cutting the doctor off. 'Hello? Down here? The one with the injury—remember me?'

The three of us pivot to see her in the wheelchair, cutoff shoe in her right hand, wardie at the ready. A long string of dribble hangs from her mouth into her lap. 'Are we out of this shithole, or what?'

Sally garbles on about George Clooney, Doogie Howser, prostitute blood and her shoe all the long way home.

Back at the ranch, Titch and I manage to haul our oldest and dearest friend into the house, one of her arms around each of our necks. It's not easy. Especially getting up the stairs. We both wince every time her plastered foot smacks against a step, pause, then start up the next step, where it happens all over again.

Step, smack, wince.

Step, smack, wince.

After we get Sally into an old T-shirt and tuck her into bed, we manage to clean up her face a little without her making too much fuss. Almost as soon as her head hits the pillow, however, she's out for the count, and before we even leave the room she's started snoring.

Outside the door, Titch and I look at each other. 'We'll probably laugh about this in the morning,' she says.

'I'm not so sure. Maybe the morning after that. Or one

morning next week. I'll check my diary and get back to you on it.'

Titch sighs. 'I think tomorrow morning I'm going to be too tired to laugh about anything.'

'You'll be fine.' I step forward and give her a hug. 'Did you want another shower? Or a bath or something?' I ask when I step back again.

She shakes her head. 'Just sleep, thanks.'

'OK,' I say as she makes for the second spare room. 'Um, Titch?' Halfway down the corridor now, she turns to look back at me. 'Don't worry about what Sally said before.'

She waves a hand, making an 'it doesn't matter' gesture. Then, ''Night,' she says and closes the door behind her.

I watch my sister's willowy form disappear from sight and then stand in the corridor by myself, a bad taste in my mouth as the doctor's words come back to me—*Are you two really sisters?* God, if I had a dollar for every time someone has asked me that. I hate it when people go on and on about Titch and I looking different. I know we don't look like much of a match. Well, we don't look like any kind of a match. Titch is tall and thin, with delicate boning—half-Japanese, we think. Then there's me. Short. Round. And, with frizzy hair, curvy body and my colouring, most definitely part Islander. How much and where from, I'll probably never know.

It always rubs me up the wrong way, people questioning Titch and my relationship. I know Titch feels the same way, though we rarely talk about it these days, now that we're grown up and it's less of an issue. Less of an issue people are willing to bring up, anyway. But back in the old days we used to do all kinds of things to pretend things weren't how they truly were. Things like covering up the mirror in our bedroom so we wouldn't be reminded how different we looked. Not just the difference between the two of us, but how different we looked to our grandparents. And to the whole of our small home town.

The phones start ringing just before six. The landline, my mobile and Titch's mobile.

Somehow, quite a substantial number of journalists have traced the darling of the weather-girl circuit to my home. It seems someone has spilled the beans and they now know about the failed IVF attempts. They know about everything.

We pull the landline out of the wall and turn our mobiles off. But we can't go back to sleep. We pace the house like unwanted ghosts. Only Fergus, trusty guard dog to the end, remains dead to the world and snoring.

The knocking on the door starts at six-thirty.

By seven the three of us have settled around the kitchen table, looking at each other bleary-eyed, heads in our hands, third cups of coffee drained before us.

'I think I might have said some…um…things last night,'

Sally says, lifting her head only marginally to meet first my eyes and then Titch's.

'You might have,' I reply. Best not to go into the finer details of the shoe, the dribbling…

'In particular, I think I might have said something about blood on a wall and a shoe that got cut off.'

'Hmm.' I remain non-committal.

'I'm taking it I shouldn't ask, right?' Sally grimaces.

'I don't remember anything about it,' Titch says kindly. 'Do you?' She directs the question at me with a 'be nice, Dicey' look in her eye.

'Not really,' I answer.

'Oh, God,' Sally groans, and puts her head down on the table, delivering a few fake sobs. 'Oh, God.' She looks up quickly. 'I can get the plaster cut off somewhere else, can't I?'

I shrug. 'I guess so.'

She sits up at this. 'I know! Maybe I could get one of those medical alert bracelets with little inscriptions?' She encircles her wrist with a thumb and forefinger. 'I could have it warning people against taking me back there because I suffer from chronic embarrassment.'

I laugh at this.

There's another knock on the door, and the three of us jump at the sound.

Raff. Fergus looks up for a second, then sighs as he lets his head drop back down again.

'The paper will be out there by now,' Titch says, putting her head back in her hands once more. 'It will be right out there on the lawn.'

'You don't want the paper,' I tell her.

'Ah, *that*. I didn't see it, but I heard about it.' Sally leans over to pat Titch's arm. But then she jolts upright. 'Oh. Oh, no!'

'What?' I ask, seeing the shock register on her face.

'Oh! I said something about that last night, didn't I? Something bad?'

I bite my lip, but find I can't be as polite on this one for Titch's sake. 'Mmm. Perhaps. A little something,' I mumble.

She leans over further, to rest her head on Titch's arm. 'I'm sorry, Titch. I didn't mean it. They drugged me to my eyeballs. After the first dose they kept asking me if it still hurt, and I lied each time and said yes. A big yes! After they asked for the third time I can't remember saying anything.'

Titch and I stare at her wide-eyed. Unusually, it's my sister who gets a grip first. 'You're terrible, Sal. But don't worry about it. You didn't say anything too bad.'

'I really am sorry. And I'm sorry in advance that I think I might have to use all the drugs. There's not going to be enough to share.' She leans across the table. 'They're pretty good, you know.'

There's silence as Titch and I look first at each other, then at Sally. 'I think we'll be OK with that.' I nod at Sally slowly. Did she hit her head as she went down on those stairs?

Titch taps her fingers on the tabletop. 'Now we've got that out of the way, I think you should show Sally the tape.' She glances over at me.

'Really?'

'Really.' She nods.

'You're the boss.'

I get up and switch the VCR and TV on while Sally swivels slowly in her seat, all the while muttering about the plaster and how cumbersome it is.

When it's all over, I come back to my chair to find Sally

speechless and quite silent. Something rather rare and worth noting.

'And that's why she doesn't want the paper,' I say, sitting down again. 'I can see it now.' I run my hand sideways through the air. *'Dyes disgrace. Sorry sisters buy two tickets to Loser City.'*

Titch's eyebrows shoot up. 'Speak for yourself!'

'OK, I guess you're right,' I say, my hand still paused mid-air. 'I shouldn't hand over my title of Sorriest Loser at the Table so readily.'

'Well, apparently I'm not going to be either driving or working for a while, so I might be a contender when all the bridal photographers start calling to gloat and pinch my clients,' Sally pipes up. 'But I don't have the energy just yet. Your title's safe for now.' She points at me. 'But only for now.'

The three of us look at each other in silence for a few minutes, then our heads return to our hands.

'I chucked Simon out last night,' I blurt out for something to say. When I'm done, I wonder to myself if this is quite true. But maybe if I think about it this way long enough and hard enough my mind might actually accept it as the truth and rewrite history.

Titch sucks her breath in. 'It's over?'

I nod.

'Well, good!' Sally says quickly, then, 'Um, sorry. I think I'm having side effects from the drugs.'

'Sure you are.' I look up at her. 'No, it's OK. He was a prat.'

'Of course he was a prat. He was your media advisor. He practically had a degree in being a prat!'

I shrug and admit the truth. 'I guess I kind of knew he was a prat all along.'

'Mmm. You *knew*, but you didn't want to *know*,' Sally

continues. 'Been there, done that. Got the all-clear from the STD clinic.'

'Sally!' Titch looks shocked.

But me—I just nod miserably. I knew Sally would understand.

'Oh, Dicey,' my sister says.

I knew Titch wouldn't. Now, she frowns at me.

'I just don't understand why you…' She stalls. Sally and I wait. 'Why you threw everything away for *him*.'

'I didn't throw away anything that wasn't limping to the bin already.'

'Dicey!' Titch looks shocked again.

'It's true. I know Simon was, um, less than perfect. But things were bad with JL. It was flattering to be wanted.' I can tell just by her expression that my words haven't helped her to understand any further. Hopefully she'll always stay as happy with Andrew as she is now. Hopefully she'll never understand what I'm talking about. 'Anyway, that's it for me,' I say far too airily. 'No husband. No lover. No job. And soon no house.'

More silence.

'You know,' I continue, 'if I was a superhero, my name would be Failure Girl'.

'Ooohhh! And your super power would be…?' Sally asks, brightening up.

I snort. 'Wallowing.'

'Would you have a dinky little T-shirt with large FG lettering?'

'Naturally.'

'Can I have one?'

'Sure.'

'With silver sequins? And matching undies to wear on the outside of my Lycra tights?'

'Whatever takes your fancy. Just no g-strings.'

'Fair enough.'

There's another knock on the door.

'What are we going to do?' Titch glances at it, then looks back worriedly.

The house is silent as the three of us think about her question—what *are* we going to do?

'We can't stay locked in here for ever,' Sally says after a while. 'There's only enough food left for about five minutes in Fergus time.'

Raff. Fergus looks up sulkily, wanting to go for a walk.

'Soon, Fergie, sweetie,' Titch calls out to him. 'Soon.'

'Well, Titch isn't allowed to have a job for three weeks, I've suddenly found myself on a six-week sabbatical from the bride biz, and you don't have a job—'

'Gee, thanks for reminding me,' I butt in.

'Failure Girl,' she adds with a laugh.

'It's always good to have friends who make you feel better about yourself,' I say.

'Well, I *am* going somewhere with this—if you'd stop interrupting me. I was going to say maybe we should go away?'

My eyes meet Titch's before swivelling to Sally's.

'Like where?' I ask slowly.

Sally continues. 'I was thinking that we need somewhere quiet. Somewhere no one ever goes. Somewhere they—' she nods at the front door '—won't be bothered coming to look for us…any of us…'

It's then that Titch and I start to cotton on to where she's going with this. Oh, no. No. Our eyes swivel and meet at exactly the same time. No. No. Definitely not. No.

And then she says it…

'Moo.'

Moo.

Where we three grew up. A tiny, green farming town.

Moo.

Famous for its Friesian black-and-white painted every-thing—telephone poles, electricity boxes, phone boxes, any-thing, really, that isn't already a cow.

Mad, mad, Moo.

My eyes remain firmly locked with Titch's.

No.

'Come on,' Sally cajoles. 'You know it makes sense. No one will look for us there.'

I don't turn to look at her; my eyes are still on Titch. 'Of course not. I mean, they only know we all come from there…'

Sally sighs. 'Well, yeah, sure. But they won't actually *come,* will they? It's too far. Too small. Too…everything.'

Still, my eyes remain locked with Titch's. I can tell exactly what she's thinking, and I know she knows exactly what's on my mind as well. There is no way in hell we're taking Sally to Moo. Because Sally… Well, Sally goes kind of crazy in Moo. It's like there's something in the air there. It's Sally to the power of ten. And Sally to the power of ten is not a good thing.

Ever.

But then it happens. There's another knock on the door and Titch breaks her gaze with me, her eyes moving quickly over to the noise.

Sally pounces. 'You know it makes sense,' she says as Titch continues to stare at the door.

There's another knock. *Rap rap rap.* This one's more insistent.

'Well, I suppose it does make sense…' Titch says hesitantly.

And by the time she turns back around to meet my eyes again I know I've lost.

We're going home.

Moo or no Moo, I can't wait to get out of here, so it takes me only a few minutes to pack.

I grab an old duffel bag out of the hall cupboard, lug it to my bedroom and start stuffing in anything that looks vaguely clean. With my indiscriminate stuffing God only knows what I'll have to wear later on (it's looking like it'll be a choice between about five hundred pairs of undies, two pairs of jeans and three T-shirts). In the *en suite* bathroom, all my toiletries get tipped into a plastic bag and, seconds later, land unceremoniously on top of Undie Mountain.

Just as I'm almost done intermittently squashing and zipping, there's a loud thump, then a long wail from down the corridor. Sally. I dump my bag on the floor and run, expecting to see her in pain, sprawled and writhing on the floor. Naturally, nothing of the sort is going on.

'What is it?' I say, leaning on the doorway to her bedroom,

my panic subsiding as I see she looks like she's still breathing. She's sitting on the bed, and the only thing wrong is her
face, looking more than a little mottled. 'What's the matter?'

'My new Sass & Bide jeans,' she puffs, digging her one
good heel into the floor with a grunt. 'I can't get them on!'

I take one glance at the circumference of the legs on those
skinny-minnie jeans, then move my gaze to Sally's cast. 'I hate
to break it to you, but it's not going to happen.'

'Maybe you could help me pull?'

Is she insane? 'Leg it go, Sally...' I start, then realise what
I've said. 'Oops. Sorry.'

'Very funny. I'll have you know Sass & Bide are *known* for
their stretchiness.' She gives another big tug, along with the
compulsory huff and grunt.

I've read as much, but I don't think the Sass & Bide girls
were envisioning most of their customers having one leg
three times larger than the other.

'How about a skirt today?' I try. I go over to the pile on
the floor and pick two. I've heard this is a good trick to use
on kids. You give them a choice between two items and it
distracts their tiny little minds away from the fact that they
didn't want to wear a skirt in the first place. 'Now, which one
of these do you want to wear?' I dangle the two itsy-bitsy
pieces of fabric in front of Sally's blue eyes.

'The denim one. I guess.' Sally pouts, her inner two-year-
old flinging the jeans across the room.

Here we go. I am so not looking forward to doing Moo
with this girl.

I pass the denim skirt to her, then stand back to take a good
look around me. There are clothes everywhere. On the bed,
on the floor, flung over the back of the room's stripy uphol-
stered high-backed armchair. 'Where'd you get all these

clothes from anyway?' As far as I remember, all Sally had last night were the clothes she was standing up in. OK, another bad choice of words—I mean the ones she was wearing in the wheelchair and the ones she'd had cut off her.

'I had a taxi bring them over from the office this morning.'

Well, there you go. I shake my head in wonder. I can't believe Sally's still one fashion step ahead of me even with a broken ankle. A thought comes to me, my mind having dredged up the fact that she's just mentioned work.

'Hey, you're not taking any cameras to Moo are you?' The last thing I feel like right now is having this trip documented.

'Not on your—umph—life.'

With one last giant heave, Sally's skirt is on. Task accomplished, she reaches down beside the bed, pulls out an enormous toiletries bag and starts to dig around inside, all in one seamless move.

'I'm not likely to get a holiday for a year after this. My old assistant, Liv, is going to cover for me, but I've promised to return the favour when she goes on her honeymoon, which means there goes my time off. Anyway, the cameras stay at the office.'

Good. I watch as she starts to hunt faster and more madly through the bag.

'Damn. Where's my Becca lipgloss gone? I know it was in here yesterday…'

This could get nasty. Time to go. 'Are you going to be OK? I've got to make some phone calls.'

'I'll whimper if I need you.' Sally eyes me only for a second before her attention's drawn back to the great lipgloss hunt.

'Rightyo.' I practise my country-speak before I head downstairs to the kitchen, pick up the cordless and dial the number I've dialed a million times before. Home.

'Dye residence—one of the cows speaking,' a rough voice answers.

'Bert!' I say with a smile. I'd know those rusty old vocal chords anywhere. It's strange to hear him answer the phone and call the house the 'Dye residence', just like he used to. After all, my grandparents have been dead for over two years now.

'Dicey, love. Good to hear your voice. How're things?'

'Great. I've got Titch here with me. And Sally. We thought we might come down for a few weeks.'

'Down here? To Moo?'

'Mmm.'

'Well…knock me down with a feather.'

I pause. 'Would that be OK with you?'

'Of course. It's your house, sweetheart. It's just been a while since I've seen any of you, that's all.'

'I know. You think the cows will mind?'

Bert laughs. 'I'll have a quiet word with them for you.'

'We'll see you in a couple of hours then.'

'Will do.'

I hang up, my smile lingering. Rain, shine, or up to my knees in cowpat, Bert always makes me smile.

I feel a touch guilty that I haven't been down to the farm much over the last few years, but that's partly to do with Bert—I never have to worry about anything while he's keeping an eye on things.

Really, Titch and I should have sold the house, land and livestock years ago, but we can't bear to do it. Not only because it would mean giving up the last tangible pieces of our grandparents, but because Bert would then be out of a job.

There's no way we're going to see that happen to our grandfather's oldest and most trusted friend and farm manager.

Thus, Bert's been looking after the place single-handedly for a while now, living in a converted stable. Titch and I have both tried to persuade him to live in the house, but he says it wouldn't be right. That he wouldn't know what to do with all those rooms and that he'd just break all of Merle's (our grandmother's) 'pretty things'.

My smile fades as I look at the phone and think about my next call. Of course, being me, I've left the hard one till last. JL. I take a deep breath as I dial the number and rest my elbows on the kitchen bench for support.

'Hello?'

'Um, JL? Hi.'

'Dicey. How are you?'

I stand up from my resting spot. 'Fantastic. Fine. Good. OK. Um, I was wondering if I could talk to you about Fergus. I know it's your week to have him, starting tomorrow, but I'm going down to Moo for a while and I thought he'd like to come. If that's OK with you…'

Raff. Fergus looks up again when he hears his name. While I've got his attention, I point to my neck. He suddenly bounces up, turns, and starts to gallop across the tiled floor (rather inelegantly, I might add, feet slipping out from under him with every second step).

'But of course! He loves it there. It will be good for him, with the cows and the beach…'

'Mmm. So, can I drop by and pick up his stainless steel bowl? And his blanket?'

'That would be good with me. Dicey, I was going to phone you today to ask about Titch. You've spoken to her?'

'She's here,' I say quickly, my free hand skittering across

the granite benchtop nervously. 'That's part of the reason we're going down. The sooner the better,' I add, as there's a faint, half-hearted knock on the front door. In my mind's eye I imagine a last lone journalist, slumped on the doorstep. 'I think we're almost ready to leave.'

'Ah. Well, I will see you soon.'

I end the call with a relieved sigh and turn just in time for my reflexes to kick into action and make me step to one side. Fergus, lead in his mouth, comes careering across the floor and hits the kitchen bench. I sigh again.

'You can't use me to stop anymore. You're too big, Fergus. You weigh more than I do.'

Raff.

'Don't you say "only just" to me, dog.' I point my finger.

There's a cough from above and behind me. I whip around to see Titch and Sally at the top of the stairs. Titch is carrying their two bags. Sally's frowning.

'You do actually know you're not having a conversation with him, don't you?'

I pause. 'Um, yes. Of course.' And then I busy myself putting the phone back on its cradle. But really he does talk. You can see what he's saying in his eyes.

When I turn back, Sally's still frowning. 'Girlfriend, you need to get out more.'

I plaster a fake grin across my face. 'So, let's go, then!'

Surprisingly, by the time we poke our four heads around the door, all of the journalists are gone.

'Well, how about that?' Sally says, hopping outside. 'There must be a birthday cake on at the office for morning tea today. Nothing else could make a bunch of journos move so fast. Except free beer, that is. And it's a bit early in the day for that.'

Beside me, I see Titch's eyes lock onto the paper on the front lawn. She starts to move towards it, but I manage to race over and grab the offending article before she even gets halfway.

'Dicey!' She stands back and crosses her arms.

If she were Sally, we'd be rolling around on the grass by now, teeth bared, wrestling for the thing. But not Titch. I go over and drop the toxic item in the recycling bin.

'Believe me,' I tell her. 'I've been there. You're better off not reading it.'

Ten minutes and some arguing later, we've managed to fit all three of our bags, my sewing machine and a whole garbage bag full of material into the boot. Titch only had to sit on everything once to compact it. Brilliant. We've also taken the roof down on the convertible, arranged Sally in the back seat, had three attempts at getting Fergus into the car (he tends to suffer from carsickness) and passed around the old bag of Minties Titch discovered in the glove box.

'Right. We're ready then,' I say. 'Happy back there?' I turn around in the driver's seat to check on Sally and Fergus.

'Yeah, I'm just loving being the Wookie's sidekick,' Sally answers, fighting for space with Fergus, her leg stretched across to his side of the car.

Fergus himself doesn't look too keen—either on being in the car or sharing the back seat, which he usually has entirely to himself. Every so often he eyes Sally's cast.

'Don't even think about standing on it, dog,' she warns him.

Titch turns in her seat to face me. 'Are you OK to drive? You don't look great, and we didn't get much sleep.'

'I feel fine,' I say with a slight shrug. I don't tell her I've pretty much been functioning on less sleep than the four hours I got last night for months now. Or that the bags underneath my eyes aren't exactly a one-off, but more part of my general look these days.

'And don't be sick either.' From behind, Sally continues scolding Fergus.

I ignore the fighting and start backing the car out of the driveway. When we hit the road, I pause for a second to look at both Titch, sitting in the passenger seat, and at Sally behind me. Unknowingly, next to her, Fergus is chewing her cast.

'Well, here goes nothing,' I say with a grimace.

And then we're off.

God help us all.

'Here goes nothing number two.' I take a deep breath as I open the car door. 'For the last time, Fergus, hang on,' I say impatiently as his feet scramble against the back of my seat. He's been itching to get out ever since we pulled into JL's street. 'Fergus!'

Too late. He's made his own way out of the car (jumping over Sally and landing ungracefully on the bitumen). A car traveling down the street slows as the driver sees him, and Fergus panics, his eyes moving back and forth from JL's house to the moving vehicle.

'Fergus, sit!' I say, in my best 'you'd really better listen to me this time' voice.

It doesn't work. The car comes to a stop and Fergus pads across slowly to the other side of the road, the call of JL just too strong.

'Sorry!' I wave at the guy in the car and run across the road in front of him as well. 'He does know better. Really.'

'No worries,' he replies, leaning out of the driver's side window. 'Hey, is that a wolf?'

I pause halfway across the road and shake my head. 'No. Irish Wolfhound.'

'Oh, right.' He nods.

What is it with the wolf thing? What would these people do if I said yes?

The guy takes off, and when I reach the footpath I sigh and lift up Fergus's head, with one hand under his chin so he's looking at me. 'Cars bad—remember?'

His expression is sufficiently guilty, and I know he knows he shouldn't have crossed the road. Still, it kind of makes me wonder who would have come off worse if he was actually hit—Fergus or the car. I wouldn't know where to place my bet. I hold onto his collar now and look back across the road.

'You guys coming in?' I call out to Sally and Titch. They both shake their heads.

'Wouldn't want to cramp your style, babe. You're on your own,' Sally yells back.

But I'm not on my own, because Fergus is already dragging me across JL's yard, his excitement building. As we make our way up the paint-peeled front steps, I wonder for a moment how JL is going moneywise. He hasn't asked for any, and I haven't noticed any moving out of our joint bank account. His part-time work at one of the local cafés is probably enough to cover his rent and food, but I'm guessing only just.

As I reach the green front door of his tiny worker's cottage I hesitate before reaching for the knocker, trying to decide whether or not we should talk about this now—the money thing. In the end I'm saved from making a decision as Fergus distracts me by starting to butt his head against the bottom of the door itself.

'Brain damage here we come,' I say, and eventually give up trying to pull him back and simply stand back and watch him.

He keeps right on at it until JL opens up. When this happens, Fergus is mid-butt. Consequently he tumbles inside, hits JL and they end up entwined on the floor, with Fergus making his usual ecstatic 'It's JL! It's JL!' noises.

As for me, I step inside calmly, close the door and lean against the wall, waiting for their love-in to end. However, this doesn't happen before boredom sets in.

'Oh, for God's sake, Fergus.' I go over and wrestle him off JL. 'You'll smother him.' With a final tug, I manage to pull him away. 'Remember, humans aren't nearly so much fun after you've killed them.'

JL sits up. 'Hello, Dicey.' He looks straight at me and instantly I feel uncomfortable. My eyes dart away from his to stare at the floor.

'Um, hi.' I reach over to give him a hand up.

'Thank you.'

'You're, um, welcome.' I pretend to be fascinated by his old navy cotton shirt as he gets up, his hand grasping mine.

Fergus wrestles out of my grasp and goes over to rub himself rapturously all over JL again.

'Look at that, will you? You know, you should keep him. All the time.'

JL shakes his head. 'He is your dog.'

'Someone should tell *him* that. In his mind I'm just the sucker who feeds him.'

JL bends down to Fergus's height and says something to

him in French. I've learned a little over the years I've spent with JL, and now I catch something about obeying and mother. Fergus watches him wide-eyed and intently—as if he's taking every word in. Sometimes that dog makes me sick. *Raff,* he says obediently at the end of JL's speech.

'He says he will try harder.' JL looks up with a smile, and I have to look away again at the floor.

Even now we understand each other where Fergus is concerned. His likes and dislikes, his funny little mannerisms. It's strange that some things between us haven't changed. I guess however we feel about each other, Fergus will always be Fergus. He'll still turn around three times, lie down, get up, turn around another three times, then once clockwise, before he's ready to go to sleep. Some things just are.

'Um, I've been meaning to ask…I mean, how's work?' I try to bring up the topic of money, which I'd been thinking about before, and fail miserably.

'Work is good.' JL looks surprised that I'm asking.

'Because, um…' I start off down the hallway towards the kitchen, still talking, but have only taken a few steps when JL jumps up and runs over to take my elbow. He turns me around.

'Er, Dicey…'

But it's too late.

'Dicey—hi!' The jolly blonde giant appears at the end of the hallway.

Oh, great. As if my life couldn't get any worse.

'How are you? Good, I hope?' she continues, in that sickeningly soft and sensual accent of hers. I'm sure she puts it on. I meet her eyes to see if she's taking the piss, but she's not.

'Fine, thanks.' I try not to sound as surly as I feel. Standing opposite her, I give her the once-over, unable to help myself. Today, as per usual, she's sporting her 'I was born with perfectly straight hair' long blonde bob. Her 'I only use soap' translucent skin needs just a dusting of powder to look made up, and her 'oh, this old thing? I've had it for years' outfit consists of midnight-blue bootcut jeans, beautifully polished black kitten-heeled boots and the most exquisite cream-coloured suede jacket I've ever seen.

I'm wearing black hipster yoga pants, a white shirt JL left behind, a black fitted woolen vest, black mules and, of all things, an old grey Gap cap that Fergus likes to chew.

I glance over at JL, who's looking worried. Like I might bite at any second.

Well, I guess he has cause for concern.

Raff! Fergus abandons JL and runs straight to the other woman in his life.

'Hello, darling!' she says, and gives him a tiny pat on the head, as if he's a Chihuahua rather than a hulking great beast of a dog. Fergus doesn't seem to mind, however, and leans against her, staring up adoringly. Traitor.

Definitely, *definitely* time to leave. 'I just need Fergus's stainless steel bowl? And his blanket?' I get down to business, finally meeting JL's eyes for a second.

'Of course.' He starts for the kitchen and I follow him, passing Ms 'I went for a run with my personal trainer at five a.m.' as I go and giving her a quick, forced smile.

Unfortunately, she hurries in after us and goes to sit at the table. Interestingly enough, she's right in front of a bottle of champagne and what looks like a whole lot of paperwork.

'We were just about to have a little celebration.' She pronounces the word 'little' as 'leetle'.

My eyes widen as I stand in the doorway. 'Really?'

'Ah, er…' JL interrupts and races over to hand me Fergus's folded red blanket. His stainless steel bowl is sitting on top.

I tuck the items under my left arm and lean in closer to him so his guest can't hear. 'Divorce papers, perhaps?' I say, one eyebrow raised.

He pulls back in shock. 'Dicey…' He reaches out for my arm, but I've already taken a step back and am heading as fast as I can for the front door.

'Fergus—let's go.' I slap my thigh twice as I go.

JL follows close behind.

It feels like for ever before my hand clasps the doorknob. I've just started to pull the door open when I realise Fergus hasn't materialised. I turn and look back down the hallway. Only JL is there.

'Fergus!' I call again, moving my head to look past him.

'Dicey, it's not what you are thinking,' JL says, his voice lowered. He takes a step towards me.

God, I just want to get out of here. My eyes jump from object to object in the hall. The walls, the floor, the ceiling. *Don't say anything else,* I plead with myself. *Don't say anything else.* The thing is, sometimes my mouth…well, let's just say it comes out with things my brain regrets later.

'Dicey…'

Where's that damn dog?

I shrug. 'Look, it's none of my business.' *Come on, come on, come on.* With a frustrated snort, I start back towards the kitchen again, shrinking away from JL's reach as I pass him. Bloody Europeans, I think. They're so touchy-feely.

I go back into the kitchen, keeping my eyes on the cracked lino, grab Fergus by the collar (of course he's still attached to his new best friend's side), and pull with all my might.

'You know what your problem is, dog?' I hiss at him under

my breath as we go. 'You've got no *loyalty*.' And maybe he understands this much, or at least my tone, because after I say this he stops tugging and lets me lead him.

'Dicey—' JL begins as we pass by.

My hand is on the brass doorknob again. I momentarily forget my vow of silence and go to say something scathing, but the words tangle in my throat. 'It's OK, JL,' I say, looking back at him. 'I shouldn't have been here. That's all.'

I walk back to the car slowly, trying to calm myself down.
I hate seeing JL. Hate it. Dealing with him on the phone isn't
so bad, but every time I see him in person I just want to
scream at him.

I want to scream the questions—'Why?' and 'How long?'
and the even more shameful, 'Do you love her?' But I can't.
I just can't. Because why shouldn't he scream the same kind
of questions straight back at me?

My fingers tighten around Fergus's bowl as I think about
it. About how I can't expect him to have any good answers.
After all, I don't have any myself about what went on with
Simon. But, still, there's no denying it's weird. Weird to be separated from your husband without any fuss. Without any discussion, or demanding of answers, let alone any screaming.

The worst thing is how OK JL seems with it all. How civil
he's being. There's no screaming going on in his head. It's as

if he expected this from me all along—expected me to take the 'we don't need to talk about this because it's not really important' emotionally constipated way out of our lives together. Out of our marriage. It's this that confuses me more than anything. Because if that's what he expected, why were we ever together in the first place?

Fergus must sense my need to double my daily dose of executive stress B vitamins, because when I pull my seat forward he slinks into the car silently, without any fuss. But it's a little late for good behaviour now.

'No mini Wagon Wheel for you today,' I say to him as I get into the car myself.

'Uh-oh,' Sally pipes up from beside my mangy mutt. 'I smell the disgusting odour of vanilla.'

I turn around and look at her, surprised. The FC always wears a gaggingly sweet vanilla-based perfume. Her one fault. I mean, really, someone needs to tell her it's not always a good thing to smell like custard.

'Well, that and the look on both your faces kind of gives it away.'

I stick the key in the ignition and start the car. 'No mini Wagon Wheel for you either.' I give her a look.

'Oh! She *was* there, wasn't she? I knew it...'

I drive, not really wanting to talk about it. About her. The FC. That's my nickname for her—the FC. The French Canadian. Juvenile, I know, but I just can't help myself. She's tall and blonde and waif-like, and comes complete with melted chocolate dinner-plate-sized brown eyes that instantly remind you of a sweet little fawn lost in the forest.

Sally keeps demanding I explain how I know what the eyes of a sweet little fawn lost in the forest look like, considering I'm Australian and we don't have fawns on every corner. Or deer, for that matter. I have to admit I'm guessing. But it sounds far more poetic than 'eyes like a sweet little frilly-necked lizard squashed by the side of the road'—don't you think?

I take heart in the fact that she's only B-grade French. I mean, French Canadian—it's hardly the Left Bank, is it? Still, it does mean that along with the height, hair and sweet scent, she also has a killer accent and a name to die for. Aimee. Not Amy. No, no, no…Aimee.

Bitch.

Every time JL pronounces that name, perfectly, a little piece of my soul turns black, withers and dies.

I take the entrance onto the freeway too fast, remembering the other things Sally has said about the FC all too clearly. And about me. Especially about how I was a complete idiot to let a tall, dark and handsome man with a French accent out of my line of sight for more than thirty seconds. Even though, yes, she knows he's actually Swiss. But his mother's French, and everyone knows Frenchness is handed down from the mother's side, and they speak French at home, so it's practically the same thing, and now he's found a French Canadian there's nothing stopping them mating and continuing the accented line.

Sheesh. I try not to think about all of this too much. Especially the last bit—the mating bit. Every time Sally reminds me of this I recall that sweet little fawn lost in the forest and my thoughts stray to the official start of the hunting season.

Eventually, I ungrit my teeth enough to share, 'She had a bottle of champagne and some paperwork. Apparently they were having a "leetle celebration".'

There's silence in the back seat.

'I suggested to JL that they were divorce papers and he practically shat himself.'

Titch gasps at my words. 'Dicey, you didn't! That's not nice!'

No, it's not. But right now I don't care. One day my sister will probably discover I'm just a 'not nice' kind of person, and disown me once and for all.

'They can't be divorce papers,' Sally pipes up matter-of-factly. 'You haven't been separated long enough.'

I roll my eyes. Trust Sally to know the ins and outs of this kind of thing. 'Gee, that makes me feel better.' I glance at her in the rear-vision mirror.

'I'm here to help.' She grins.

'So what *were* the papers?' Titch asks.

I shrug. 'Maybe something to do with their writers' group?' That's how JL and the FC met. Through their writers' group.

'Writers' group, my arse,' Sally belts out.

'Oh, please. Not this again,' I say.

I've tried to convince her a million times that there really is a writers' group. A serious writers' group. And that I've seen it with my own eyes. That I've seen all the members and even spoken to some of them. Still Sally refuses to believe me. She seems to think JL picked the FC up somewhere. At a bar, or a café, or online, or maybe hanging out at the local baguette shop. Who knows?

'I did warn you,' she continues.

Here we go…

'About what?' Titch takes the bait.

'Well, come on. You don't let a man with a French accent out of your sight for more than fifteen seconds. It's asking for trouble. And now he's found a French accent to match. I don't know. I think you really stuffed up this time, Dice. You've surpassed yourself.'

'Why don't you tell me what you really think?' I throw
her a look.

'I always do, darling.'

Silence.

'Just leave her alone, Sally.' Titch turns around for a second. 'Here. Choose a CD.' She passes her back the case.

'Ooohhh! I love picking the CD!' Sally instantly forgets
all about what she was saying.

I want to throw Titch a 'thank you' glance, but my eyes
are glued to the road and I start to repeat my 'I don't want
to think about it; I won't think about it' mantra, which I
seem to have been using frequently lately. However, I only
make it through a few repetitions before Sally's fingers start
to slow in their rifling through the CDs. Soon enough, they
stop altogether.

My hands tense on the wheel, waiting.

'Still, at least you both stuffed up,' she muses. 'That's something to be grateful for. You with Simon and JL with the FC.
The guilt cancels out that way.'

'Sally!' Titch roars, and she turns around fully in her seat.
Titch never roars.

'Sorry,' she says meekly, and goes back to her rifling.

'Put the Bangles on,' I bark, my eyes still glued to the road.
I'm suddenly furious—not just with Sally, but at Titch's moment of weakness that's led to the four of us being in the
car together at all. 'I need some sisterhood, and I'm certainly
not getting any at the moment.'

Silently, *Different Light* is passed over to me from the back
seat. I shove it hard into the CD player and put my foot down
on the accelerator.

After approximately fifteen minutes—or three tracks of 'sisterhood'—Sally and I start to bicker again. Mainly over which CD to play.

This continues all the long way down the coast. CDs go into the player, and CDs come out. Every so often Sally quits bickering to yell, 'Fergus!' and then something along the lines of, 'Oh, my God, what are you feeding that dog?' Each time, I try to look innocent. I neglect to tell her about the leftover beef vindaloo he helped himself to a few nights ago, and how I won't be letting him do that ever again.

Before long, we turn right and start to head inland. I start to relax as we travel up and through the hills. The landscape starts to get greener and more lush, the houses become further apart, separated by steps of banana trees and fields of cows. Honesty boxes start to pop up—five mangos for a dollar, a bag of tomatoes for two dollars, huge jars of honey on the comb for two dollars fifty. The rust-red dirt lifts up an earthy, wet, just-rained smell…

'Fergus!' Sally screeches from the back seat.

Well, OK, an earthy, wet, just-rained beef vindaloo smell.

Finally, *finally,* we get to Moo. We drive over Quint's Bridge, over the railway track, turn left and there we are. On the main drag. This is it. Cow Mecca.

It's strange how I always forget just how weird Moo is when I'm not there. It's only when I make that left turn that it comes back to me.

Moo really is, um…weird.

A town that makes no sense.

Because Moo is kind of a car crash on the freeway of towns. It's smack bang in the middle, stuck between the coast and its cashed-up yuppies, the hills with its hippies, and the land with its farmers. Moo brings them all together in a black-and-white splodgy mess. And usually, despite their differences, they all get along OK.

We've only zipped past the Moo name sign, a few black-and-white-painted telephone poles and a matching Friesian electricity box when, for some reason, my stomach tenses and I feel the urge to pull the car over to the grassy verge beside the road and turn the engine off. I sit for a second, and then let my eyes travel all the way up the road before I turn to look all the way back down the other end.

There is not a person in sight. A lone cow, however, runs over to the fence bordering the opposite side of the road and moos, its eyes suddenly wide, sensing there's something big going down that everyone needs to be alerted to—three new people and a dog in town.

Whoopee.

My face, I think, as I glance at it in the rear-vision mirror, looks frozen in horror, with the questions I'm asking myself written all over it. What am I doing here? Why did I think coming back to Moo was any kind of an idea? Slowly I move my gaze over to Titch, and then, after that, back to Sally. No one says anything, and I note their faces look exactly the same as mine. Only Fergus is smiling as he checks out the cow and starts to scratch eagerly on the back of Titch's seat. A new friend! Heaps of new friends! He starts to scratch harder as the whole herd begins to make its way over to see the show that's come to town.

When I can't bear the silence or the scratching any longer, I get out of the car, pull my seat forward and let Fergus jump out. He runs straight across the bitumen and over to the cow, where he starts to vie for the grass she's eating, gulping it down in great chunks. He'll be sick in approximately fifteen minutes. I know I should yell at him for running across the road, but frankly I don't have the energy. Instead, I close the car door without looking back, take a few steps forward into the middle of the road and just stand.

I stand there, without even listening for a car, for what feels like for ever. I am on a highway. A *highway*. And I'm not checking for vehicles. I'm no better than my idiot dog. I could be killed at any moment.

If anyone ever drove down here.

Eventually, behind me, I hear a car door open, and Titch comes to stand beside me. A few seconds later Sally hobbles up as well.

'Depressing, isn't it?' her voice booms. 'I always thought when we came back there'd be a ticker-tape parade and streets named after us.'

I look over at her blankly. I'd forgotten how different her voice sounds down here—like it's echoing off the hills.

Fergus turns around and howls, making me jump, but when he finishes all is silent again. The three of us stand in the middle of the highway, looking for all the world like a scene from a bad spaghetti western. In my head I laugh hysterically at this, thinking that at any moment a tumbleweed will roll down the road and some music will sound overhead—*Da, da, daaaaa…* Except that it won't. Because that, of course, would mean the inevitable epic battle between good and evil, a bit of excitement with some horses and guns and a wardrobe of dapper clothes.

Things like that don't happen in Moo.

Sally's right. Depressing is the word. Because all I can think about, all that keeps circling round and round in my head, is that I've failed. I've failed and come full circle. From Moo—to Moo.

I turn around and look at Sally and Titch. 'Can you guys give me a minute?' I ask. 'I just want to run up to the bridge.'

'Sure,' Titch says, looking at me strangely, and she bites her lip for a second before she continues speaking. 'Dicey, I hate to ask again, but are you OK?'

I nod. 'I'm fine! Really, I'm fine. I won't be long,' I say, hurrying off, trying to outrun my claustrophobia and telling myself it's OK to be back. It's OK. At least there'd been some kind of a life in between for me. Some people never got out of Moo in the first place.

I half run all the way to the wooden bridge, where I grab onto the top railing and swing my legs out in front of me, landing my butt on the bridge itself and ending up with my legs dangling down below. Just like the old days. The river gurgles away below, like it always has. Breathe, Dicey, breathe, I tell myself, not being able to quite grasp why hitting *chez* Moo is affecting me the way it is this time around. Old memories, I guess. Memories that for the past few weeks I've been trying to deny, to push down the back of the sofa and forget about. Memories about the last few years. About my business. My business that is now all in the past.

It all started with a trip to one of Moo's neighbouring towns. To a fabric remnant shop housed in an old church. It was great, that place. A dusty old church filled to the brim with rolls of fabric no one really wanted and tubes of buttons dating from the fifties onwards. I'd finished high school the year before, done a year at the local community college learning how to manage businesses (not that we really had any in Moo to manage), and was working as a part-time waitress at the Moo Inn—the local café. I was broke and, with plenty of spare time on my hands, decided to make everyone pyjamas for Christmas for some reason or another. I think maybe I found a pattern in an old women's magazine at the doctor's office and ripped it out as quietly as I could.

Anyway, it was right up at the back of the old church that I found it—rolls and rolls and rolls of black-and-white cowprint flannel. It had been there so long that the dust was centimetres thick on the top of each roll and, if I remember correctly, it was marked down to around about nothing. I laughed when I saw it. Over the past few years our town had been trying to cash in on its cowlike name to attract tourists, and had been slowly painting everything that didn't move (and some things that did, like the town's one taxi) black and white. I stood there, in front of that fabric, and thought, What a scream! I'll make Moo pyjamas. Everyone will get a laugh out of that.

So I bought a roll. Enough to make a pair of pyjamas for Titch, Sally, my grandfather and even myself. Nan I splashed out on, and went next door to the chemist to pick up a violet talc, soap and perfume set. Nan was never going to wear pyjamas. Hell, Nan still wore the candy-pink bedjacket she'd bought to wear in hospital when she gave birth to my mother. Novelty pyjamas probably weren't what she was looking for in a gift.

Over the next few weeks I sewed my spare hours away. As it turned out I had enough material and time left over to make little padded slippers, eye masks, complete with closed pink satin eyelids and embroidered eyelashes, and, as a whimsical afterthought on Christmas Eve (OK, so I might have had a little recreational smoke with Sally before this), I added a tiny fringed tail to the behind of each pair.

The pyjamas were the hit of Christmas. Nan even felt left out, so I spent Boxing Day making her an eye mask and slipper set as well.

Within a week news got around about my bovine fashion creations, and I had orders for five pairs. Hildy, a local who ran a tiny craft shop and Devonshire Tea business out of her home, even called around to see my wares and ask if I wanted to sell some through her.

Soon enough, I was back at the old church. I took all ten rolls of cow-print flannel off their hands for $199.50 (I drive a hard bargain), and sewed until I practically lost my eyesight.

It was Hildy who convinced me I should reach for the stars and try my luck at the markets in Byron Bay. After all, it was summer, the tourists were plentiful and cashed up, and the yuppies loved the kind of product no one else back home would have. I wasn't sure I had enough time to sew. I wasn't sure if the markets were for me. I wasn't sure about anything much, but then Hildy asked me if I really wanted to work part-time at the Moo Inn for the rest of my life and I became sure about a lot of things quick-smart.

She helped me change my product a little, so that the pyjamas, slippers and eye mask were all encased in a matching drawstring bag. I sewed until my fingers were actually bruised, and within two weeks we were at the markets in the thirty-two-degree heat.

I couldn't imagine why anyone would want to buy flannel pyjamas in thirty-two-degree heat.

But they did.

I had thirty-five sets to sell—four extra small, eight small, fifteen medium and eight large. At eight-thirty we priced them at $75 a set; at eighty forty-five we priced them at $95 a set, at five past nine we priced them at $120 a set. At ten-fifteen, we had sold out.

At ten-fifteen and twelve seconds I slumped down behind the stall in shock. I had made $3730 in less than two hours, for the princely outlay of $200 and a week and a half of convictlike hard labour. Hildy, grinning like a maniac, came and sat down beside me with the cash box.

'The yuppies. You never can guess what'll take their fancy.' She shook her head in wonder. 'It was the tail, you know.' She nodded at me. 'They couldn't get enough of the tail.'

As I looked at her, the thought flashed into my mind that I should seriously consider moving further up the drug hierarchy. It had seemed to work for the Beatles, after all. If I'd come up with the tail on dope, imagine what I could do on LSD? Hooves? A neck bell? A co-ordinating feedbag for the yuppie on the go?

Hildy and I packed up after this and headed out of the heat. I tried to pay her for helping me out, and for working on the stall, but she wouldn't have a bar of it. In the end I took her out for a slap-up seafood lunch.

The next day I resigned from my job at the Moo Inn and

Hildy and I got down to business. Within the month I'd hired two girls from my old home economics class to sew for me. Boutiques in the area started ringing and asking if I could sell some of my stock through them, and all four of us were sewing like crazy in between sourcing any kind of cow-print fabric we could get our hands on.

Another month after that and things were still hectic. The school holidays were ending soon, and we were trying to make the most of the last-minute holiday boom before things quietened down until Easter. On a whim, one day one of the girls made a then-teenaged Fergus a pair of pyjamas from a bunch of remnants.

It was the day that we took him to the markets at Byron Bay, dressed up to the (ca)nines, that it happened.

Fergus had been trawling the crowded market all morning, hamming it up, looking for attention and leading people back to the stall (for which he received a reward). It must have been around mid-morning that he dragged her up, alternately pulling on the front hem of her skirt and then running around to nudge her backside. I watched his antics from across the other side of the market, all the way to our stall. Even from far away I could see she didn't fit in there. Not even with the yuppies. She was a class above the yuppies. The sort of thing yuppies aspired to be. She had some kind of a black linen loose top and skirt on, huge black Jackie-O type sunglasses and perfectly smooth honey-blonde hair peeping out from underneath a gigantic black hat.

With one sweeping look at her, I wrenched my price list off the front of the table and mentally doubled all my figures. Finally Fergus reached his destination, sat down, now ignoring the woman beside him, and waited for his mini Wagon Wheel.

'Hi!' I said to the woman as I unwrapped the chocolate and flicked it at him.

She watched as he snapped it up and swallowed it without chewing.

'That's quite a dog you've got there.'

American. The Australian dollar was low. Trying not to scrunch up my face at the maths, I tripled my prices. I didn't feel too bad about it. After all, the price of one pair of pyjamas, even tripled, was probably less than she'd pay for a two-course business lunch special in New York.

'And what are we selling here? Pyjamas?'

'Yep. Pyjamas. Pyjamas from Moo. You probably drove through on the way from the airport. It's very, um, cowlike.'

The eyebrows rose a fraction at this. 'Ah, yes. The black-and-white town. I wondered about that.'

'Would you like to see a pair?'

I grabbed a pair of small-sized pyjamas from underneath the stall. I couldn't exactly see her wearing a garment that included a tail to bed, but, hey, you never knew what people were really like beneath their façades. Maybe she'd once let that smooth brow of hers furrow for a few minutes and pushed out a child? I passed her the set and, surprised, stood back in wonder as she whipped it out of its drawstring bag in an instant and started to inspect each item, bringing the pieces up only centimetres from her face.

'The fabric's good quality,' she said after a while, turning the pants inside out and running a finger over the stitching. 'These are well made.' She glanced up for long enough to look me over.

'Um—thanks.'

She was about to say something else when a matching

black-outfitted red-haired woman came over to stand beside her. Suddenly her whole demeanour changed.

'Look, darling. Little cow pyjamas from the little Moo town we passed through.'

The other woman took the pyjamas from her and went through a similar inspection routine as Fergus and I looked on. Eventually she placed them back on the table.

'What do you think, Candace?' the first woman said to her when she was done. (As for Candace herself, I don't think she ever once looked at me.)

She nodded slowly. 'Maybe. Maybe.'

Maybe? Maybe what?

'Right, then.' First woman snapped to attention and turned to me. 'We'll take one in each size and a pair of the doggie ones.'

Raff. Fergus looked up at her.

'Sorry, the dog ones are a sample. And he says they're not for sale.'

She paused for a second, as if she was thinking of chucking in the whole thing, but then made her decision and continued. 'Fine. One in each size, then.' She opened her cherry-red leather chequebook.

I didn't take cheques.

Until now.

'How much is that?' She glanced up, matching pen poised.

'For four pairs?' Four pairs at triple the price, that was... Ouch! $1440! A little bit steep. I took myself back down to double. '$960.'

To her credit, she didn't even bat an eye-lifted eyelid. 'That sounds fair.' She nodded and leant back down.

Was she serious?

'I like to keep the punters happy,' I said, practically drooling as she wrote out the cheque. She was a left-hander, and as she wrote I stared, my eyes mesmerised by the glow of her boulderlike, probably from Tiffany's on Fifth Avenue, solitaire diamond ring. With the last flourish of her signature I woke up to myself and started stuffing the pyjamas into the largest screen-printed black-and-white canvas bag I had (the town's hippies tended to hassle you if you used anything easy and plastic).

'Nice doing business with you.' I grinned as I handed the bag over to her and she passed me the cheque.

'Yes,' she said as she took it from me. 'Do you have a card?'

'It's printed on the bag.'

She turned the bag around to see. '*Moo to You*. Adorable. I should give you mine.' As if from nowhere (maybe she kept them up her sleeve?), a card appeared in her hand and she passed it to me.

'Thanks,' I said.

And then the two of them were gone.

Raff, Fergus said.

'You're right. That was a bit weird,' I answered him. 'But it'll keep you in mini Wagon Wheels for a couple of years, so I wouldn't complain.'

It was only after I'd fed him another one that I looked at the card properly. A name, her title. And her company…

Vogue.

She was from *Vogue.*

If I'd known that, and where her five-minute visit to my stall was about to take me, I would have given her the pyjamas as well as the promise of my firstborn child for nothing.

I get a few weird looks for my lengthy absence when I stroll back over to the car. 'All done,' I say breezily, trying to avoid any questions, and thankfully I don't get any. We pile back in, I start the car and, quite unnecessarily, check over my shoulder and indicate.

The cows watch us and give forlorn 'moos' as we pull out.

It's as I negotiate the car up the last steep hill, which will lead us over and into town proper, that I suddenly realise what made me stop and pull over before. I'm petrified. Petrified that things will be the same. Or different. That everything will have changed. Or nothing will have changed at all. It's been almost a year since I've been back to Moo. God knows what's gone on here since then.

I hold my breath as we reach the crest of the hill, not knowing what I'm going to see on the other side. And it's then that, as one, Sally and Titch raise their arms above their heads and ride the hill like it's a rollercoaster. I'd forgotten about how we used to do that. And, with a laugh, I exhale and take us down into town.

The closer we get to the Moo version of civilisation, the slower I go. By the time we pass the dusty feed shop and the tiny federation-style post office I'm only doing around forty kmph—although legally this road is still classed as a highway and I could zip past at a hundred if I wanted to. Beside the post office, the grocery store is dead for a Saturday early afternoon. The Moo Inn seems a little more active—with, I notice, a fresh coat of paint and a new attraction. It's one of those kitsch boards where tourists can stick their heads in the back and have their photo taken. This one is situated outside the alleyway that leads to the toilets, and has four cows painted on the front (Mr Moo, Mrs Moo and two kiddies Moo). A word bubble proclaims 'We did a wee-wee at the Moo Moo!'

'Classy.' Sally whistles as we pass by.

There's a gap between shops, then four or five old wooden houses which our eyes skip over and then move on to the next attraction. Because there, further down the road, is the pub.

Several concrete benches line the awning-covered footpath outside, with three or four people at each one, enjoying their Saturday afternoon beer. As we get closer I notice the bar seems pretty busy as well. I can see the dark outlined forms of people inside, and, lining the window so they can see out, people are seated on pretty much all of the high-backed stools. I get the same stomach-clenching feeling that I had only minutes before, and my foot automatically presses down a bit harder on the accelerator.

'Oh, no, you don't.' Sally reaches forward and places a firm hand on my shoulder until I slow back down again. In fact, her nails dig in until the speed drops to even slower than we were travelling before.

Titch turns around to look at her. 'Sally, you're not going to…?'

I watch in the rear-vision mirror as Sally rolls her eyes dramatically. 'Do I look like I'm in any state to do that today? Anyway, I only ever did it once, and I was *drunk.*'

Titch gives a 'you never know when Sally's in Moo' shrug, but doesn't turn back around. I take one last glance at the road (still, of course, car-free), slow down even further, and then glue my eyes to the rear vision mirror, not wanting to miss the show—whatever it's going to be. After all, she may not be drunk today, but she's *drugged.*

'Fergus—paw, please…' Sally says formally, extending one hand to him.

Sitting next to Sally, minding his own business, Fergus swivels to eye her, unsure. I don't blame him. They've had a rocky relationship at best up until now, and he probably thinks she's going to cut off said paw and sell it as a good luck charm from an oversized rabbit. *Raff,* he says. Which in this case means, *I don't think so, lady.*

We're almost in front of the pub now, and Sally huffs impatiently, realising she's losing time. 'For God's sake, dog, get over here.' She grabs him in a large bear hug, pulling him against her like some overly hairy boyfriend, then takes his front right paw, lifting it up. What is she doing? 'Now, smile for the crowd.' She begins to wave his paw slowly in a wide arc, from left to right, right to left, a bright, fixed smile on her face.

The royal wave.

Outside the pub, the patrons gawk, their beers stuck in various positions in mid-air.

Solemn-faced, beside me, Titch starts to wave too. Slowly and steadily in the same wide arc. Left to right, right to left.

As for me, I drive with all the dignity I can muster, my hands in a perfect 'ten to two' position on the wheel, back straight, cap jaunty. A 'my father was a driver, my father's father was a driver, and his father was a driver before him' kind of look.

By the time we reach the other end of the pub everyone has poked their heads either out of a window or door to see the show.

'Now what?' I say between my jaw-clenched teeth (for that chiseled, handsome driver expression).

'Right. Now, pause…' I hear Sally say from behind me.

I stop the car for a second.

'…finish the wave, Fergus…and *floor it!*' she yells.

And I do.

We laugh hysterically pretty much all the way up the last few hills to Nan and Pop's place.

'What do you give it? Five minutes before everyone knows we're in town?' I ask Sally and Titch when we've calmed down a bit.

Titch eyes me incredulously. 'What are you talking about?'

Sally wiggles forward in her seat. 'Yeah. You're in Moo, remember? That *was* everyone.'

'Ah, true.' I nod as I pass the old steel milk churn that serves as the Dye letterbox and turn left into the farm's mustard-coloured dirt driveway. We pass under the thick glossy canopy of mango trees, and then suddenly there it is. Nan and Pop's little white wooden house.

For a moment the relief in the car is almost tangible. Until it's broken by Fergus, who begins to scratch at the back of Titch's seat, excited about seeing Nan and Pop. He always forgets they're gone, poor lamb. I steer the car around to the back of the house, pull up, and Titch jumps out to let Fergus alight and bound around like a mad thing. I help Sally out of the car and the three of us come around the front to rest our behinds on the bonnet and take in the sweeping scenery.

It really is the best view in town.

The Dyes have lived in this area for just over a hundred years. They came to log and stayed to farm. As my eyes travel across the countryside I don't blame them for not going back whence they came. Spread out in front of me is a dairy farmer's dream—acres and acres of greener than green grass, rolling gently over perfectly curved hills. It looks more like the English countryside than rural Australia, but rural Australia it is (the cow's accents always give it away).

'Smell that.' Sally takes a deep breath in.

'Grass,' Titch says.

'Cows,' I add.

'Weird.' Sally makes a face.

'What's weird?'

'I'd almost forgotten that smell. But now…it's like it just slapped me in the face.'

'How long since you've been back?'

Her eyes scrunch up as she counts back. 'Not since the funerals.'

'Two years,' Titch and I say together.

We stand in silence then, each thinking our own thoughts. And after a while, as I listen to the leaves rustle in the breeze, the occasional cow mooing in the distance, I begin to think to myself that maybe it won't be so bad to be here—in Moo.

When I start to get chilly, standing in the shade, I push myself off the bonnet. 'Let's go inside.'

We leave the keys in the ignition and our bags in the car without a second thought and head across the short expanse of lawn to climb the five thick and wide wooden stairs.

On the third stair Titch pauses and looks up at the exterior walls.

'What's wrong?' I ask. She looks anxious.

'The house needs painting.'

I glance past Sally, who's thumping up the steps beside me, to see that spots of paint are peeling off the exterior of the house like a bad sunburn.

'We've got to get it painted. Nan and Pop wouldn't like it,' she says quickly.

I take my sister's arm. 'It's OK. We'll get it painted. I'll ask Bert about it.'

Sally's already crossed the shady verandah and is standing waiting by the door. I go to tell her it's unlocked, but she speaks first.

'After you,' she says, and I realise she's thinking it's important that Titch and I enter first.

It's me who turns the knob on the door and pushes it open. For some stupid reason the thought flits through my head that the first thing I'll see is a scene of dustsheets thrown over furniture and cobwebs hanging from the ceiling. But of course I don't. And I'd bloody well hope not too, because Titch and I have been paying for a cleaner to come in monthly and keep the place like Nan would have wanted it to be kept.

So, no, I'm not presented with dustsheets and cobwebs. What I'm presented with is…

…a time warp.

In keeping with my feeling of hesitancy, the temperature drops a good few degrees as I step inside the house onto the cool black-and-white checkered lino. I start down the hall-way at a snail's pace and come to the lounge room, my mouth hanging ever so slightly open. Everything about this house makes my heart's frantic city-style beating slow down—the clashing items, the collection of royal cups and saucers, the milk jug with its crocheted cover, the old wooden radio. Everything about this house comforts me.

I keep going, passing the blue guest room on my right. The wall begins on my left then, and instinctively I stick my hand out, like I've always done, and run my fingers over the cream-coloured vertical joins that run all the way down till we get to the kitchen.

The kitchen.

I pause, my hand still resting on the wall, and peep slowly around the corner. It's this bit that always makes me sad. Because the kitchen was Nan's territory. Women only. And even now it's hard to believe that a plate of her home-made peanut biscuits and special 'welcome home' Monte-Carlos, complete with a room temperature glass of fruit cup cordial won't be waiting on the table for me. For all three of us.

'That smell…' Titch pipes up from behind me, and I jump.

I sniff. She's right. The place smells… Well, all wrong. It should smell like baking. Baking mixed with Nan's lavender-scented furniture polish. But it doesn't. Instead it smells like lemon toilet cleaner. Cheap lemon toilet cleaner and bleach.

'I'll open the windows,' she adds, and as I watch her go I think how strange it is that we're smelling everything more acutely today.

'Do you think Bert's here?' Sally asks as Titch moves around the house opening windows.

'He must be busy with the cows. Or out. He would've

come in if he'd seen us.' My eyes, still searching the kitchen for something, move over the fifties-style formica table and matching chairs and come to rest on the stove. Tea. Tea made with tank water. The best sort of tea in the world. 'Tea?' I turn to Sally.

'I thought you'd never ask,' she sighs.

I don't have to ask Titch. I know she'll be dying for a cup.

We take our tea out onto the verandah and squish into the three-seater swing chair. It's a gorgeous day—blue skies, a few fluffy white high clouds and a gentle breeze. The three of us sit in companionable silence, finish our tea, and then decide we'll all have a second cup. I even find us an old tin of shortbread in the pantry. It's well out of date, but seems OK.

We're onto our third cups and fourth, only slightly stale, biscuits when Bert's ute drives around the right side of the house. All three of us spring up, Sally spilling tea on her shirt as she hops around.

'Bert!' we say, as one.

With a lurch, the ute stops and Bert jumps out, Fergus appearing after him. Eight years old again, I clap my hands and run down the steps to give my old friend a hug. He feels exactly the same—sun-bleached thick cotton shirt and jeans that have been washed a million times. I look up at him and smile. There might be a few more deep-cut lines on the brown face above me, but it's still the same old Bert. I'm glad to see he's another thing around here that hasn't changed.

'Look what I found down the bottom paddock, harassing the cows.' He lifts his bushy eyebrows and tilts his head to indicate the grey wonder.

'I'm sure he was a great help.' I laugh. 'The ultimate working dog.' Right on cue, Fergus starts to chase his tail, running round and round in ever lower circles until he falls onto the grass. After this, he gets back up dizzily and starts all over again.

Bert laughs a hearty laugh as he watches. Fergus is the least useful, softest city dog ever made.

'Come on.' I grab Bert by the arm and start to drag him up the stairs to see Titch and Sally.

'Still full of energy, eh?' He laughs again as he's pulled along.

This makes me pause slightly. I haven't felt full of energy for ages. Bert, however, doesn't seem to notice my surprise. His gaze is focused up on the verandah.

'Ladies.' He tips his hat when he gets to the top of the stairs.

'Bert!' Titch says again, and goes over for her hug. 'It's great to see you.'

'You too, sweetheart.'

Sal hobbles over to give Bert a kiss on the cheek.

'In the wars again, Sal?'

'You should see the other guy,' she laughs.

'Would you like a cup of tea?' Titch asks.

'We're only on about our eighth cup each,' Sally snorts.

'Love to, girls, but no time. Must be off. I've got a cow to see about another cow.' Bert nods out into the greenness.

'Can you come up for dinner?' I ask. 'Maybe tomorrow night?' I add quickly, thinking about the amount of food in the pantry (none).

'That'd be great, Dice. See you then, eh?' He tips his hat again and is off.

Raff. Fergus stops chasing his tail for a second to say goodbye.

'Watch out for those hooves, Fergus,' Bert warns him, pointing a finger.

Fergus has a bit of reputation for being kicked by the odd cow.

Raff.

With Bert gone, we return back to the swing chair and our silence, the only punctuation being the occasional noise from Fergus, infuriated by his tail, or a bee, or a moth. He also finds, and eats, a rather large spider. Ah, well. At least the vets around here are cheaper than in the city.

Soon enough, it starts to get dark, and Titch offers to drive to one of the nearby, larger towns to pick up some takeaway Thai food. Sally heads inside to have a shower (after I've garbage-bagged and rubber-banded her plastered leg) and I remain on the swing chair.

It's then that depression sets in. And fast. I'd been happy the last few hours, sitting and drinking my tea, not thinking, but I should have known it wouldn't last for ever. Now my regular thoughts return, like a veil over my eyes. By the time Titch returns with the food and Sally appears, smelling powder-fresh, my funk has found its way back to me.

We take the food inside and set it out on the kitchen table. But even before we open the containers all three of us seem to know it feels wrong. It would be sacrilege to eat anything other than meat and three veg, followed by jelly and custard, on Nan's table. So we dish up and then haul our loaded plates back out to the swing chair—our new home.

Just as we're settling in, Titch gets up again.

'I forgot. I got you guys some wine. Some Chardonnay.'

'God, you're an angel,' Sally says, her mouth full of food. 'Chardonnay. The perfect wine with Thai. And painkillers.'

'I'll just run in and open it.'

'No…' Sally and I both start to protest, but Titch is already gone.

'It's OK,' she calls from the hallway. 'I need a glass of water anyway.'

Sally looks over at me and shakes her head. 'That girl is too good for her own…good.'

Titch returns with a tray and three glasses. Two large glasses of white for Sally and me, and a tumbler full of water for herself.

'So…' Sally holds her glass up.

'To…um…' Titch holds her glass up as well.

Eventually they both turn to me.

I pause, then shrug. 'Failure?'

Sally snorts. 'Oh, that's nice. Really cheery.' She turns to Titch, shutting me out with her shoulder. 'To old times.'

Titch smiles. 'To old times.' They clink glasses.

Sally and I manage to polish off both the rest of the Thai and the bottle of wine, but Titch, I notice, doesn't eat most of the first helping on her plate. Before long she says she's tired and just wants to have a shower and go to bed. She's not even halfway down the hall when Sally turns to me.

'I want to talk to you,' she says, her eyes narrowed.

I get up and go over to lean on the balcony railing, leaving some distance between us. Who knows what kind of a dangerous weapon she could turn that cast into?

'Mmm?'

'Oh, don't *mmm* me.'

'Sorry?' I decide it's safer to play dumb, even though I know exactly where she's headed. I didn't, even for a second, think I'd get away with it.

Sally sighs. 'What's with the failure comment? That was a nice thing to say to Titch.'

I wince. 'I know. I didn't mean it like that. It just popped out from nowhere…'

'Oh, sure. From nowhere. Don't give me that. I know what you meant. Titch certainly didn't need to hear it though.'

Silence.

'You're a touch obsessed with this failure thing. You were going on about it this morning as well. Failure Girl. Loserville.'

I slide my right shoe on and off. I don't want to think about it. I won't think about it.

'Well?' Sally pushes me for an answer.

I turn around and stare out into the darkness. 'Well, in case you hadn't noticed, I just lost my business.'

'No? Really?'

'Yes. Really. And, just to rub it in, I had it splashed around in every paper, magazine, news programme and bad current affairs show in the country.'

'Oh, cut the crap. You know everything they said was bullshit.'

Was it? I think to myself.

'Well?' Sally says from the swing chair.

I turn around to face her again. 'Maybe you wouldn't be so blasé about it if you'd been there yourself.'

'Been where?'

'Failure.'

Sally laughs now—really laughs. 'Have you lost your mind? Failure? Yeah, I've never been there. What about my ex-husband line-up? You think everyone sees me as some big success story?'

I shrug when she says this, because in some ways I do think of her like that. Sally always makes setbacks look like a breeze. Like she always knew things were going to turn out the way they did.

'I'm the queen of failure!' She laughs again.

This comment pisses me off. Perhaps because it's my crown she's talking about. Or maybe because I knew it was a mistake to bring her here. I knew it was a mistake right from the start and now I'm paying for it. 'Well, maybe that's the difference between us. You do failure with style and grace.'

'Oh, that's me. Failure with panache.' She makes a flowery gesture.

'Failure with panache,' I repeat as I turn back around once more. 'That's pretty funny. You wear failure *with* panache. I wear it *like* Panache. Like a cheap perfume from the chemist's bargain basement bin.'

'Hey, that's a bit harsh. Panache is my mum's favourite perfume.'

'Oh. Sorry.'

Sally sighs again then. 'Look, Dicey…'

Through the open front door I hear the shower turn off. 'My turn, I guess.' I push myself off the balcony railing.

'Dicey, sit down and we'll talk about it. Properly.'

'No, I… It's boring.' I wave one hand, finally managing to close my mind off to what we're discussing with the gesture. 'I'm sick of talking about it. There's nothing left to talk *about*.'

As I head inside I think about how clichéd that sounds, but it's true. I've been talking about the loss of my business for almost three months now, and thinking about it for even longer. I never want to think or talk about it again if I can help it. People keep telling me that it's cathartic, that talking will get it all out of my system, but they're wrong. I think it can only be that way if you've already come to grips with what's actually happened to you. If you've taken it in. Frankly, I don't think I'm there yet. Right now the hurt is still too raw, like a nail bitten back too far, exposing the soft pink skin underneath. Maybe some day my protective coating will grow back and I'll be able to sit around and chat about where I went wrong.

But not yet.

The guilt hits me in the shower—almost as hard as the jets of water from the huge, old-fashioned shower rose.

Sally's right.

I can't believe I said that in front of Titch. How could I be so insensitive? And Titch is the last person in the world I can bear hurting. I mean, Sally and I—we can say anything to each other, apologise in the morning and it's all forgotten. But Titch…Titch stores hurt like a badly treated cat. If you treat her wrong, she'll flinch whenever you come near her again.

When I'm done in the bathroom I help Sally make up the guest bedroom for herself, and then tiptoe down the hall to the room I shared with Titch. I'm grateful for the fact that it doesn't look the same any more. There was some storm damage to this side of the house a number of years ago and the room needed to be recarpeted and repainted and a new wardrobe installed. The two single beds are in a different position and most of our old things have been packed and stored under the house.

I stop in the doorway to the dark room and listen. Titch is asleep. Really asleep. Not pretending. After years of sharing a room with her I can tell in an instant when she's faking.

I pad across the room and slip into bed. And then I stare at the ceiling and wait for sleep to come.

I wait.

And I wait.

And I wait.

After an hour I give up and haul myself out of bed. I tiptoe out to the living room, where I locate my sewing bag, take out the bag I've been sequining—a beautiful little seashell-pink concoction—and set myself up in Nan's rocking chair, next to the stained-glass lamp.

As I rock, my needle going in and out, in and out, slow and steady, I remember the woman from *Vogue*'s comment— 'These are well made'—and I smile. Of course they're well made, I think, becoming more aware of the rhythm of my rocking. 'If a thing's worth doing, it's worth doing well,' Nan always told me, and now I can see she was more than right. 'These are well made…' The words echo in my ears once more, and, just like on the bridge this afternoon, I can't help but think back again.

It didn't take long for *Vogue* to get excited. Very excited. Within a month they sent a photographer and a stylist out to the house to meet me, to discuss some kind of fashion story they were doing on sleepwear. The stylist did a lot of talking, the photographer ate a lot of Nan's biscuits, and when they left I had absolutely no idea what was going on.

As it turned out, I ended up on the beach in the next town

over, in the middle of winter, emulating a cheesy old sunscreen ad. You know—the one with the little pigtailed girl making the 'Oh!' face and the dog trying to pull her bikini pants off? Well, that was what Fergus and I became. I wore a pair of my now much in demand Friesian pyjamas with the tail, pigtails and the 'Oh!' look, and Fergus... Well, Fergus pulled on the tail. In fact, Fergus enjoyed pulling on the tail so much we went through three pairs of pyjamas.

I almost died of shame doing it, but I had to admit that when *Vogue* sent over the pictures before they published them they were actually pretty funky.

And everyone else must have thought they were too because, as soon as the issue came out, business went insane.

I still had Hildy, the two girls from my home ec class and myself sewing. But when the tidal wave of calls hit us I think we all realised instantly that it was time to seek out a manufacturer. The next realisation was that manufacturers cost money. A lot of money.

Even though everything panned out beautifully, I wince now thinking back to it—the day my grandfather stepped forward and offered me his savings, all $80,000 he and Nan had, as an investment. An investment in my company. Naturally, I balked. There was no way I was taking Nan and Pop's money.

And that was when he pulled what he liked to call one of his 'fast ones' on me—he acted offended, like I thought his money wasn't good enough, and then went on to say it damn well wasn't charity. He expected a decent return on any money he invested in a business one of his granddaughters had started up. I wasn't ten any more. I saw beneath the song and dance. But what really made my world stop spinning for a second was the fact that I could see in his eyes that he *did* believe my business would be a success.

This absolutely floored me, after what he and Nan had been through with my mother. After all, he would have had a lot more than $80,000 in that bank account if she hadn't traipsed up the driveway once or twice a year and taken however much he'd give her. That was, of course, after she'd stolen whatever else she could get her hands on.

So, I let him lend me the money. And it made me even more determined to work hard. To make my business a success. Within a fortnight a manufacturer had gone into production and we were able to start filling our back orders. And there was no denying we had back orders. We had back orders like these things were Birkin bags. Back orders for pyjamas! Pyjamas with tails! I couldn't believe it.

Within six months I paid my grandparents back $88,000, which they took with grandparently reluctance, bargaining me down from my offer of $100,000.

Things stayed insane. I got an accountant (the money side of things just wasn't my forte) and then really got stuck into running things. The rest of the year passed by in a daze of orders from the *Moo to You* website, phone calls from boutiques, and meetings with department stores. I think it was just after New Year that the accountant took me aside, white-faced, and said he'd never seen anything like it. The company's percentage growth from January to January was nine hundred per cent. Not only that, but we hadn't spent a cent on advertising, other than the website.

After *Vogue,* more magazines than we could count had got on board, wanting to feature our product, which meant that supply still couldn't meet demand. This was when the accountant suggested I take it all the way. I had no idea what he was talking about. My head was swimming with designs I'd been busy making up—summer, winter, pants, boxers—

I hadn't had time to think about anything else. So he sat me down and explained it to me like I was in business kinder-garten (which I may as well have been).

The talk was all about how small companies became big companies. What I needed to do was to find an investor. The first thing I thought of was Nan and Pop again, but this sug-gestion was gently brushed aside. My accountant had been thinking of perhaps a little more money than, say, $80,000. He went away and made some calls, and arranged for me to meet Harry.

As soon as I met Harry I knew he was the answer to my prayers.

Harry was a businessman in the true sense of the word. He made his money selling medical instruments. Now, Harry wasn't a doctor. In fact he didn't know any doctors, other than his GP, and he didn't know anything about manufac-turing either. All Harry knew was that hospitals needed medical instruments and that if he made better ones and sold them at the same price the hospital administrators were al-ready buying at—or, hopefully, made them cheaper—they'd buy his. That was all Harry needed to know.

He got himself some investors, consulted with some doc-tors about what they did and didn't like about—hell, I don't know…scalpels?—then he did the rounds to find a manu-facturer, made some test products, finalised some changes and started selling. That was how Harry made his millions.

It shocked me when he told me this over lunch—that he made millions of dollars from a product he essentially knew nothing about. All he'd started out with was some simple logic and the gift of being able to persuade rich people to part with their money (before his meteoric rise in scalpel-dom Harry used to be a BMW car salesman). Apparently people do this all the time—pick a product, make it better and market the hell out of it.

Over dessert, I told Harry we were from different planets—galaxies, even. That I'd never be able to do something like he'd done. After all, *Moo to You* was all about where I came from and who I was. Harry just laughed at this. Later on, I'd laugh too. Bitterly. I'd been right. We were from different planets. It was just that Harry was from one I hadn't heard of yet—Planet Tyrant in the Asshole solar system.

The next day, as the papers put it, there was a 'sum of money invested in *Moo to You* in order to grow the company and expand its product line'.

That sum was three million dollars.

What that meant was, overnight, I became the face of a multimillion-dollar company. Some days I used to sit in my fancy new leather chair in my fancy new city office and wonder if soon I'd be discovered. If a reporter would come charging past my assistant and through my heavy wooden office door and demand to know what I thought I was doing.

The thing was, it was all a bit of a shock. Things had happened fast—it was only a little over two years ago I'd still been ordering jammy pikelets and chocolate milk at the school tuckshop for morning tea. The biggest decision I'd had to make then was whether or not I was going to scam my way out of sixth lesson phys ed and what kind of an excuse I could use. Now I was hailed as the pyjama queen, and given the crown of Young Australian Businesswoman of the Year to boot.

But somehow, despite all this, that leather throne of mine still felt wrong.

After Harry, I didn't have nearly so much to do. I was paid

a fantastic amount of money simply to be the face of a company that wasn't even really my own anymore. I was product branding and marketing. Harry was money. 60/40. How I wanted it. And things were fine. For a while...

Over the next year we expanded into bedlinen, bathrobes, towels, hot water bottles, and a range of milk-based bath products. And things were still fine.

It was the year after that when Harry went a little bit mad.

For a start, he wanted to move the company headquarters to London. And he wanted concept stores in London, New York, Sydney and Tokyo. (Paris, I think we both knew, was never going to happen for *Moo to You*. I couldn't exactly see Parisian women lining up to look like cows. It just wasn't their scene.) Anyway, worse than both these things put together was the fact that Harry also wanted to move into lingerie and make-up.

When I heard this, my heart filled with dread. I really, really didn't want to go there. I loved pyjamas and lounging around in the bath, but I knew nothing about make-up and tended to wear white cotton undies until they went grey in the wash. I wasn't the make-up and lingerie type, and women would sense this in a minute. I couldn't sell those kinds of products and I didn't want to try.

Also, I'd seen other women with my kind of cult company go down that path. I'd bought some of their wares in the 'Eighty per cent off!' discount bins in the after Christmas sales.

Scarily enough, at the time Harry hit me with his bombshell I'd been secretly planning to hit him with one of my own—I wanted to cut back a bit, downsize our range of products. The economy wasn't good. People might need pyjamas, but we weren't living in the eighties any more and thus they weren't interested in buying a $55 clear hot water bottle filled with floating plastic cows to go with their nightwear. Stupidly, I hit Harry with this piece of information, thinking he'd take it OK.

He didn't. Instead he turned beetroot-red and went off his nut. What would I know? Did I have a degree from Harvard Business School? How many companies had I run before? Etc., etc., etc…

I let him have his say, but I didn't budge. I wouldn't budge. I couldn't sell those products.

After this we started to argue. More and more. And more and more and more. It got to the point where one day, while we were screaming at each other across the ridiculously large boardroom meeting table, I asked him what we were going to sell next. Little plastic cowpats to leave around the home?

He thought this was a good idea.

And that was when I was sure that I wanted out.

Now, back in the present, I gulp, remembering, and I try to concentrate on my beading, forcing my fingers to move faster and faster.

It's this bit, the downhill slide of my business, that I still have trouble thinking about, that keeps me awake at night and tends to bring on my 'I don't want to think about it; I won't think about it' glazed stare. Anyway, it's not like I don't have plenty to be going on with in the present. Soon enough my car will have to be returned. The townhouse too.

I'd stood firm on those. Both these things are held in the company name, but I fought to keep them for twelve extra weeks. The thing is I need to figure out what I'm going to do with myself. With my life. I need to work out what's going to happen next. It's coming close to the end of those twelve weeks and I still don't know. I've been avoiding thinking about it, as if I can somehow put the future off. And I've been quite successful at it so far. The last few weeks have flown by in a hardly memorable haze of bad daytime TV and bag-making.

With this thought, I look up from beading the last delicate pink crystal into my swirled design and wait, blinkingly, for my eyes to adjust. As a child, I used to lounge around in this room and dream about what my future would be like. But now—now I'd love to put off thinking about the future for ever if I could.

I take a deep breath and then exhale slowly, putting the bag down into my lap. It's then, still looking around me, that I feel one final gulp rise in my throat. Because something tells me that being back here, in Moo, and being kept in close quarters with both my sister and Sally means that, as much as I want to, I may not be able to hide from the future much longer.

It's the crashing coming from the direction of the kitchen that wakes me up. Reluctantly, I drag myself out of bed and squint my way out there.

'Hey, raccoon face.' Beside the stove, Sally looks up, and at the same time manages to drop the anodised metal teapot she's holding onto the floor. Tea leaves spill everywhere. 'Bugger.'

'Here.' I go over to the kitchen table and pull out a chair for her. 'You sit down. I'll make the tea.'

She doesn't argue, but hobbles her way over. 'Sorry. Is the teapot OK?'

I pick it up and perform a quick inspection. 'It's fine.' I grab the tea canister, refill the pot and add the already boiled water. Leaving it to infuse, I locate the dustpan and brush and sweep the mess away. 'All done,' I say to Sally as I tip the pan into the sink.

'Didn't you get any sleep?' Sally asks.

So that's what she meant by the 'raccoon face' comment. I turn away from the table and busy myself with mugs and sugar. 'Um, of course I did. Where's Titch?'

'In the shower. Again.'

'Hey, it's better she showers too much than not at all.'

'True.'

'Did she go down to the cemetery this morning?'

'Um…' Sally suddenly becomes interested in the kitchen tabletop. 'Yeah, I think so.'

'So you didn't go with her?'

'No. I fed the dog, though,' she says, quickly changing the subject.

'Hmph.' I watch her for a moment or two, then decide to let the change of subject slide this time. Especially because I don't think I've taken the dog food out of the car yet, and Sally sounds a tad too cheerful about feeding Fergus. I give her a look now. 'You fed the dog *what* exactly?'

'Mini Wagon Wheels.'

Oh, great. I glance out of the window to see Fergus streaking across the yard like a thing possessed. 'Let me guess. A whole packet?'

'Maybe. He looked hungry. Sugar-hungry.'

I look back at her now. 'Right. Sugar-hungry.' Please, God, don't ever let her have any children. I send up a quick prayer as I pass Sally her tea and yesterday's tin of biscuits. 'You know too much chocolate can kill dogs?'

Sally nods. 'Yeah. I was hopeful. But it doesn't look like it's going to happen. Is that tea ready yet? I'm starving.'

It's midday before we get ourselves together and hit the shops. I'd forgotten we're on country time now. In Moo, everything takes twice as long as it does in the city. It takes twice as long to have a shower, twice as long to iron a shirt, twice as long to drink a cup of tea. It's as if the air itself becomes thick and treacle-like, turning your movements into something resembling slow motion.

Thus, we trawl the aisles of the tiny supermarket in the neighbouring town, picking up and turning over every item on the shelves, deciding whether we need three packets of Tim Tams or two will be enough, and bickering over the merits of the Tia Maria version over the good old-fashioned original.

We've finished that discussion and have moved on to arguing over salt and vinegar crinkle-cut chips versus nacho cheese-flavoured corn chips when we hear it.

'Lavender? Cinnamon? Sally?'

The three of us freeze, our bags of chips held in various positions. What was that?

'Yoo-hoo!'

'Mrs Tuddle,' we hiss under our collective breath.

'There's no time to run,' Sally whispers urgently. 'And anyway, I'm not leaving the Tim Tams. They're on special, and these are the last three packets.'

'Oh, don't be silly,' Titch scolds the two of us. 'She won't bite.'

'Unless you're chocolate-coated.' Sally waggles her eyebrows at me before Titch grabs our elbows and whirls us around.

'Mrs Tuddle, how nice to see you!' Titch says kindly to the huge approaching flower-frocked form.

'Well, well, well. If it isn't Sally Bliss and Lavender and Cinnamon Dye.'

Aaaggghhh! No! Not again! My brain screams and my

teeth start to grind at the second mention of my real name. As if once wasn't bad enough.

Beside me, Titch gives my arm a 'be good, please' nudge.

'I thought it was you three.' Mrs Tuddle huffs and puffs at the effort of walking down the whole of aisle four to reach us. 'And of course I'd heard you were in town.' She brings her cart to rest beside ours.

'Of course.' Sally gives me an 'I told you so' glance.

'It sounds like you made quite an entrance.'

'Mmm,' I say, my teeth still grinding away. Cinnamon? And Lavender? No one's called us that for years, and she knows it. Titch gives my elbow another nudge and I get a sideways 'stop that awful teeth-grinding noise!' look.

'Just down for the weekend, are you?' Mrs Tuddle's eyes run over the groceries in our cart and come to rest on our prize possession.

Back off those Tim Tams, lady!

'No, no. For a fortnight or so.' Titch does all the talking while Sally and I look on like a pair of sulky teenagers.

'Ah, because of the...' Mrs Tuddle pauses for a second and my eyes widen as for the first time in her life it seems she's going to use a little something the less gossipy among us (that's everyone, where Mrs Tuddle is concerned) like to call discretion. But she simply coughs—'Oops, almost swallowed my Tic Tac!'—and continues her sentence. 'The unfortunate events of the past few months.'

That's it? I glance from Sally to Titch. We're going to get away without an embarrassing run-down of what we've done wrong lately in screaming Technicolor?

No, of course not.

Mrs Tuddle steps up to me now and grabs my shoulder. She's so close I can see the whiskers on her chin. Shudder.

'You know, I thought it was a shame, dear, about your company. All those little sets of pyjamas going to waste. They were lovely, even if they were a touch overpriced.'

It's Titch she turns to next. 'And you, darling. With the television thing…' She sucks her breath in.

'Yes, I know,' Titch says sadly, and I want to take that arm of Mrs Tuddle's, which is doling out conciliatory pats, and rip it right out of its arthritic socket.

'And you, Sally.' She turns again, dropping the rippling jelly-like dimpled appendage before I get my chance.

'What can I help you with, Mrs Tuddle?' Sally says brightly, and both Titch and I give her a 'keep it clean' glare.

Mrs Tuddle gives her a long, hard once-over, taking in the cast. 'You've obviously been up to no good again, my girl.'

'I do my best!'

'Hmm.' Mrs Tuddle doesn't look impressed. 'Two weeks did you say, dear?' She turns back to Titch—always her favourite where the three of us are concerned.

Titch nods. 'At least.'

'Hmm.' There's another assessing look. 'Maybe you girls could do something for me. For the Moos, actually.'

'The Moos? But of cour—' Titch the do-gooder starts to answer, but ends with an 'Ow!' as I kick her leg behind the trolley.

'You see, I'm having a bit of an operation.' Mrs Tuddle leans in closer to us. 'I won't say what—it's a ladies thing, you know…'

'That's OK. You don't have to,' Sally pipes up.

'Oh, I'm sorry to hear that, Mrs Tuddle.' Titch really shoots Sally a look now. 'What can we do?'

I suddenly have horror visions of helping her to and from the toilet during the Moos meetings. Oh, please, no.

'I'm looking for someone to run the meetings. Just till I'm back on my old feet again.'

I breathe a large sigh of relief (it wasn't the toilet thing after all), and everyone turns to look at me.

'Sorry. Um, I mean, um—it's just that I don't think we can commit to anything long-term. We don't know how long we're going to be here. It could be a couple of weeks, or it could be a couple of days.'

'Oh, but it wouldn't be long-term. I'd only need someone for two weeks. Or maybe three.'

'Um, well…that's what I mean. Like I said, we might only be here a few days.'

Mrs Tuddle gives me a long, hard look. 'That's a real shame. The Moos could learn a lot from three successful girls like yourselves. Though, again, it *was* a shame about your pyjamas, Cinnamon. And about your television programme, Lavender.'

'She's going back to work, you know,' I cut in. 'She's just on holiday.'

There's a pause.

'Yes, yes—of course,' Mrs Tuddle says, and then nods a little too hard and non-believingly.

'She is!'

'Dicey!' Titch says out of the side of her mouth, and gives my sleeve a pull.

'Well, you are…' I mumble to myself.

Mrs Tuddle pauses again. 'I'd best get back to my shopping. I wouldn't want to keep you. Perhaps I'll give you a call…'

Typical. Lay on the 'you think you're too busy and important to help us out in little old Moo' guilt. She'll be mentioning Nan next. Mrs Tuddle was a good friend of Nan's, though I can't say I ever really understood what Nan saw in her.

'Bye, Mrs Tuddle. It was lovely seeing you. Do give us a call.' Titch waves slightly as Mrs Tuddle backs her cart away.

As she passes, Mrs Tuddle gives one last, lingering look at our Tim Tams. For a moment I think Sally might throw herself over the cart to save our precious bounty. The three of us watch her closely until she turns into aisle five and is gone.

'Saved.' Sally reaches in and pats our stash of chocolate biscuits, still resting safely on top of my haul of pistachio nuts (I'd cleaned the store out of those as well).

'You two…' Titch shakes her head at us.

'Arse-kisser.' Sally puckers up and starts to chase her around and around the cart as fast as her cast will take her—which isn't very fast at all. '"Bye, Mrs Tuddle. It was lovely seeing you. Do give us a call…"'

'Stop it!' Titch gives her a swat. 'You'll break something else.'

'Like the Tim Tams,' I laugh.

'Shut up about the Tim Tams or I'll put them back.' Titch hides behind me.

'Yes, ma'am.'

Sally stops and rests both hands on one side of the cart. 'No, no, no. You mean, "Yes, Lavender", don't you—Cinnamon?' She lets out a loud cackle.

Both of us groan. Not our real names. Anything but our real names. They had doled out to us during our mother's happy-hippie phase. That was when she was living in a commune in a nearby hippie town, and obviously experiencing a great deal of free love.

'Thanks for bringing that up again.' I try to emulate one of Titch's looks, but don't quite pull it off before I break out laughing again.

Titch and Sally join in, and we egg each other on until everyone in the shop is looking at us and we're holding onto the cart for dear life.

'Cinnamon with her dead business, Lavender on an enforced holiday, and Sally the temporarily crippled whore, who finally made it out from behind the school bike shed.' I'm practically wetting myself now.

'Oi!' Sally gives me a whack. 'If I wasn't so happy on painkillers I might be offended by that.'

'Still, there's no denying it. Right now the Moos could probably learn more about life from Fergus.'

The three of us look up to the front of the store, where Fergus is chained up outside the plate glass window. He gives us a toothy 'don't forget the mini Wagon Wheels' grin and we start laughing again.

When the phone rings that evening, and Titch spends a good half-hour talking to the person on the other end of the line, of course I assume it's Andrew.

I've been away from Moo too long.

I should have realised that the meeting in the supermarket today, the small guilt trip, and the mention of giving us a call was just the beginning.

It takes Titch another fifteen minutes or so after hanging up to raise the courage to slink outside to the verandah and break the news to me.

'Um, Dicey?' She sidles up beside me.

'Mmm?'

'About that Moos thing…'

I sit straight up in the swing chair. 'No. Oh, no. No, no, no, no, *no.*' I grab both her arms. 'Tell me that wasn't Mrs Tuddle on the phone.'

Titch's eyes mosey off down the garden path.

'Oh, Titch.' My shoulders slump now. 'Why didn't you pass the phone over to me? Or even to Sally?'

Titch looks trapped. 'I couldn't help it. She started talking about Nan. About how she'd be so pleased to see us back. And to see us helping out in the community.'

Ooohhh. I knew it. And using Nan like that. Nasty. 'That woman!'

Titch bites her lip for a second before she continues. 'She's not really that bad, Dicey. She just…'

I shake my head. 'You are too nice. Way, way too nice. She just played us. She's probably got her flunky monkeys out there with binoculars right now. She probably waited until she saw you near the phone so she knew you'd be the one to pick up!'

'Oh, Dicey. I don't think she's got any flunky monkeys. Nan really liked Mrs Tuddle, you know. And it won't hurt. You loved being a Moo. Remember?'

I snort.

It's all I can do.

So thanks to Titch that, as they say, is that. For the next three weeks we will join together and take Mrs Tuddle's place, collectively, as Big Moo. Leader of the Moos.

What the hell are the Moos? A fair question. The Moos are the Moo version of the Brownies, or the Girl Scouts, or the Campfire Girls, or whatever you like to call them. Of course in Moo (we used to call it Cowpat in our own younger Moo days…) nothing is allowed to be straightforward. Instead of the usual branch of the usual organisation most normal kiddies are allowed to join, we have the Moos—because of the large resident hippie population. In the Moos you learn to read tea leaves and hang crystals, to make fash-

ion from recycled hemp bags, rather than collect badges, re-
cite prayers and bake chocolate-chip cookies. Boys are more
than welcome to join as well. Being a Moo was an education, to say the least.

I have to go and lie down with some pistachios as I recall
more about my childhood years as a Moo. Reach for nut,
pick up nut, open nut, put nut in mouth, chew, swallow.
Reach for nut, pick up nut, open nut, put nut in mouth,
chew, swallow. I start to eat faster and faster as I recall something else as well—Mrs Tuddle's mention of our real names.
I hadn't been called Cinnamon in such a long time I'd almost forgotten the name might crop up again once I got
back on home soil. Like I said, the names had been bestowed
upon us during our mother's hippie phase. Lavender and
Cinnamon.

Yikes.

Our mother must *really* have been on some drugs to come
up with a couple of corkers like that. And I can't even begin
to imagine how she persuaded the local authorities to type
the names onto our birth certificates. After all, we weren't
from the hills. We were from farming stock. They were only
used to spelling things like Susan and Jane for people like us.

Over the years Titch and I had almost managed to leave
the two most hated words in the dictionary behind. Titch
had become Titch—at first, I think, because she was always
so tiny. So frail. It had been kind of funny when she'd finally shot up at thirteen to become the tallest kid at school.
And me—somehow along the line I became Dicey, because
of our surname—Dye. Dicey Dye. Get it? Pretty funny, huh?
Still, it's better than Cinnamon. Though I guess that's not
saying much, because just about anything's better than
Cinnamon.

Reach for nut, pick up nut, open nut, put nut in mouth, chew, swallow. Reach for nut, pick up nut, open nut, put nut in mouth, chew, swallow.

Moo. You've got to love it. And as an adult at least you can look back and laugh. But, oh, God. Those poor kids. I was joking when I said it before, but they probably *could* learn more about life from Fergus. Reach for nut, pick up nut, open nut, put nut in mouth, chew, swallow. Reach for nut…

'Dicey?'

'Oh, JL… Um, hello. I mean, hi.'

'Hi. I thought I would call and see how you are going.'

'Well, um, good. Fergus is having the time of his life, of course.'

'He has been kicked by the cows yet?'

'Not yet. But only because he's been lucky.'

'And Titch? And Sally? She is being a handful?'

'Titch is doing OK. Sally's still taking as many painkillers as she's allowed, so she's pretty docile—even by Sally in Moo standards.'

'And you?'

'I, um, I'm fine. Thanks.'

'Dicey, I wanted to say I am sorry about the other day. I should explain…'

'It's OK. You don't have to explain anything to me.'

'But I want to explain…'

'No, really. I don't want to know. It's just easier that way. Look, I've…I've got to go. We're kind of busy down here, and I think my mobile's ringing…'

'Sally!' I yell down the hall for the third time. Behind me, Titch gives up waiting and takes a seat on the swing chair. *'Sally!'*

'I'm coming already! I'm coming!' Finally she limps her way out of the bathroom and down the hallway, still applying her lipgloss. 'Where's the fire?'

'We're going to be late.'

She leisurely applies a little more gloss and smacks her lips together before she speaks. 'Yeah, and I'm sure they'll start on time. They always did when we were kids.'

I sigh. 'Well, maybe we can start a new trend. Punctuality comes to Moo. Who knows? It may even catch on.'

Sally goes to open her mouth again, but Titch beats her to it. 'Sally, just get in the car. Please. And keep it down. For my sake. I'm begging you.'

We both turn around. Titch looks tired, her face white

and pinched. I think she's been getting almost as much sleep as I have—and eating about a fifth.

'OK. Sorry,' Sally says meekly, putting away her pot of lipgloss. She starts the slow journey down the stairs with her cast.

'You all right?' I go over to Titch. 'You sure you want to come?'

Titch simply nods. 'Let's go.'

Silently we pile into the car, yell for Fergus, who bounds in at the last minute, and we're off. It's our first Moos meeting tonight, and I head down the driveway and aim the car for Moo Central (read: Moo community centre hall). Thankfully, from what we hear, the Moos already have their monthly project worked out and began it last week, so all we'll be doing is a bit of glorified babysitting. Even the three of us should be able to handle that.

We drive down Moo's main street, turn left at the pub (again, full) and, around two hundred metres down the road, turn right to get to the hall. Not the slightest thing about the place has changed, I note as we approach it. The grass at the front of the hall is still brown and patchy, with spots of prickles, the same potholes remain in the car park area, and the flag, flying high, looks just as worn as it always has, and still clink-clinks against the silver flagpole in the same distinctive way.

'Wow. Blast from the past.' Sally whistles as we all sit in the parked car and look around us.

'Guess we'd better start getting things ready.' I swing my door open.

As it turns out, the inside of the hall hasn't changed either. The wooden floors are still vast and wide, the joins in between each plank are still ever-widening, the kitchen is still clean, but desperate for a makeover, and the storage area is still locked and stuffed full of Moo treasure.

Titch and I unlock the storage area door and take out a pile of chairs, unstacking them and placing them around the hall. We've just set the last two down when the first car pulls up, and the three of us make our way outside to greet the new breed on the block.

We chat to the first set of kids and parents until a whole lot of cars turn down the street and make their way into the community centre car park. As it turns out there will be eight Moos tonight, quite a normal number as the Moos go, but, while things might have stayed the same on the hall and the numbers front, as far as everything else goes the Moo world is a different place.

For a start, the car park is now an interesting, eclectic, confusing mix of vehicles. Two four-wheel-drives (one a Mercedes, the other a Lexus), a beat-up old cream-coloured Holden station wagon with a large dent in the front bumper (stray cow?), and a working ute that smells rather like a cow.

Like I said, eight kids. Camilla, Hamish and Madeleine, Rainbow, Leaf and Sorrel, and Tom and Jo. And, it's funny, but you can match the kids to the parents and the parents to the cars in an instant. Camilla, Hamish and Madeleine belong to the shiny four-wheel-drives. Their parents are the newcomers—yuppies from the gated communities near the beach, who've sea-change retired with their second families and botoxed foreheads. Rainbow, Leaf and Sorrel have been environmentally station-wagon car-pooled from their hippie community in the hills, and Tom and Jo are ute-travelling farm kids all the way in their stiff jeans, sturdy boots and thick shirts.

What really makes me laugh, however, is how the kids fall

out of the cars and sprint off onto the grass *en masse* not giving a damn. Not about us, their names, the cars, where they come from or their parents. They run straight over to Fergus and start to alternately roll on the grass with him and try to ride him. With so many new friends, the dog is in ecstasy.

'Dicey?' One of the mothers touches me gently on the arm and I turn to look at her. It's the second look, however, that confirms it.

'Rachel?' I say slowly.

She smiles now. 'I didn't think you'd remember!'

'Of course I do. We're not that old, are we?'

Rachel laughs. 'Sometimes it feels that way.'

I look over at the kids for a second. 'Let me guess. Rainbow?'

'That's right—the loudest one. How'd you know?' She laughs again as Rainbow yells something at the top of her lungs.

I shake my head. 'It's great to see you again!' God, I can't have seen Rachel since, I don't know…a year or two after school?

'You too. Are you staying up at the farm?'

I nod. 'Just for a couple of weeks. A bit of a holiday. It's a little strange. I kind of keep expecting my grandmother to walk out of the next room. But it's good to be back, even if it does make me miss my grandparents.'

'Everyone still misses them, I think.' There's a pause before Rachel reaches out to touch my arm again. 'Look, I just wanted to say it's a shame about your business. I really felt for you.'

'Oh, thanks.'

'And Titch. I read about it in the paper on the weekend. I hope everything works out for her. You know, I didn't expect my Rainbow at all, but I don't know what I'd do without her, really.' Rainbow yells something else now, and Rachel laughs again, that easy, throw-your-head back laugh she's always had. 'No, I do know. I'd probably get a lot more sleep and I'd never have spoken to a school principal at all. I'd better let you get on with it, hey? Tell Titch I said hi. I'll have a chat to her later.' Rachel walks off with a quick wave.

I wave back as Rachel heads for her car (the Holden). The other parents seem to be ready to make a move too.

Titch comes over. 'Ready to take them inside?'

I nod.

'Was that Rachel Sorenson?' She watches the car drive off.

'Mmm. She said to say hi.'

Titch glances over at the group. 'Rainbow's mum?'

Now it's me who laughs. 'That's what I said.' I grab my sister's arm. 'Come on—let's go herd some cattle.'

Rainbow, it seems, is the spokesperson for the group. When we've got all the kids sitting in a semicircle in the middle of the hall, Fergus in the centre, she gets down to business, explaining exactly what's going on here.

Their monthly project is 'wish books'. Last week they decorated their books (plain old school exercise books from what I can see) with pictures from magazines and fabric scraps, and this week it's time to start writing in them. She continues filling us in on just what a 'wish book' is. Apparently it's a book in which you write down your hopes and dreams so you can be more mindful of them. When you're upset, or frightened, or simply lose your way, you can come back to the book, read what you've written and remind yourself about who you are, what you want and what's important in life.

I try not to laugh. Rainbow *is* Rachel. It's the serious set of her brow and her talk of being 'mindful' and 'losing your way' that really get me. It's too much. I wouldn't be surprised if the wish books were Rachel's idea in the first place.

'My dad thinks wish books are—' Camilla starts, but is quickly interrupted by Rainbow, who sighs loudly, for everyone to hear.

'Camilla's dad always thinks something.' She rolls her eyes at Titch, Sally and myself, and we look at each other and try not to laugh.

Camilla's dad was the overbearing number who drove the Mercedes four-wheel drive. He asked me the 'wolf' question, just like the guy driving past JL's place the other day (again, what *is* it with the wolf thing?). Anyway, he wanted to know if that was a wolf I had playing with the kids. *Of course,* I was dying to say to him. *I always bring a wolf when I host Moos meetings. Keeps the kids in line!*

'And then we're supposed to make organic muesli slice,' Rainbow continues, and my attention slides back to her. 'We've all brought our ingredients. Except for Hamish. He forgot his prunes.'

'Prunes?' How many prunes can there be in a batch of muesli slice?

'You make up some prune puree and substitute it for butter. It's much better for you,' Rainbow informs us. 'But I've got enough. Hamish can use some of mine.'

Again, I try not to laugh. 'Well, that's very generous of you, Rainbow.'

'It's not a problem.' She nods, still completely serious.

Sally looks over at Hamish. 'I'm sure Hamish's bowels will be forever grateful.' For this, she gets a look from Titch and a pinch on the arm from me.

The prune situation sorted, we set up a few trestle tables for the kids to write on and they get down to their wish book task—some of them staring at the ceiling, some of them staring at the floor, others writing furiously—their little brows furrowed. Fergus stalks from table to table, begging for pats and attention.

After about five minutes, Titch, Sally and I hold an emergency meeting in the kitchen.

'Well, here are our three exercise books.' I pass one each to Sally and Titch. 'Mrs Tuddle brought them for us. So we can write as well, and set a good example.'

'Can't we just decorate them?' Sally looks at hers forlornly.

'I think we're supposed to be old enough and wise enough to skip the decorating part and just write.'

'Oh. Pity about that. I'm much better at cutting and pasting.'

Titch pokes her head out around the kitchen door to check on the kids. 'I guess we'd better go and set that example then.'

'On the count of three.' I hold one finger up and begin the countdown. 'One, two…three.' Together we head out to the nearest trestle table, where only Hamish is sitting, biting on his pencil. The three of us sit down.

'How's it going, mate?' I ask him.

'OK.' He nods. 'I can't decide if I want a yellow Labrador or a black one.'

I puff my cheeks out. 'Well, that's a hard one. A big life choice.'

Hamish nods again. 'I know.' He pauses. 'Do you think you'd have to wash the yellow one more?'

I shake my head. 'Probably the same amount.'

'Oh.'

'You'd think you wouldn't have to wash Fergus much, being grey and all, but he's a very dirty dog.'

'He rolled in some cow poo before. I saw.'

'That really wouldn't surprise me, Hamish. It really wouldn't.'

There's a lengthy pause from the seven-year-old beside me. 'If you'd have to wash them the same amount, I think I might get the yellow one, then.'

'Good for you.' I nod, and Hamish goes back to the picture of the dog in his exercise book. He picks up a yellow pencil and gives me a grin before he starts colouring the creature in.

What a sweetheart, I think, turning back around to my own exercise book.

Which is still, not surprisingly, blank.

I fill in my name in the space on the front, and then look over at Titch and Sally. They've also filled in their names and are now looking at me.

'Hmm,' I say.

'Yes, hmm,' Sally says back.

The three of us give each other 'now what?' stares.

'So…?' Sally asks.

I shrug. 'Don't ask me. Now we write, I guess.'

'I don't know what to write,' Titch whispers.

'Same here, sister.' Sally puts her pencil down.

I'm about to agree, when something makes me pause. 'What's the matter with us?' I whisper back. 'How hard can it be? I mean, we must have something to wish for, right?'

Silence.

Then, 'Um, yeah—sure,' Sally says.

'I suppose,' Titch seconds.

More silence.

'How long till muesli slice time?' Sally picks up her pencil again and starts to tap it against the wooden trestle table.

I check my watch. 'Another twenty minutes.'

'Oh.'

The three of us sit out the next twenty minutes saying absolutely nothing. I can hardly believe how well-behaved the Moos are. Either they're totally into these wish books, or there really is something to be said for cutting additives and preservatives out of kids' diets.

As for Titch, Sally and myself, for the first ten minutes or so our pencils hover hopefully over the first blue-ruled lines in our books. Then we put the pencils down. For the last five minutes we just sit, arms folded. I count down the last minute, second by second on my watch.

'All right! Muesli slice time!' I stand up and clap my hands.

'Ooohhh…' The kids look up with one of those 'what a disappointment, I'll never be happy again' sighs that only kids know how to give out. They've obviously been having a fantastic and productive wish book evening. Lucky them.

I stop. 'You don't want to make muesli slice?' Oh. Now what? 'I guess we could always…'

'Yeah!' As one, they push back their seats and bolt for the kitchen, wish books forgotten. I turn back around to Sally and Titch, probably looking more than a little confused.

Sally shrugs. 'I'm the last person you should ask what's going on. Their attention spans are better than mine.'

'So, um, how do you do this muesli slice business?' I turn to my sister.

Titch busies herself pulling her chair out and getting up. 'I suppose you think I'm some kind of an expert at making prune puree?'

'I was hoping…'

'Well, as it happens, you're in luck. I learnt all about cooking with prune puree when Andrew had to lose that bit of weight a few years ago. It's not bad, actually. Not as good as butter…'

'But better than heart failure?' Sally butts in, pushing herself up from the table.

Titch smiles. 'That's pretty much it.'

As it turns out, Titch has almost as much of a ball making the organic muesli slice as the kids do. Sally and I stand back, lending a hand when we're needed, but mostly gas-bagging about nothing.

'There's one more, Titch,' Rainbow calls out loudly, making both Sally and I look over. She takes the tray over to Titch, who's standing by the industrial-sized oven and placing the goodies inside.

'Thanks, Rainbow.' Titch takes it from her, pops it inside and closes the door. 'Now, do you want to set the timer for twenty minutes, Hamish?' Titch guides him to the front of the group, her hand placed lightly on his head.

'OK!' He reaches up and Titch puts her hand gently over his in order to guide him. Together, they push the timer over to count down twenty minutes.

Up at the back of the kitchen, I glance sideways, and Sally catches my eye.

'I know,' I say. 'I know.'

After a quick outside kick-around with a football (Moo colours, black and white, of course), a piece of organic muesli slice and a glass of milk each (that's non-genetically modified organic soy milk, of course), the Moos' parents start to turn up again.

'Bye, Hamish.' Titch waves her favourite off and then walks over to have a chat with Rachel, who's trying to wrench Rainbow away from a surprisingly tired-looking Fergus.

'He'll be here next week, love,' she sighs.

Rainbow grips on tighter, and Rachel opens her mouth to say something else, but is drowned out by a car entering the car park. It's the ute—Tom and Jo's mother. Except it's not Tom and Jo's mother.

'Dave?' I slap my hand onto my thigh when I see the dark-haired figure get out of the car. I can hardly believe my own eyes.

'None other.' He comes running over and gives me a hug. 'My wife said there was a Dicey down here,' he says when he pulls back. 'I knew it had to be you. Thought I'd come and pick up Tom and Jo myself and check out your wrinkles.'

I laugh. 'Great—thanks for that. Did you want a closer look?' I turn my head sideways. 'Crow's feet good enough for you? Or did you want to see my forehead as well?'

'Crow's feet'll do for now.' Dave takes a look around and then whistles. 'Oi!'

Out of nowhere, Tom and Jo come running up.

'How about a "Hi, Dad"? "Thanks for picking us up, Dad"?'

'Hi, Dad. Thanks for picking us up, Dad,' Tom and Jo chant in unison.

'Grrr—come here.' He grabs a kid on each side of himself, pulls them in and proceeds to rub his knuckles on the top of each of their heads.

'Dad!' both the kids yell, louder and louder, until Dave finally lets them go.

'I'm an embarrassment.' He looks at me with a shrug. 'Sad Dad. That's me.'

'So I see.' I laugh as I watch the kids run off to join the others, getting their last spurt of running around for the evening out of their systems. I shake my head when I turn back to him. 'I can't believe you're a dad. I mean I'd heard, from my grandparents and everything, but I hadn't actually seen the, um…'

'Products themselves?'

'I didn't know they were yours, but now I have to say they look…'

'Exactly like me?'

I nod again. 'And the rest of your family.'

There had always been a bit of a town joke that the Thompson men were too scared to cheat on their wives just in case a child ever resulted. The Thompsons were practically clones of each other.

'Hope they haven't given you too much trouble.'

'Oh, come on.' I give Dave a look. 'They're lovely kids. The peacemakers of the group.'

There's a moment's silence.

'Dicey, the business thing…' Dave starts.

I wave a hand. 'It's OK. You don't have to mention it.'

'No, really. I'm sorry it didn't work out for you. It made me so mad reading all about it. That guy—your investor—he was a bloody crook!'

'Mmm.' I look away. But Dave waits until I look back at him again, and then he smirks that smirk of his that I know so well. 'OK, he was a bloody crook,' I add, and can't help but smile.

'That's better. I knew you wouldn't let it get you down. I see you're still standing.'

'Looks like it.'

'Can't say as much for Sally…' Dave glances over. 'What happened there?'

'A very high and expensive pair of shoes lost their lives.'

'Ah. That sounds like the Sally I used to know. I'm, er, very sorry for her loss.'

'So are we all. We've heard about it for *days.*'

In front of me, Dave crosses his arms. 'Look, why don't you come by one night for dinner, so we can catch up properly?'

'Um…' I begin, and even though I'm looking directly at Dave my eyes glaze over on hearing this phrase. I almost forget where I am and open my mouth to do the 'sure, that would be great' air-kissing thing that I'm so used to.

'Really—any night's fine,' he adds.

I start then, realising he means what he says, and my eyes focus again. 'Oh, um, that'd be great. Thanks.'

'We bought the old King farm, so I'm sure you'll find your way there. Or anyone'll give you the number. You know how it is.'

'How could I forget?' I smile.

Dave turns and lets out an ear-piercing whistle that makes the kids sprint back over to him like a pair of obedient kelpies. I laugh. 'Bye, Tom—bye, Jo.' I wave at them.

'Bye, Dicey,' they call back from under their dad's arms.

Sally waddles over to stand next to me. 'Bye, Sally,' they call out to her, and she gives them a wave before she elbows me in the ribs.

'Ooohhh, the ex-boyfriend!' She gives me another dig.

'Sally! Don't be stupid.'

'I've got to say, he's a real dad at a barbecue, isn't he?'

'What?' I look over at her. 'What's that supposed to mean?'

'You know—he's totally in his element.'

'Oh, right. Well, yes. The kids obviously adore him.'

'Not feeling like you missed out?' There's another dig with this.

'No!'

'Ah, well.' Sally looks disappointed and hobbles off. 'I'm just looking for some hot gossip, that's all.'

Typical. I shake my head as I sit down on one of the large logs that border the car park. Now the kids are all gone I think a quick breather is in order before we tidy up.

It's nice and cool outside now, and I sit for a while just taking in the peace and quiet, breathing in the grassy-smelling air. Thinking back on this evening, I smile. It's been a nice night. To be honest, this afternoon I was worried I'd see people I'd know here. People like Rachel. And Dave. I was worried about what they'd say. But I'd forgotten how different things are in Moo.

Back at home I've spent the last three months talking, talking, talking about my business. About why it failed and trying to justify the fact that it did. But here…

Well, I really must have forgotten. Because the thing is, in Moo businesses fail all the time. Farms especially. Dependent on the weather, and on what other people are growing, stock health and diseases, it's no great surprise when things go badly. And when they do the neighbours help out a bit and life goes on. What Rachel and Dave said tonight wasn't just lip-service—they meant those few words. And now, sitting outside in the calm, with my arms crossed for warmth, I realise that in Moo I might just be able to take off a piece of the heavy armour I feel like I've been wearing for months. Not all of it. But maybe a piece…

'Hey, slacker,' Sally calls from the hall door, making me swivel in my seat. 'Come and give us a hand. Fergus ate a whole tray of the slice and he's been sick. Twice.'

Oh, great. A whole tray. And with all those prunes something tells me throwing up isn't going to be his only bodily function problem tonight.

'Coming!' I yell, and jump up to run inside.

Sally and I tidy up, and listen to Titch talk about the kids. Then we get in the car and drive home, and listen to Titch talk about the kids. We park the car, and listen to Titch talk about the kids—about what a sweetie Hamish is, how Rainbow's a bit of a handful, and how Camilla's dad needs to stop telling her what he thinks quite so much.

It looks like Titch might have taken a piece of armour off as well. Either that or it's fallen off by accident.

She's still chatting away happily as she enters the house, Sally and I trailing after her.

'I'll get us a cup of tea, shall I?' Titch pauses in her thoughts about the Moos for a second.

'That'd be great. Scotch, thanks.' Sally groans. 'A double.'

I laugh. 'Tea's fine with me, thanks, Titch.'

At the bottom of the steps, as I hold Sally's arm to steady her, the two of us watch Titch breeze down the hallway and turn left into the kitchen. It's then that I glance sideways again, and Sally catches my eye in exactly the same way she did an hour or two ago, in the hall's kitchen.

'I know,' I say for the second time tonight. 'I know.'

Titch and I may have each taken off a piece of armour and stored it safely, but the rest we have on quickly starts to rust.

After the initial running around of grocery shopping and Moo minding, our first week 'back home' crawls by in a dreary blur of rain. Stuck inside, the three of us haunt the house—Sally watching bad daytime TV until her eyes turn square, Fergus begging for mini Wagon Wheels, me sewing, beading, sequining and pistachioing until my fingers hurt and my mind is suitably numbed, and Titch—well, the organic muesli slice seems to have had a different kind of effect on her from the rest of us (don't ask what it did to the rest of us…). Because Titch raids Nan's cookbooks and takes over the kitchen.

She cooks all the old favourites until the house is a confused mix of breakfast, lunch, afternoon tea and dinner smells. Banana pancakes, date loaf, sunshine pie, braised lamb chops, streaky bacon meatloaf and corn chowder appear at all times of the day and night.

Sally and I gorge ourselves, but I see Titch eat barely anything.

After day four, when we're beginning to crawl the walls, and Sally is starting to heckle and throw things at *Dr Phil,* I back Bert into a shed corner and demand to know who's still around to entertain us. It's looking like slim pickings. Hildy, I know, has moved to Tasmania, and it seems that most of the people we were close to at school have moved on as well. And most of my grandparents' friends have passed away.

We go back to crawling the walls, skirting each other, because it's simply easier not to talk and the conversation isn't that spectacular anyway. Not knowing how to help either Titch, Sally or myself, I dig the trenches of my funk even deeper. As for Sally, she moves on to checking up on how things are going at the office far too often (in between frustratedly pushing a ruler down her cast in order to scratch her itches), and Titch starts jumping whenever the phone rings, and Sally and I try to pretend we haven't heard her awful midnight calls.

The truth is, however, we have. We've heard them all, including the tears that she keeps telling us she doesn't want to talk about.

For the past few nights Titch has been up late on the phone to Andrew, her husband, who's still located in the middle of nowhere. Like I said, unfortunately for both of them his month on had just started when Titch found herself with ferret problems on TV. Being the guy he is, I know he must be desperate to get home to Titch and her worries. But without another mechanical engineer to replace him, and a plane and a pilot's licence up his sleeve to get him out of there, he's kind of stuck.

After the third night in a row of hearing Titch cry down the phone, I can't bear it any longer. I wait till she hangs up and has made her way outside to sit on the swing chair. Then I get us a pot of tea and two pieces of date loaf, spread thickly with butter, load up a tray and carry it out to her. Fergus is asleep at her feet.

'Here you go.' I sit down beside her, placing the tray on her lap.

'Oh, I'm…'

'Not hungry? Well, I'm going to watch you eat it anyway. All of it.'

Titch gives me a weak smile. 'Thanks.'

I notice again how painfully thin she's becoming, and the thought comes to me that she looks like she's dying emotionally—being eaten away from the inside out. Sitting beside her, trying not to stare, I realise there's no way she could sustain another life form right now, however many fertility drugs the IVF clinic have her on. And it's not that she's sick. This is not a cold, or flu. It's something else entirely—it's worry. Titch's forte. Right now I'd bet that it's Titch's mind holding her back from what she really wants. Not her body.

'Did you want to talk about it?' I try.

Silence.

'Titch?'

She shakes her head slowly. 'I…can't.'

I'm shocked at how defeated she sounds. Whatever this is, it's worse than I first thought. 'Um, well, that's OK. We can just sit. As long as you eat your date loaf.' I place the small plate in her hands, and after a while she complies.

For the next half-hour or so we sit without saying a word, listening to the bats fight in the nearby mango tree and watching the ringtail possums crawl across the electricity wires.

'I'm just so tired, Dicey.' Titch eventually speaks, not looking at me. 'I'm just so tired.'

I know what she means. I don't say anything, though. Instead, I take the tray away and put my sister to bed, with Fergus standing guard beside her.

I wait till I know she's asleep.

And then I tiptoe straight to the phone and dial the number.

'Andrew? Sorry for ringing so late.'

'Dicey? What is it? Is Titch OK?' He sounds stunned. I realise I've probably woken him up. Amazing how men can sleep through anything and everything.

'No, no,' I reassure him quickly. 'She's fine. I just put her to bed. Look, I don't want to pry, but I'd like to help if I can. It's just that I don't really understand what's going on. She's my sister. I'm worried about her.'

There's a pause. 'I…I don't know either. Not really. She's not making much sense. I'm trying to arrange another engineer, but there's just no one, Dicey. No one. She keeps calling up and just crying, not saying anything at all. I'm starting to get scared something's really going on. That Titch is losing the plot—'

I cut in as Andrew begins to lose the plot himself. 'What was she like before you left? Had something happened?'

'That's the weird thing. I mean, the last round of IVF failed, but she was OK, you know? We were dealing with it. Titch was dealing with it.'

'So there was nothing out of the ordinary?'

'No, not really. Well, I suppose there was one thing she said that caught me off guard, but I thought it was just her way of coping.'

'What was it?'

'Er, something about fate. That maybe it was all better this way. I didn't think much about it at the time, but the last couple of days it's kept coming back to me for some reason…'

Fate. This makes me stop and think for a moment.

'Dicey?'

'Hmm? Oh, sorry. It's just that she said something like that to me as well. But she wouldn't explain what she meant.'

'She won't explain anything to me. She won't talk about what's going on at all.'

I sit down in Nan's rocking chair.

'I told her we'd stop the IVF if she wanted,' Andrew continues. 'You know—not go the next round. I mean, it's not the end of the world if we don't have a baby.'

Now I stand up again. Fast. 'You said that to her? To her face?'

There's no reply.

'Andrew?'

'Was that the wrong thing to say?' he says quietly.

Yes! I want to scream. Christ, the poor girl needed encouragement, to be convinced that it was worth continuing to fight for their dreams. That had been the plan from the outset. Didn't he understand that not having a baby *was* the end of the world for Titch?

'Oh, no,' Andrew groans. 'It was the wrong thing to say, wasn't it?'

I shake my head. 'Um, no, of course not,' I say quickly. 'Not if that's the way you really feel.'

'But it's not. Not really. I think we *should* try again, but if it's too much for her I don't want to push. I thought maybe she just needed a break. And I wanted to give her an out—you know, if she didn't want to continue but didn't think she could tell me.'

Silently, I shake my head. He's such a darling, Andrew. I adore him—and the gilded pedestal he puts my sister on.

'Just…don't fret,' I tell him. 'She's having a good rest here. She's cooking up a storm. We'll see how she goes. I'll see if I can get some sense out of her. Get her to talk about things.'

'OK. Thanks, Dicey. And can you call me again? So I know everything's all right?'

'Sure. Of course. And if things… Well, if things get any worse, I'll take her to the doctor.'

When I put the phone back down carefully, quietly, a feeling overwhelms me—shame. I'm ashamed of myself. All this time I've been in Moo I've been wallowing. Wallowing like a pig in the mud of despair. And all the time I've been doing this my sister has been here, right beside me, needing me. Needing my help. Probably needing my help more than she ever has before. And while no one could say I haven't tried, the thing is I haven't tried hard enough.

I stare down at the phone in front of me, really worried now. She won't talk to me and she won't talk to Andrew.

I may be stuck in the mud, but I'm starting to feel like my sister is standing in something different and more threatening. Something like quicksand. And she's sinking fast.

The next day sees us still a reasonably unhappy threesome. Even with the rain finally gone, and not a cloud in the brilliant blue sky, as we sit around the breakfast table there is no 'all for one and one for all' spirit. Not even after Sally and I sugar up and share a second piece of Titch's caramel slice.

It's me who cracks first. Mainly because I can't bear to see Titch like this.

'Oh, come on.' I suddenly push my chair back noisily across the floor. 'Let's get out of here.'

'And go…?' Sally asks.

'Who cares? Anywhere. Anywhere but here.'

Sally shrugs. Titch shrugs. Fergus grunts.

'Oh, come *on*. We'll go out and do something touristy. There's plenty of touristy things to do around here.'

'Yeah. Like Avocado Land,' Sally pipes up.

'Or Macadamia Land,' Titch seconds.

I see her smart-arse answer as a good sign, but don't say anything. 'Well, do you have anything better to do?'

Over the next hour I goad the two of them into the shower, out of the shower, into clothes and out the door. It's no easy task, and I start to think that if they're not careful I *will* take them to Avocado Land. Or Macadamia Land.

Or worse.

'Where are we going?' Sally finally asks, when we're all sitting in the car.

'Byron Bay.' I nod decidedly. 'We're going to get a massage and then we're going to sit on the beach. After that we're going to have lunch and a double scoop ice cream, and then we're going to come back. If we feel like it.'

And that's what we do. We hit the main street of Byron Bay, the three of us have a stress-busting aromatherapy neck and scalp massage while Fergus has an aromatherapy doggie wash, and then we float our way down to the beach, where we lie down on our towels and soak up a bit of sun.

'Well, this isn't so bad after all.' Sally rolls over as best she can.

'Gee, thanks. Anything to add to that, Titch?'

'The massage was nice, but people are staring,' Titch moans forlornly. 'They always stare.'

Sally and I turn our heads to look at her. Then we shade our eyes from the white glare and laugh. Poor Titch is covered from head to foot in thick white sunscreen, a long white linen shirt covers her body, and a floppy white cotton hat is pulled hard onto her head. Poor thing. With her half-Japanese skin, a ray or two of the Australian sun hits her and she turns beetroot-red.

'Have you even got a swimsuit on under there?' Sally asks.

'Somewhere. I think. It's one of the SPF50 ones.'

'Well, so what if you're kind of white? I say let them stare.' Sally waves a hand. 'Go on—take a good look. It'll cost you a dollar!' she yells at a couple of passers-by.

'Sally!' Titch hisses, but then lets a small giggle escape.

'Ooohhh, careful.' Sally turns back. 'We almost had a good time for a second there. If we don't watch ourselves Dicey will get cocky on us.'

The bright, breezy day, holiday atmosphere and sun seem to do us all a bit of good. We share a couple of pizzas and a Greek salad for lunch (not to mention cocktails for Sally and me and a shared bottle of wine) and are strolling down the main street slurping on some vivid sorbets when, in front of Titch and myself, Sally stops dead in her tracks.

Titch and I stumble over our feet, and then over Fergus. 'What is it?' I ask.

Sally looks up at the sign above her head and points with her cone. 'Let's get our cards read.'

'Tarot cards?' Titch says dubiously, her eyes moving to mine.

'Come on—my treat.'

'Well, OK, why not?' I check back with Titch, who's shading her eyes and trying to peer inside the beaded curtain entryway.

Not being able to see anything in the darkness, she stands back again. 'Um, OK.'

Big mistake. Big, big, mistake.

Because as it turns out the tarot card reader is having an off day. (When we leave, I wonder if she knew she would in advance…).

We finish our ice-creams, and then Sally goes first.

When she returns, fifteen minutes later, she squints in the bright daylight.

'Well?' Titch and I both ask at the same time.

Sally snorts. 'Whatever. And talk about weird…'

It seems like this is as much as we're going to get out of her, so Titch leaves us to go in next. When she returns, it's with a worried expression on her face. She doesn't look at either of us.

Well, I guess that means it's my turn.

I hand Fergus's lead over to Titch and push through the beaded curtain with trepidation. After all, Sally and Titch haven't exactly looked impressed on exiting. Surprisingly, when I get into the small inner room I'm not met by an ogre, but by a voice. A gravelly voice.

'Come and sit down, dear,' it says.

'Hello?' I bring my hand up to my eyes. It was bright outside, but not that bright. 'Can we have a light on?' I can't see a thing. What is this? The bat cave? 'Um, hello?'

After a second or two, the room gets a tad brighter. But not much. 'Is that better?' the voice rasps.

Not really. But my eyes are adjusting to the low light now, and I make my way over to sit down at the sarong-covered rickety card table in front of the gravelly-voiced woman. As she begins, asking me a number of questions—my age, where I come from and what's brought me to Byron Bay—I get a better look at her. Or at her eyes. Because that's all I can see. She's fairly well covered up, with a sort of spangly purple turban on her head complete with a veil-like attachment that runs down from one side of the turban, hides her mouth and flicks back up the other side.

Sally's right—this is weird. I've had my cards read twice before and I've never seen anything like this. Come to think of it, both the other people who read for me before wore the same thing—jeans. As she asks me another question, I'm struck again by her voice. Again, weird. It's like she's putting it on.

I butt in. 'Um, are you OK? Do you need a glass of water or something?'

There's a quick shake of her head at that. 'Oh, no. No. It's just a cold, dear.'

'Oh. OK.'

I soon forget that this is all a little bit weird, however, because the woman in front of me starts placing the tarot cards on the table. I'd forgotten how much I love having my cards read and now, flip, flip, flip, they're laid out in front of me on the silky purple cloth, some of them back to front. When she's finished placing them down and has adjusted a few of them, she moves in and inspects them closely.

'Hmmm. Hmmm,' she says softly.

Hmmm. Hmmm. What? I want to ask. And just when I think I'm never going to find out she begins speaking, the fingers of her right hand skating over the top of the cards as she goes.

'This has not been a good year for you.' It's a statement, not a question, but she looks up anyway, her eyes peeping over the veil, piercing mine.

'Um, no, not really.'

As for *my* eyes, they move quickly back down to the cards. Most of them seem rather bleak. There's a dark one with a tower on, flames licking out of it. I can't stop looking at that. And then, of course, there's the one with 'Death' written in great big letters on the top. A lovely drawing of the grim reaper underneath is rather eye-catching as well. Only two—a bright yellow sun and, further along, an angel—seem promising.

'Um, what does the Death one mean?' I ask quickly, needing to know right away.

The woman chuckles, the raspiness of her voice gone for a second. 'Yes, sometimes that one worries people a little. But don't fret. It's a good thing. It means the troubles you've had are ending. Did your problems all happen quite quickly? One on top of the other?'

I nod. Did they ever.

'Yes, I thought so. It was all rather dramatic?'

I nod again. 'My business…kind of failed.' And my marriage, I add to myself.

'Yes. Well, it doesn't seem like it was very fair, and you won't forget what's happened. Ever. However, I am happy to tell you it's almost all over. It's quite an interesting spread you have here, you know. Quite interesting indeed. As I see it, over the next few months you've got some choices to make. Some big choices. And the choices you make can take you in either of two directions. One of these would be the right direction and the other would be—well, not so right. But it is your choice to make, just the same.'

I watch as she scans the cards again, touching one here and there.

'What about this one?' I point hesitantly at the card that reads 'The Lovers'.

'You're married, yes?'

I hesitate, glancing down at my wedding ring. 'Yes.' Despite my answer, the hesitation is obvious, and there for both of us to see.

'That's part of the choice you have to make.'

'I guessed as much.'

'The cards say you already know what you want to do about it.'

I look down at them. Do they? 'Can you, um, tell me some more about these two paths?' I ask.

'Of course.' She takes away a few of the cards and starts flipping again. 'If we concentrate on this area in particular, we should be able to learn a little bit more…'

There's those eyes again. And, this time, they seem even more piercing, if possible.

'He's a good man, your husband.'

I pause. 'Well, yes. Yes, he is.'

Her eyes don't move from mine. 'You are not being true to each other.'

I almost laugh as a picture of Aimee zaps into my mind. You can say that again.

'You are hiding things. Both of you. And that is not good.'

This wipes the smile off my face.

'You should—' she starts talking quickly, her hand reaching out to grab onto mine. But she then stops herself just as fast as she started and her hand pulls back, as if she remembers she shouldn't be touching me. As if I've burned her.

I lean forward. 'What? I should what?'

The woman coughs. 'Talk to him. You need to talk to him.'

Talk to him? That's it? I could have sworn she was going to say something else. 'Anything else?' I try and extract it out of her. But that's it, it seems. If there *is* something else, she's not telling me what. The cards are put away and I start to make my way back outside.

It's only when I'm almost at the door that it hits me again. She really *was* going to say something else back there. I know she was. I spin on my heel, ready to make my way back inside, when I see the figure walking down the hallway. Well, not walking, but waddling.

I stop in my tracks. The movement of the figure is familiar to me. I shake my head and look again, but the figure has turned a corner and is gone. Again, weird. Or maybe this time it's not so weird after all—after the cocktail and two glasses of wine I had at lunch, I'm probably waddling myself. Then, my question forgotten, I turn around once more and head back outside, to squint just as the others squinted before me.

'Well?' Sally asks immediately.

'You're right. It was all a bit...strange.'

'Strange how?'

I shrug. 'The lighting, for a start. That voice. And she certainly rubbed it in a bit.'

'I know!' Sally pipes up. 'I told you so! But what do you mean? About rubbing it in?'

'Yes. What did she say?' Titch's forehead wrinkles.

As we walk back to the car we share our readings. As it turns out, the cards said a variety of things. They told me my husband and I are being untruthful (like I said, rubbing it in!). They told Titch she'd have two children, both girls (ouch). And they told Sally she needed to 'behave herself'.

Huh. Like we needed any cards to tell us that...

'Dicey?'

'JL. Hi.'

'I thought I would call and ask if it is OK to come down.'

'Here?'

'Well, yes, to Moo. I have booked a place.'

'Booked?'

'At a hotel.'

'But you can stay here.'

'No, no. I cannot. Anyway, it is all arranged. And I can see Fergus. And you, of course. That is the important thing.'

'Um, OK. Sure.'

'I will see you tomorrow, then? Sunday?'

'Tomorrow? I mean, um, great…'

It's around four-thirty a.m., when I'm finally getting to sleep, that I sit straight up in bed, suddenly realising why JL's staying in a hotel and not at the farmhouse. It's because *she's* coming. The FC. Oh, great. And how embarrassing. I'd been about to insist that he stayed with us. I thought he was just being stoic, keeping his distance. Now I'm grateful I kept my (usually wide open with two feet planted firmly inside) mouth shut. How cosy would that have been?

At five-thirty I give up and get up. Sleep isn't something that's going to happen. Maybe ever again. Back in the good old days I used to fall fast asleep for a good eight to ten hours as soon as my head hit the pillow.

Not anymore.

These days I can only dream of dreaming. Now, for something to do, I have a shower, blowdry my hair, iron my jeans and the only decent shirt I've brought with me—a white linen number—and slap on a little make-up in the hope of hiding my 'What? Me? Sleep?' under-eye shadows.

'So, what time's he coming?' Sally leans up against the doorframe.

Sitting on the swing seat, dressed and ready to go, I almost drop my third cup of tea. 'God, you frightened the life out of me!' I say, turning around.

'I'm guessing the answer to that question is "early". When were you going to tell us?' The smirk is practically plastered from ear to ear.

How did she know? And why does she always have to be so damn right? 'Um, when you got up, I suppose.'

Sally inches her way over to the seat and sits down beside me. 'And here I was hoping you'd got all dolled up to take me out on a date.'

'I'm not all dolled up!' I splutter. 'And there's no date. As far as I'm concerned he's only coming to see Fergus.'

'He's staying? Overnight?'

I nod. 'At a hotel.'

'Oh,' Sally says. But then she pauses, and I see her work out instantly the same thing it took me approximately eight hours to realise. 'Ohhh…'

'Mmm. I know.'

'I'm surprised. I didn't think she'd be able to "do" the country, you know? I didn't think she'd have the shoes for it.'

I laugh at this because it's quite true—the FC will look ridiculous in the country. For a start, I don't think Louis Vuitton make wellies. And she'll probably be surprised to find out the true connection between cows and where her little FC-sized portions of fillet steak come from.

A couple of hours later, at a more friendly hour, I hear

the car drive up. Quickly I sit up from my relocated slouched position on the couch in the lounge room, throw my book down without marking the page, and I'm up. Within seconds I've grabbed my bag, smoothed my shirt down and am on the front verandah.

It's only then that I don't know what to do.

JL takes his time getting out of the car, while I hold my position on the verandah, moving from foot to foot and occasionally trying to lean casually against the wooden post on my right.

'Um, hi,' I finally say, with a small wave, when he meets my eyes. 'Should we just go?' I start down the steps, stopping halfway to glance back and be thankful that Sally and Titch are nowhere in sight. 'I'm going!' I yell over my shoulder, and then run the rest of the way down the steps.

Minutes later I'm sitting in the driver's seat of my own car beside JL, Fergus barking joyfully in the back seat. It's another gorgeous day, so we've decided to leave JL's car behind and take the convertible.

'So, where are we going?' I turn to JL when we get to the bottom of the driveway.

'Kingshill.' He nods. 'That would be nice, do you think?'

I nod back and turn left. It's the perfect day for Kingshill, a tiny nearby seaside town that, like all of the New South Wales North Coast, is currently being gentrified by retirees with money. When I was a child, Kingshill consisted of a beach, a bowls club, a Chinese restaurant, a fish and chip shop, a newsagent and a whole heap of boring, two-storey brick apartments. Not anymore. Now, you can swim a few laps in your rendered Mediterranean-style penthouse lap pool, go downstairs to the restaurant below to order a skinny de-caff latte and some gluten-free blueberry eggwhite pancakes for breakfast and then meet your personal trainer for a quick ab workout on the beach after lunch.

It doesn't take long before we're parking on Marine Parade, the street that runs along the park which borders the beach-front. The three of us jump out of the car and head across the grass, only stopping to kick our shoes off and roll our jeans up when we hit the first stretch of sand. Fergus bounds ahead until I look up, realise he's taken off, and yell after him. He turns around and comes back sulkily to see JL holding up his leash.

Raff.

'Yes, you know what will happen,' JL says sternly. This is Fergus's official warning. If he goes too far ahead of us, or too near anyone else on the beach, the leash goes on and there's no mini Wagon Wheels for a week. Legally, the leash is supposed to be on the whole time, but I'm pretty sure I'd drown if I followed Fergus into the surf with his leash on, so we bend the rules slightly—as does just about everyone else with a dog.

The rules laid down, we set off. It's reasonably windy on the beach, so we cross the dry, stinging sand quickly and run down to the water.

'God, it's freezing,' I say, sticking one foot in. The water has to be practically lukewarm for me to get in, and that stage of summer temperature has yet to hit. A few more weeks and we should be there. Fergus doesn't seem to mind, however, and dives straight in. 'Not too far,' I call out to him. He ignores me.

'Fergus!' JL yells, and the head turns back.

That dog. I huff.

JL laughs. 'He knows you are easy, that's all.'

My eyebrows rise at this. 'You say that to all the girls?'

'Ah, sorry. I mean, er, a soft touch.'

I laugh now as well. 'Well, OK, then.'

The wind means it's hard for us to hear each other, so we wander the beach not saying much, turning things over with our toes, poking dead jellyfish, taking sly looks into fisherman's buckets and picking up sticks to throw for Fergus, who runs around like we've had him chained up for the last four years.

The further we walk, the more the knot in my stomach, which had been winding itself up tighter and tighter since JL's call last night, slowly starts to unravel. I feel like I could walk for ever, but after a while even Fergus begins to look tired.

'Hungry?' JL asks.

I think about it for a second and then nod. I hadn't noticed—my mind was busy with other things—but I am, in fact, starving.

So we turn around and begin the trek back to civilisation. On the way, we decide on fish and chips for lunch.

'With extra chips,' I add. 'And extra salt. And extra vinegar.'

'And a potato scallop.'

I make a face at this, sorry I ever introduced JL to the revoltingly greasy things. 'I can't believe you actually like potato scallops. I thought the French were supposed to know something about food?'

He shrugs and smiles.

'OK, then. If you insist. A potato scallop for you. But if you ever move on to kabana or crumbed sausages, I'll have to call the embassy and have you deported for your own good.'

Back in the park, it turns out the taps aren't working because of water restrictions, so we wipe our feet on the grass as best we can and lope over to the fish and chip shop.

'Hey, Bernie,' I call out as we push through the waterfall of plastic rainbow-coloured ribbons that keep the flies out of the shop.

'Dicey!' Bernie turns around from his deep frying. 'Haven't seen you for donkeys.'

'My arteries won't let me come too often,' I joke, then proceed to order a disgusting amount of food—way, way too much food for two people, even with a dog. 'Oh, and a potato scallop,' I add at the end.

'For your arteries?' Bernie nods, his pencil poised.

'Well, vegetables are important for good health…'

'Two potato scallops, then?'

I shake my head. 'One's fine. They're not *that* beneficial.'

'JL's up to his old potato scallop tricks, then, hey?'

I laugh. 'You've found us out.'

'What's he doing out there?'

I glance out beyond the ribbons to where JL is sitting at a white plastic table. 'Holding Fergus. He's absolutely disgusting. While we're waiting do you mind if we use your hose? I've got to give him a rinse off.'

'Sure, sure. You know where it is.'

We give an unwilling Fergus a good hose down, getting half soaked ourselves, then grab our order from Bernie.

'Want to see the pelicans, Fergus?' I ask him when I return outside with our white paper parcel.

Fergus loves the pelicans. Ah, who am I kidding? I'm the one who loves the pelicans. I adore the way they float up and down the estuary without a care in the world, their little feet paddling like crazy beneath the water. I glance at JL, who nods at my suggestion, and we start the walk down towards the estuary, all three mouths watering as we go. We end up climbing over a few rocks and down onto a sheltered sandy patch, where we sit and don't waste a second diving into our lunch.

'How is it?' I look over at JL, who's inspecting half a potato scallop.

'Hmmm. Not so good as I remember.'

'That's because every other time you've eaten one you've generally had a lot to drink the night before. How much did you have last night?'

'One glass of red wine.'

'Expensive?'

He nods.

I try not to think about which French restaurant he and the FC went to. 'Well, it's probably not your day for potato scallops. Try again after you've had a bottle. To yourself. And make sure it costs under ten dollars.'

JL laughs and throws the other half of the potato scallop over to Fergus, who swallows it in one gulp. Before he can start begging for more, however, a dog starts barking loudly over to our right. It's an over-excited German Shepherd who leaps into the water and starts chasing the pelicans. Fergus shakes his head sadly. He knows better. With the strong current in the estuary, chasing the pelicans is a mug's game. Sure enough, the dog starts to float off slowly downstream while the pelicans paddle off easily.

'So, how's the writing going?' I ask, after all three of us have watched the German Shepherd make it safely to shore.

JL nods. 'Good. Very good.'

'The manuscript's all finished? It's with your agent?'

He nods again. But it's a final kind of nod, as if I shouldn't ask anything more, so I back off. 'And, um, work? How's the café?'

'Also good.'

'And Aimee?' I'm getting desperate here. Anything not to talk about the burning issue.

JL gives me a strange look.

We eat in silence then, every so often flicking a chip at a very grateful Fergus. As the minutes pass and the clouds move in, the tiny sheltered bay becomes more and more quiet. I remember back to last night and this morning, how I was trying to convince myself that I could do this today. That I could go out with JL for the day and act normal. As if this is a normal thing to do—it certainly doesn't feel like it is right now. And there's that knot again, slowly but surely winding itself up tighter and tighter in my stomach, until it's a hard ball of twine.

Beside me, JL is talking, saying something about the weather, but I can't listen. My attention keeps straying, my mind desperately searching for something I can say next, so there aren't any awkward pauses. I nod my head, hoping he's not going to notice I'm losing it here, hoping that he hasn't already noticed. I can't check though, because I can't look at him, can't turn my head and look at his face.

His face—that's something else I thought about last night. I tried long and hard to come up with a mental picture of JL's face and couldn't do it. I couldn't do it! I couldn't remember what my own husband really looked like. The truth is, I don't think I've really looked at him for ages. Not straight in the eye. Not since before that night in the restaurant. Or maybe even before then. Because, the thing is, if I don't look at him, I can pretend our problems don't exist. That everything is normal between us. That he hasn't been sleeping with someone else. That I haven't been sleeping with someone else.

Now, sitting beside him, all these thoughts circle in my

mind, whipping themselves up like the small choppy waves in front of us. I shiver. It's awful, us sitting here, talking about the weather, me frantically searching for something to say next. What did the card reader say? That we were hiding things from each other. That we needed to talk. Well, good luck. We're hiding so many things from each other now that there's nothing left to talk *about*.

I dig my nails into the sand and let the grains push hard under my fingernails. Ugh. This is just awful. When we met, those first few months we had together, God I could never have believed we would end up like this.

Never.

As stupid as it sounds, we met over a bad bagel. And when I say that, I don't mean a bagel that had turned on society, but a horrible little food poisoning incident—mine, unfortunately. And when I say food poisoning, I mean food poisoning, not the 'I drank a bottle of champers by myself' kind of 'oh, dear, I think I have food poisoning' excuse. It was a learning experience—I'll never order room service half an hour before they close for the night ever again. Or at least I'll never order a smoked salmon and cream cheese bagel from room service half an hour before they close for the night ever again.

It was somewhere in the airspace between Melbourne and Sydney that the bad bagel decided to make a curtain call. I'd been feeling queasy ever since I'd hauled myself out of bed that morning to catch my plane, but in those final few 'God, where the hell is my sick bag?' fumbling moments, I knew I was done for.

The guy on my right froze in terror at my first retch (even though we were in Business Class and he was an aisle-length away). But the guy on my left, against the window, simply said a quiet, 'Oh', handed me *his* bag and then calmly held my hair back as I emptied the contents of my stomach into an envelope that would never see film processing.

Yes, that's right. That's what I said...

He held my hair back.

I think I fell in love before I even looked over at him. And when I did finally look, he looked back at me—as if I was the most desirable woman in the world. The goddess of the used sick bag.

So how did we get here? To this?

'Dicey?'

Caught unawares, I look over at JL. Straight into the brown eyes that I used to know so well. The brown eyes that saw some poor sick girl on a plane once and the man who was kind enough to help out. Quickly, I glance away again.

'Are you OK?'

'Sure,' I say. 'Of course.'

'Is there anything you would like to talk about?'

'No, no. Not really.' The words stick in my throat and my eyes suddenly become full.

'Dicey....'

I get up—fast—and whip off my T-shirt and jeans, leaving only my bikini on. 'Let's go for a swim,' I say, without looking back. Within seconds I'm down at the water's edge and wading in.

It is *freezing*.

Behind me, still on the beach, Fergus barks an 'are you crazy?' bark. When he went in before, it was at least sunny. Now the sky is grey and the water uninviting. I ignore him and keep going. But JL follows. I can hear him following me, pushing through the water, though I don't turn around to check.

When I'm up to the middle of my thighs, I take a deep breath, count to three, and dive in. The cold envelops me. Resurfacing, I swim out a short distance and then over to my left, around some rocks and into a small private pool that's always been one of my favourite spots. Surrounded on three sides by a black rocky outcrop, the water is always crystal-clear, and on a sunny day you can sit for ever and watch tiny, brightly coloured fish swim lazily in and out of the pool's crevices.

Today, however, the mood is different. I stand in the waist-deep water, shivering, and look up to see the sky has become even more ominous, and, beneath it all, the rocks seem to tower over me menacingly.

I've almost forgotten about JL when I feel his hand on my right shoulder and I freeze. Again my eyes fill up, but I don't move, don't say anything, don't turn around. His hand stays there for what feels like for ever, small pieces of sand gritty between us. It's the first time we've touched in...I don't know how long.

When his hand begins to move, slowly, I think he's about to pull away. But he doesn't. It moves down, down over the top of my arm, up again to my back and then down my side to my waist, where it moves around my front. With one swift movement, so fast I barely realise what's happening, he pulls me back a step, closer to him. Before I can respond, before I can even breathe, his hand moves again, up this time, pushing under my bikini top to my breast. My nipples are hard and I'm still shivering—though whether it's the cold or his touch I'm now not so sure. His face moves in close. So close I can feel his breath on my neck. And there's another pull then, with his other hand, bringing me closer to him again.

This time his groin presses hard into my back. I groan and,

without caring what I'm doing, move my own hand up to grab his. I take it and thrust it down, underneath the water, down between my thighs, pushing aside my bikini pants.

And then I turn around.

Within seconds we're fucking. There's no other word for it. It's not making love; it's not having sex. We're fucking. And there's no thought about stopping, or what we're doing, or why we shouldn't be doing this, or the fact that we're in a public place. There's just fucking. JL pushes me back against some of the smooth rocks and we fuck. Fast and hard and rough. Not caring who sees or hears. Not caring about anything.

Foolishly, at one point I open my eyes, and I'm paralysed for a second as I see the expression on JL's face. It's then that I realise what we're doing isn't right. It isn't good. It isn't good and it isn't healthy. That look on his face—it's like I'm taking something from him and he's taking something from me. It's not right, but still we can't stop. I can't stop. And, as he pushes inside me, my eyes close once more, involuntarily, and I don't open them again.

We come together.

It's strange that even now we manage this. We always have.

And, even more strangely, it's this one moment that we choose to look at each other. Properly. Straight into each other's eyes. Pupil to pupil. For the first time in months.

Sally is hanging around the verandah like a very bad smell when I trudge up the front steps, Fergus following forlornly behind me, howling away. 'Well, JL certainly left in a hurry,' she humphs.

'He said to say hi,' I lie quickly, wanting to slip under her radar unnoticed. 'He had to go.'

Sally snorts. 'He had to be somewhere in a hurry around here? Like where?'

'Um, he said he had to meet someone.' This much is true.

'Oh. Ah. Sorry. So she *is* here.'

I shrug.

'Gawd, what's the matter with you, dog?' Sally looks behind me and I breathe a sigh of relief as her attention focuses on something else.

I glance down at Fergus's face. 'That's his "I come from a broken home, pity me" expression.'

Fergus howls again.

Sally sighs. 'Well, I guess we're in for another cheery evening at the homestead,' she says over the noise.

Speaking of which… 'Where's Titch?' I ask.

'Probably still in bed. That's where she's been all day.'

Oh, no. 'Has she eaten anything?'

'I made her eat a bowl of porridge and an orange.'

That's something, at least. 'Thanks.'

'She looks…really unhappy, Dicey.' Sally lowers her voice. 'I know that sounds obvious, but it's more than just work and the lack of a you-know-what, isn't it?' She pats her stomach.

I nod, concentrating on my sister's problems now and pushing my own as far back in my mind as possible. 'I'm not quite sure what's going on. You're right, though. It's different this time around. Almost like she's ready to give up. Andrew thinks so too.'

'That's terrible.' Sally looks truly distressed. And when I see this my heart sinks even further for Titch—to *Titanic* depths. For Sally to be serious and worried, things have to be bad. Maybe even worse than I'd been viewing them up until now.

'I've been thinking maybe I should run her down to the GP?' I whisper.

Sally pauses for a moment. 'More doctors?'

'I don't know what else to do.'

'Maybe give her another day or two.' She glances inside. 'See how she goes.'

I nod. 'You're probably right.' I take the final two steps up to the verandah and feel the tiny bit of energy I'd had left drain out of me and sink through the floorboards. Fergus doesn't even make it this far. Instead, he falls into a heap on the middle step and refuses to budge.

'Would a bath make it better?' Sally suggests as, together, we walk inside slowly.

I sigh. 'Nope. But a bath and a large glass of wine propped on the side might be a small start.'

The thoughts begin in the bath and continue all through dinner.

They nag at me while I'm watching TV. Haunt me through a packet of pistachios. Shadow me into bed. Creep up from behind and scare me while I'm trying to distract myself with some late-night beading.

I can't stop thinking about JL and what happened between us today.

I particularly can't stop thinking about that moment in which I opened my eyes and saw the expression on his face. I really, really wish I hadn't done that. If I hadn't, I think the whole thing would be easier to discount. But that look…and that awful feeling—the feeling that we were both taking something from each other. But what, exactly? For me, I think it was any kind of affection JL was offering. And for him? Who knows? Any dignity I had left? That was what it felt like, anyway. And then—oh God—the way he'd had to scoot away from it all afterwards to get to his 'appointment'. Sure. Most likely to his hotel room and…her. Probably to an appointment they'd made with their king-sized bed and spa bath.

And dirty talk in French.

I almost make myself sick, thinking about how tomorrow they'll get up late and breakfast on something fabulous, feeding each other and gazing into each other's eyes, make love again and then get out their respective notebooks and write something meaningful in French that they can share with their writers' group next meeting. Or just with each other, if it's really personal.

Ugh.

It just makes me—shit—I don't know—furious. Which is ridiculous, I know, because what gives me the right to feel this way? Nothing! I get up now from Nan's rocking chair and try and walk out my anger, pacing with my beading.

I bead from one end of the house to the other. And back again. Forward and back. Back and forward. But instead of my muscles relaxing, with each step they become more and more taut, until they start to ache. When this happens, I sit down on the floor and stretch. I stretch every muscle in my body until each one hurts. And then I get up and pace again, beading as I go.

But nothing manages to distract me. My previous thoughts trace my footsteps, never far away, and confusion continues to fill my head, not leaving any space for sense or reason. The thing is, I knew—even when things were going badly with JL, even when he moved out—that I'd always love him. But now... Oh, Jesus, the way I can't stop thinking about him, it's like... Well, it's like I'm *in* love with him again. It's starting to remind me of when we first started seeing each other. Back then, I'd have these vivid, vivid dreams. I'd be asleep, but then I'd remember something—a conversation we'd had, a moment we'd shared—and sit straight up in bed, thinking it was really happening. I've never had that with anyone else before. Or since. And definitely not with Simon.

No. *Definitely* not with Simon.

At two-thirty I give up, pull a jumper over my pyjama top and tracksuit pants and sneak out the front door. Quietly, quickly, I tiptoe across the verandah and start down the steps towards my car. Fergus gets up from his sleeping place outside and follows me.

Maybe if I can see their room…even if it's just from a distance…

'Going somewhere?' a voice calls out in the dark.

I freeze.

Behind me, there's the clip-clop, clip-clop, clip-clop of someone who isn't one of the three billy goats gruff.

Sally.

I turn around slowly, as does Fergus. 'I was…um…'

'My guess is you were about to participate in a little bit of stalking.'

'Um, ah…' I take another step down towards the car and Fergus pads along behind me.

'I'd stop right there, if I were either of you.'

'No, really, I…' beside me, Fergus is silent. Obediently he takes a step back upstairs.

'That's better. And another.'

Mesmerised, our four eyes locked on Sally's two, we step up.

'And one more.'

We do as we're told.

'Now—heel.'

Both of us slink over to Sally, our eyes on the floor.

'You've kept me up since eleven, waiting for this. I was starting to think you weren't going to be stupid enough, but here we are…'

'How did you…?' I finally look up, my eyes wide.

'Dicey, sweetheart, how long have I known you?'

'Um…' I think hard.

But Sally cuts in fast. 'Now, let's not go naming the number of years, or showing our age, or anything rash. Let's just say long enough.'

'OK. Long enough.'

There's silence as we size each other up.

'Oh, come here.' Sally reaches over and drags me in under her arm. 'Gorgeous, you'd only embarrass yourself. You know what'd happen.'

'Do I?' I gulp.

Sally presses me in harder. 'You'd get there. You wouldn't be able to see enough from the lawn, so you'd creep up to the door like some kind of an axe murderer. That wouldn't be enough, so you'd peer in through the window. Then you'd do something like try and blow the curtain aside. It's all sickeningly downhill from there. She'd probably hear you and be startled, running out naked with a perfect "men can't resist me and now you know why" Brazilian and not a spot of cellulite on her.'

I groan.

'That's what I mean. There's certain information you just don't need to know. And, just in case you forget about our little talk and feel like another midnight stroll later on, I might just tell you something now.'

'What?'

'I'll be sleeping with these under my pillow.' In the darkness I see Sally swing something around one index finger.

My car keys.

'You stole my car keys?'

'No. There was no stealing involved. I like to call it safe-keeping.'

I reach out for the silver dangling in front of me, but Sally's too fast, snatching the bunch back into her palm. 'You gotta get up early, kiddo.'

'What's going on?' Titch says from the doorway behind us, and Sally and I both jump. 'What are you doing out here?'

'Just, um…'

'Having a chat.' Sally slides the keys into her pocket. 'We were just having a chat.'

'Oh.' Titch rubs her eyes.

'But now I'm going to bed,' Sally adds, giving me a sideways look. 'I've been up long enough, and I don't get any more drugs until eight.'

'Sorry,' I mumble as Sally lets go of me and heads inside. She waves behind herself.

Titch and I watch her go.

'You up now?' I ask when Sally's gone.

'I think I slept all day.'

I nod. 'Your body probably needs it.'

'What do you mean?' Titch frowns at me.

'Nothing. I just mean that you're probably winding down. You know—on holiday mode.' I think fast, not wanting to upset her.

'Oh. I see.' Titch rubs her arms and I move forward to guide her inside.

'Come on, you're cold. Let's go in and see what's on TV.'

'At three a.m.?'

'You're right. Probably not much. But who knows? We might get lucky.'

We move into the lounge and both take a seat in front of the TV on the comfy old couch that's been Sally's domain all this week. Titch passes me the remote and I flick through the channels. It's an abysmal ode to programming. And the depths of Titch's stomach must agree, because they let out a loud grumble, making me look over and Fergus glance up from his sprawled sleeping position on the floor.

'I think I might be hungry now,' Titch says, staring down at her stomach.

'Just a bit.' I stare at her stomach as well, just in case an alien or two is about to pop out of it (with the noise I've just heard, it's a definite possibility). 'I think there's still some stir-fry in the fridge. Want me to heat some up for you?'

Titch shakes her head as she gets up. 'No, it's OK. I'll get it. Cup of tea?'

'Sure.' I nod. 'But only if you're having one.'

While Titch is gone, I keep flicking channels. Around and around and around. As if something interesting will magically appear. I know for a fact that it won't—lately I've been up enough at this time of night to realise that much—but there's something soothing about hitting each button in turn and then coming full circle to start again.

Well, until the five hundredth time around, that is. On that attempt I give up, turn the TV off and flick the remote onto the other end of the couch. I mustn't know my own strength, however, because it jumps off the cushion, hits the arm of the couch, falls, skids across the floor and lands beside Nan and Pop's buffet cabinet where all their good china and other treasures are kept. I hold my breath as I watch it move towards the glass, then breathe a sigh of relief as it lands firmly on the carpet. That was close. Too close.

Not wanting Titch to see, I kneel up on the couch and lean over until my stomach's resting on the opposite arm. I reach my hand out and go to pick up the remote, but before my fingers grasp it something catches my eye—Nan and Pop's photo albums. I pause for only a second before I get up properly and take myself over to sit cross-legged in front of the small sliding glass door. When I open it up, I know exactly what I want to look at. My fingers skim past the vinyl covers of my childhood and reach further over to the right. To the heavier, leather-bound albums. The oldest albums in the cabinet. I pick the last one up and bring it out carefully.

The black pages creak and the protective paper crinkles as I open up the cover, resting the album in my lap. My eyes take in the pictures before me—Pop's parents standing in a garden, three of their children at their feet with Pop, the youngest, in short shorts and thick boots, his hair sticking straight up at the back (it always did that), held by his mother. Pop's father at work, one foot resting on the hugest tree trunk I've ever seen, his braces holding up his heavy wool pants.

Further on there are childhood birthday parties and fancy dress dances. I flip over the pages carefully, smoothing down the thin white pages in between as I go.

Finally I find what I'm looking for. Nan and Pop's wedding photo. They're standing outside a small church with their arms linked, by themselves. I've seen the picture hundreds of times before, but this time I really study it. I bend over the album and stare into their eyes. Pop looks like—well, like Pop. Just young, and in a stiff-looking suit that I just know he's dying to get off. And there's Nan, of course, in her beautiful cream lace drop-waisted dress.

My eyes move down the photo, studying every tiny detail, until I sit back for a second, surprised, because there's something I haven't noticed before. One of Nan's delicate shoes that match her dress is turned at a sharp angle to the right, her ankle bent awkwardly. It's as if she's uncomfortable being the centre of attention. As if she can't wait for all this fuss to be over and to 'get on with it' as she used to say. I stare at the foot, then back up at her eyes, which aren't giving away anything of the sort, and I smile.

I wish she was here to give me some advice. I look up suddenly to the walls of the house. It's not the same here anymore. It's not the escape it used to be for me when my grandparents were alive, and I realise why now. It wasn't the place—it was the people. Still, it's grounding in some ways, just being here and forcing myself to slow down. At home all I could concentrate on was the fact that my business had failed. But here, in Moo, it doesn't feel like it's the end of the world. People are more interested in the other pieces of my life that have gone astray.

Like my marriage.

I look back down again when I think of this. Back at the

image of my grandparents. They'd be so disappointed to know that I'm separated. And shocked that, up until now anyway, I didn't think it was that big a deal. At least three-quarters of my friends who married in the last ten years have now separated or divorced. Not to mention that Nan and Pop would have been ashamed if they'd been the ones to catch me tonight, trying to spy on my husband. Because there's no other word for it. That is what I was going to do. Spy.

That's the worst thing—that my grandparents would feel ashamed of me. Disappointed in me. Not once did they ever yell at me, or raise their voices. They didn't need to. It was always that look in their eyes that would trip me up. The few times I failed to meet their standards. It was like quick stab through the heart, being on the receiving end of that kind of look from them.

And, remembering this, I realise that I have to stop. I have to stop thinking about JL. I have to let him go. I had my chance and I threw it away, and—well, that was that. As Pop would have said, 'You made your bed, girl, now you have to lie in it.'

By myself.

At least before today, JL and I were able to be civil to each other. But the sex—like I said—there was something about it that was just plain wrong. Like our relationship was souring even further.

I keep flipping though the album, turning over page after page, following my grandparents' lives. Their first home. Their friends. Pop's family history of heart disease slowly and cruelly picking off his siblings until he was the only one left. That always made him desperately sad—the loss of all his brothers and sisters. I think, being the youngest by ten years, the cherished baby of the family, he took it especially hard.

Finally, a moment of joy appears in one of the last photos in the album. Something Nan and Pop never thought they'd have—a child. My mother. Their faces beam out from the picture; they're overjoyed at their luck. I feel another quick stab in my heart, knowing the pain that she'd cause them later on. Why couldn't it have always been as good as in the picture before me? Why couldn't things have stayed like that for them? They deserved more. Not that they ever so much as hinted at that.

'What are you looking at?' Titch leans over the top of me, making me jump.

'Old photos.'

Titch places my tea on the floor and sits down beside me.

'Look at their faces,' I say. 'I mean, really *look*.'

Titch leans over the album so our heads almost touch. After a while she glances up at me. 'Dicey, Nan and Pop, they're…they look…so old.'

I nod. There's no denying the wrinkles, formed from years in the Australian sun without any kind of sunscreen or age-defying night lotion.

'Nan was thirty-nine when she fell pregnant. I guess thirty-nine then looked a lot older than it does today.'

'Thirty-nine,' Titch whispers, almost to herself, and I know what she's thinking. The thought had just flickered through my mind as well.

Thirty-nine. Four years older than Titch.

My sister takes the album from me now, almost in a robotic motion, as if she has to have it. She holds it in her lap and stares, her eyes not flicking from the page for a second.

'Andrew says if I don't want to try again, we don't have to.'

This time I keep my mouth shut, wanting her to explain further what's been going on in her head.

'Maybe…maybe he never wanted a baby in the first place?' she continues.

This, however, is just too much.

'That's not true, Titch.' I reach over and touch her on the arm. God, I *knew* that had been the wrong thing for him to say to her.

She glances up at me. 'Do you really think so?'

In her heart, I'm sure Titch already knows the answer to this question, but I answer it for her anyway. 'Andrew's desperate for a baby. You don't go through what you two have been through unless you are. And you can see it. You know you can. You know he wants it almost as much as you do.'

Titch sighs and nods. 'I suppose.'

'I think…I think he was just trying to be kind, Titch. To give you an out if you needed one, you know?'

She nods again, and runs a finger over the album page. 'I know. Oh, I wish they were here, though. They'd know what to say. They always knew.'

I look at the photo again. At the lines around my grandmother's eyes. Thirty-nine. Of course, I'd always held hope knowing this—that Nan was older than Titch when she had our mother. But I'd never really thought about it this way. That Nan might have felt everything Titch has been feeling. Everything, maybe, except hope. In Nan's day there wasn't the hope that IVF gave, the expectation that something could be done. Back then, if you couldn't have a baby—well, that was just your lot.

Suddenly Titch turns to me and grabs my knee, making me gasp. But it's not the quickness of her gesture or her tight grasp that sends the shock through me, but the look I see in her eyes when I move my gaze to her face. For the first time in days—months, even—she looks as if she feels something inside.

Her eyes—they're wide and frightened—and her fingers push past the fat on my legs and grip bone. It's almost like she's seen a ghost.

'I'm just scared that I'm tempting fate, Dicey. Maybe I'm not meant to be a mother. What if…? What if…?' She pauses long enough to shove the album onto the floor in front of her. As if she can't bear to hold it for a second longer.

'What if *what?*' I prompt, knowing that she's not going to cave this time.

She turns back to me, seeming both disgusted and destroyed by the thought at the same time. 'What if I was like *our* mother?'

My voicemail. Ten-fifty-six a.m.:

'Dicey? It's Jean-Luc. JL. Er, I think we should talk about…about the beach. I am sorry…I should not have… Please, call me back. Any time…'

'Sally!' I scream at the top of my lungs. 'Sally! Stop with the bloody lipgloss and get out here.'

'Yeah, yeah, yeah,' she grumbles, thumping down the hall-way, and I flash back to this time last week, when I was screaming exactly the same thing. Sally pauses in the entry-way for effect when she finally gets there.

'Does it always have to be like this?' I shake my head at her.

'What? You hollering at me like a banshee?' She applies a bit more lipgloss (I knew it!) belligerently. 'Looks like it, doesn't it?'

Sitting on the swing seat, Titch moves position, making a noise, and we both turn to look at her.

'Shall we continue this in the car?' Sally snaps her pot of gloss closed, stalking past as best she can with her cast. She gives me the eye as she goes. She knows something's gone on between Titch and myself—she knew the minute she saw both of us at breakfast.

Since then—all day, really—she's been badgering me to tell her what it is. But so far I haven't. I can't. Or won't. I'm not sure which. Even if I wanted to, I couldn't think of a place to begin, to tell the truth. After Titch's reaction to the photos last night, and what she said about our mother—after seeing that look in her eyes—I'm not convinced it's something I'd be able to articulate. Anyway, because I won't tell her what's going on, Sally's peeved. And this, combined with the fact that she wouldn't give me back my car keys last night, however much I begged, cajoled and tried to steal, means that we're currently not playing best friends.

The three of us climb into the car wordlessly. Even Fergus knows enough to shut up when Sally's in one of her moods, and he slinks in after her, sitting as far away on the back seat as he can.

Five minutes later we're back at the community centre hall, ready for round two: Return of the Moos. We open up and do a quick run around, putting out chairs and tables like we did last week.

Titch prepares the kitchen for later—this week it's organic strawberry smoothies (again, complete with non-genetically modified organic soy milk and non-genetically modified organic soy milk ice-cream for extra flavour. Mmm. Yummy. Hippies sure know how to show kids a good time).

At six on the dot the kids begin to bounce inside, their voices ricocheting off the walls at the excitement of seeing each other again.

Slowly, as the minutes pass by, Titch begins to smile again. Single-handedly she gets the Moos sitting down with their wish books and pens, pencils and crayons of choice.

'Here we are.' She finishes by sitting down next to Sally and myself and passing us each something.

'Oh.' I look at it. It's my wish book. Great.

'I second that "oh" and raise you a—'

'Sally,' Titch warns her, guessing she's about to come out with something tender Moo ears probably shouldn't hear.

'Right. Sorry.'

'So we're in for another great forty minutes or so of blank-notebook-staring, are we?' I look from one side of me to the other.

'We could write in them,' Titch suggests.

Silence.

And then the three of us laugh.

All the Moos raise their hard-working little heads to look at us.

'Sorry, kids,' I say. 'It's OK. Sally just forgot how to spell something.'

'What?' Rainbow asks.

'Oh, um—Porsche.'

Rainbow snorts at the mention of this soulless consumer goodie.

'My dad has a Porsche,' Camilla pipes up. 'And a Jag. And a—'

Rainbow snorts again. Louder this time.

'It's yellow,' she adds. 'My dad's Porsche.'

'That's nice.' I nod. 'Maybe you can wish for one like it for when you're older.'

Camilla shakes her head. 'Oh, no. Girls don't have Porsches. Girls have four-wheel drives.'

Beside me, Sally starts to cough. Titch's eyes have popped out and are now resting on the table in front of us. And, as for Rainbow, she looks like she's about to have an aneurism.

'Plenty of girls—I mean, um, women—have Porsches,' I say quickly. 'Or other kinds of sports cars. Sally's got a red Ferrari back at home.'

I watch to see how Camilla takes this piece of wisdom. I mean, hasn't she ever seen a woman driving a sports car before? But Camilla's expression just reads like she doesn't really believe me. A few seats away from her, Rainbow remains silent and stunned. I shoot Sally a quick 'what are they teaching that kid at home?' look, and she shoots a 'to ask for a nose job for her sixteenth and implants for her eighteenth birthdays' raise of her eyebrows.

I'm about to open my mouth to say something else wise (I hope…), when something surprising happens. Rainbow's sidekick, Leaf, pushes her chair back, scraping it loudly on the wooden floor, then jumps up and runs out of the room.

It's Sally who gets it together first, closing her mouth, pushing her own chair back and heaving herself to her feet. 'I'll go,' she says.

I stand up as well.

'No, it's OK,' she says. 'I think I know what it is. I overheard something before…'

'What?' I whisper.

She waves a hand as she starts across the room. 'Just let me check it out.'

'Can I come?' Rainbow jumps up in her seat.

Sally waves again. 'No, it's OK, kiddo. I've got it.'

It seems like an eternity before Sally appears at the door and beckons Titch and I over to her. The two of us tiptoe across the hall, not wanting to disturb the Moos now they've got back to their wish books.

'Is Leaf all right?' Titch asks.

Sally nods. 'It's like I thought. Women's problems.'

Titch nods knowingly.

'What?' I say, confused and obviously too loud, because I get a *'shhh'* from both Titch and Sally.

Sally rolls her eyes at me. 'Come on, Dicey.'

Titch nudges my arm. 'She's got her period.'

That's what I thought they meant, but my confused look stays put. 'She must be...what? Ten? Eleven?'

'It's like everything else. They start early these days. Anyway, have you guys got any supplies?'

Titch shakes her head.

'Only a few tampons,' I say.

'That's no good,' Titch says. 'We'll have to go to the shops. Unless you think we should call her mother?'

Sally snorts. 'And have her skip down from the hills with something filthily earth-friendly like those disgusting reusable sea sponges? No, thanks. The kid's got enough problems without her mother stepping in right now. We'll go to the shops and get something bad for the environment.'

Titch nods. 'You two take her now, and I'll get the other Moos started on the smoothies before you get back.'

'You sure you'll be OK by yourself?' I turn to Titch.

Her eyes widen. 'I doubt they're going to tie Fergus and myself up and dance around us.'

I shrug. You never know. It only takes one rotten Moo...

'I'm sure Rainbow will help you out,' Sally smirks, and the three of us glance back inside the room. Funnily enough, Rainbow has one eye on her wish book and the other fixed firmly on what's going on by the door. I shake my head. That kid doesn't miss a beat.

'OK, let's go.' I look over at Sally. 'Where's Leaf?'

'Hiding in the toilets. She wouldn't come out.'

'I'll close the door and you can take her around the side,' Titch says. 'Have you got keys? Money?'

I nod on both accounts.

'Well, good luck, then!' Titch closes the door behind her.

Sally and I start towards the toilet block, a small wooden building just down the end of a winding cement path.

When we get to the entryway, we stop.

'Leaf?' Sally calls out hesitantly.

There's a noise from inside.

'Leaf?' I try. 'We need to take you down to the shops. Is that OK?'

'Is there anyone else out there?' a voice calls back.

'No. It's just Sally and me. Dicey.'

'Really?'

'Really. I promise. Cross my heart and hope to die.'

There's a pause. 'No one says that anymore.'

Sally suppresses a snort.

'Sorry—I'm a dag!'

Silence.

'Well, OK, then. If there's really no one else out there, I'm coming out.'

Sally and I wait, and eventually there's a few small footsteps. A head appears around the door.

'Ready?' Sally asks.

Leaf does a quick scan of the surrounding area.

'It's OK. Everyone's inside,' I say. 'And Titch closed the door.'

'All right.' Leaf nods and scampers off across the grass and around the side of the hall to where the car is parked. Sally and I follow.

When we get to the car, I open it up and help Leaf into the back before I get in myself.

'Everyone set?' I turn around and look at Leaf. 'Seatbelt on?' Leaf nods. 'Great.' I start the car and pull out onto the road.

'I'm glad you're here,' Sally huffs as we leave.

'What do you mean?'

'Well, I've practically forgotten what to do. I haven't had a period in years.'

My foot slips off the accelerator. 'What?' I look over at her.

She gestures me on. 'They've got pills for it, baby. You just skip the white ones.'

I can't believe what I'm hearing. 'You mean you skip *all* your periods? All of them? For how long?'

'Three years. At least.'

I shake my head. 'But don't you get…?' I pause for a second, remembering Leaf in the backseat. 'B-r-e-a-k-t-h-r-o-u-g-h b-l-e-e-d-i-n-g?'

'God, no. I take another lot of pills for that. Wonders of modern medicine and everything. That's why I don't date doctors.'

'Huh?'

'It's my little offering towards science. You know—let them trot along with all that drug development stuff.'

'What's breakthrough bleeding?' Leaf pipes up.

Shit. 'Um…ah…' I stall.

But Sally doesn't blink an eyelid. She pushes herself around in her seat to face Leaf. 'So, you're a woman now, hey?'

In the rear vision mirror, I see Leaf stare back at Sally, the ultimate 'strange lady'.

'You know what that means?' Sally continues.

There's no reply.

'It means you're suddenly extra good at making grocery lists, organising household chores, and can rest comfortably in the knowledge that there's one certainty in life.'

'And what's that?' I take the bait.

'That it will always be you who scrubs the toilet.'

Wisdom imparted, she hoists herself around again. I try not to laugh. Frankly, this is pretty rich coming from Sally, who, all her professional life, has had a cleaning lady. But before I can say anything she's reaching forward to the glove box.

'What are you looking for?' I ask.

'These.' She fishes a packet out.

'I thought you'd quit!'

'Not likely. Only around Titch. Nicotine withdrawal is less painful than her sad "you're killing yourself" looks.'

'Well you can't smoke now.' I tilt my head towards the back seat.

Sally swivels once more. 'You've seen it in all the movies, right?'

Leaf nods.

'You know it's bad for you and you should never do it?'

Leaf nods again.

'You know smoking kills you?'

'Yes.'

'Well, you're a pretty smart kid by all accounts. Here you go—read this…'

'Sally!' I can't believe she's passing Leaf the packet of cigarettes. What planet is this girl from?

'"Smoking when pregnant harms your baby,"' Leaf reads out obediently.

'That's right!' Sally points at her. 'And I should add that it's a filthy, dirty habit that never looks good on a Moo.'

'But you were a Moo. Titch said so.'

'Yes, but I was a very bad Moo. I always have been, I'm afraid.' And, with this, she lights up and blows the smoke up and out of the car.

'We're dead.' I shake my head as I pull into the supermarket parking lot. 'Dead, dead, dead. Dead Moo meat. Steak.'

But that would be organic steak, of course.

'So, what do we get?' I glance at Sally as we stand in front of the feminine protection section. I almost crack up every time my eyes meet that sign. The only feminine protection Leaf needs right now is protection from Sally.

'One of everything, I suppose.' Sally reaches forward and starts to pull boxes of pads from the shelves. 'I thought you'd know what to get.'

'It's been a long time since I used anything that resembles a nappy,' I say, then remember the small figure beside me. 'Sorry, Leaf. Did you want to go choose a treat? A chocolate bar or something?'

'I'm only allowed to have non-genetically modified organic soy chocolate.'

'Oh, Christ.' Sally rolls her eyes. 'Do you *like* other sorts of chocolate?' she asks.

Leaf nods. Hard. 'I like Snickers bars the best.'

'Hey, sister, me too! Pick one up for me while you're at it.'

Leaf trots off happily in the direction of the candy aisle.

'Moo meat,' I say again. 'Moo meat.'

'Oh, for God's sake. Her mother will never know. And what kind of a psycho brings their kid up like that anyway? When she hits eighteen and leaves home she'll turn into an obese fast food and television addict—you watch. Right. That's it, then.'

I look down at the basket, now crammed full of pink and purple packaging. 'Regular, super, maxi, wings, no wings and g-string,' I read. There's a pause as the last item hits home. 'Hang on. G-string?'

'Yeah. So?'

'Something's telling me Leaf's mother doesn't buy her daughter g-strings.'

Sally snorts. 'I guess. They probably don't make them in hemp.'

The two of us squirm just thinking about it.

Sally puts the g-string labeled packet back on the shelf. 'That lot should keep her going for a while, anyway.'

'Almost until she can buy her own g-strings, I'd say.' There's a lot of feminine protection in that basket.

'Oh, that reminds me. Peanut butter. Here, hold this…' Sally thrusts the basket at me and hobbles off.

Hmm. I really don't want to know why g-strings remind her of peanut butter, I think, as I look down into the basket again.

'That's quite a stash you've got there,' a voice behind me says, making me jump. 'Stocking up for the nuclear winter?'

I spin around. 'Dave! Oh, um—hi.'

He takes a closer look at the basket, then moves up to meet my eyes. 'Sorry. Don't mean to be nosey.'

'I, um—I—that is…' I start, but then realise I don't quite know how to explain what's going on. 'There's been a…a situation.'

'Right.'

'With the Moos.'

Realisation dawns across his face. 'Ah.'

Sally starts to hobble back down the aisle then, and a little early warning alarm starts to go off inside my head. I need to get rid of Dave and I need to get rid of him fast.

'Right. Well…'

But Sally can move a lot faster than usual when she feels the need to.

'Ooohhh, the flames of old love are flickering in aisle five, hey?' She dumps the peanut butter into the basket. 'Sorry. Didn't mean to interrupt.'

Annoyed, I shoot her a look. 'You're not *interrupting* anything.'

'Is that so?'

I turn away from Dave now, embarrassed. 'Yes, that's so. Don't be stupid,' I hiss at her.

'I'd, er, best be off, then…' Dave says from behind me.

I swing back around. 'Sure. Nice seeing you again,' I say, a bit too brightly.

His eyes move from mine over to Sally and back again, and he gives me a funny look before he speaks. 'You too. And I meant what I said the other day. That you should come up and visit.' With a slight wave of one hand he's gone.

Furious, I hurl myself back around one more time and grab Sally's arm.

'Ow!'

But just as I'm about to start in on her Leaf comes running back up the aisle.

'I got three.' She holds out the chocolate bars in her hand. 'In case Dicey wanted one too. And I got king-size. Because I thought you might be hungry.'

'Thanks,' I say, trying to compose myself.

'Is that OK?' Leaf looks worried.

I exhale. Act composed. Act composed. 'Of course. It's fine. Whatever you want, Leaf.' Anyway, who am I kidding? I was never one to say no to a Snickers bar, let alone a king-size one (as much as I don't want to admit it, it seems Sally is probably right about Leaf and the fast food addiction thing).

I exert some frustration by leaving Sally and Leaf and making a quick dash for the pistachios. I also stock up on mini Wagon Wheels and then join the two of them in the checkout queue, where we polish off our illegal chocolate rations as we wait. I say nothing as Sally reads brain-rotting, non-mother-sanctioned bits and pieces from assorted women's magazines out loud.

We've paid, and are heading back to the car, when a guy approaches us. 'Sally? Sally Bliss?' He takes a few steps forward, halting us in our tracks.

Sally looks at him blankly.

'It's George. George Bryson.'

Another blank look.

'I never saw you again. You know—after that night.'

Oh, great. Another Sally moment, I think, as I see the lights come on behind her eyes. I look down at Leaf and wonder if I've got time to drag her away. But Sally's got a firm grip on her hand and is already speaking.

'Oh, yes. *That* night. Well, the thing is, George. I was sort of busy. I had to leave town.'

'Oh. Oh, that's too bad. I had a, er, great night that night.'

He pauses, looking like he doesn't know what to say next. 'Er, is this your daughter?' George looks down at Leaf.

There's another pause. 'I guess you could say I might ask you the same question,' Sally says mysteriously, leaning forward to tap George on the chest with one finger.

It's got to be a full thirty seconds before the shock of recognition hits poor George's face. His eyes move from Sally to Leaf and back again. Then he makes a kind of a woofing sound, where every last bit of air is expelled from his chest, and chokes. Standing beside him, I can see the arteries in his neck. His pulse must be running at about one hundred and eighty beats a minute.

'But, we—' he starts.

Sally shrugs.

'I—'

She shrugs again, this time adding a small smile for good measure.

'You coming?' a guy calls out from across the other side of the checkouts. A very cute guy, actually. I see Sally's eyebrows register a nine on the interest scale.

'My housemate,' George's face drains of colour when he sees Sally's expression. 'Yeah, I'm coming!' He swivels around before turning back to us again. 'I've got to go. He's a good friend of the family, you see, and if my parents found out… Er, they're very Christian, you know…' There's a beseeching look directed at Sally, who looks back at him innocently. 'Look—here…' George reaches into his back pocket and brings out his wallet. He opens it up and takes out all the money in it, pressing it into Sally's hand.

'Gosh,' Sally says, surprised.

George gulps. 'Er, can we…can we just pretend we never met tonight? That everything is how it was before?'

'Sure!' Sally replies. 'No worries. See you around, then?'
But George is gone.

'Let's go!' Sally grabs my arm and Leaf's hand even harder and we move on, out through the sliding doors and into the car park.

'What the hell was that about? He just gave you $400!'

'Nice touch, huh? I wasn't expecting $400. And that, my dear, was about revenge. He was terrible. The worst. I'd almost forgotten. I mean, hello? It's called an orgasm. And, despite what he might have heard in the football club showers, we're *both* supposed to get one.'

'*Sally!*' I bellow. Right. That's it. Leaf's vocabulary has probably expanded tenfold tonight. I pull the kid towards me and cover her ears.

But it's too late. The muffled question is already escaping the innocent—before tonight anyway—rosebud lips. 'What's an orgasm?'

'Wait right there,' I tell Sally as she begins to move towards the passenger side door. 'No. I mean it. Right there.'

And she must realise I do mean what I say, because she does stop moving, and waits right on the spot I point to, next to the boot of the car. I then take a minute or two putting Leaf in the car and watching her buckle up before I make my way back to that pointed-out spot. And when I get there I'm no less furious than I was those few minutes before.

'What?' Sally says innocently.

I almost want to cry, I'm so worked up.

'What?' she says again. And it's this that pushes me over the top. As if she doesn't know!

'What is it with you?' I ask. 'What is it with you and Moo?'

'Hey, that kind of rhymes!' Sally says. Then her grin fades as she clocks my expression. 'Ah, um…'

I turn my face away for a second so I don't have to look at her.

'What?' she says again.

I turn back slowly. 'What is going *on* with you, Sally?'

In the pause that follows she slowly loses any hint of the smirk that's been on her face. 'You're serious, aren't you?'

'Yes, I'm serious!'

'Stop yelling! You're making a scene. Now, what are you talking about?'

'A scene? *I'm making a scene?* What am I talking about? Are you kidding me? If you really don't know, I'll tell you—whenever we come back here you turn into…some kind of freak. You go crazy. Off the planet. You drive everybody nuts. You can't tell me you haven't noticed.'

Sally says nothing, but she doesn't look impressed.

'Well?'

'Well, what?'

'Well, what was that with Dave back there? And with that George guy? Would you care to explain any of that?'

'I didn't think there was anything *to* explain.'

I stare at her now, incredulous. 'You've really got to be kidding me. Are you trying to tell me that's normal? How you behaved in there? You're acting like a two-year-old. No. That's not true. Two-year-olds behave better than that. Every time we're here, in Moo, it's like you just can't help yourself.'

'Is that so?' Sally gives me a withering look.

'Don't look at me like that.'

'Like what?' Her expression turns from withering to innocent again.

I've really had it now. 'Just stop it. *Stop it!*' I yell, making people in the car park turn around and look at us. And when they do I want to yell at them too. But I don't. Of course I don't. The last thing I need in Moo is a reputation for being crazy. So, instead, I turn around and make my way over to the driver's side door. 'Forget it. Just get in the car, Sally,' I say. And I can't even look at her as I say it.

Apart from my, 'Sorry about that, Leaf', we drive back to the Moo community hall in complete and utter silence. The poor kid scrambles out of the car in seconds flat, making me even more furious with Sally. Like she hasn't had enough to deal with tonight as it is.

As for me, I go to follow close behind her, pushing my door open milliseconds after I've turned the keys off in the ignition.

But, beside me, Sally grabs my arm, stopping me. 'Dicey…'

I sit back down, but I don't turn around to face her.

'I'm sorry. About before. I just…'

As she speaks, there's something in her voice that completely defuses my anger. A vulnerability. I turn my head to look at her.

She shrugs a small shrug.

'Just what?'

There's that shrug again.

And now Sally looks smaller, and more tired than I've ever seen her look before in her entire life.

'What is it?'

'I just…I can't explain.'

'Try me.'

Another shrug.

I can't believe what I'm seeing. It's like she's not even the same person. The person sitting beside me—it's not the Sally I know.

'I won't do it again,' she says, not looking at me, but star-ing out of the window now.

Silence.

I keep looking at her. It feels like for ever before she can bring herself to look at me again.

'Forgive me?' she says quietly.

I don't understand. I don't understand at all. However, words exit my mouth. 'Of course.'

I still don't understand, but what else can I say?

Sally skips over the weird bits. The bits Titch won't understand, just as I don't understand. As for me, I stay out of it
and say nothing. When Sally's finally done with her story-
telling, Titch only manages a very poor and short disappointed look before she starts laughing.

'So what did you tell her?'

'The truth.' Sally takes a slug of her beer. 'Complete with
a small but anatomically correct diagram.'

'You didn't? No. Don't answer that. Of course you did.'

'Hey, she's better off knowing early. Share the knowledge,
I say. If it eases your mind any, I also gave her a quick run-
down on condoms.'

'I stopped her from going back to the supermarket and
buying a packet and a hand of bananas,' I add, trying not to
sound sour.

Titch sighs now. 'You're evil, Sally. I can't believe he gave you $400. What was that supposed to be for?'

'I think it was "go away, I never want to see you again" money,' Sally suggests. 'But I like to think of it as compensation for services not rendered.' She laughs loudly then, and everyone in the pub turns to look at the noise.

Even Fergus sticks his head in the door from his tied-up position to see what all the fuss is about.

So much for 'I won't do it again', I think to myself. What is it about Sally and Moo?

'Anyway,' Sally adds, raising her beer to them, 'just like the baby that never was, I'm not keeping the money. I put it in the Moos donation tin. I'll tell Mrs Tuddle it's there when we see her next.'

'That's nice,' Titch says.

'Hopefully it'll save them from doing another one of those bloody biscuit drives. Christ, I've never tasted anything so bad.'

'Oh, come on. The mint ones were quite nice.'

'Says the sister of the girl drinking *crème de menthe* and lemonade.' Sally looks at my glass as if I've got poison in there.

I make a face as I stare into my glass. She's got a point— it *is* a pretty crap drink. I bought it in a salute to the old days, and my first trips to The Spotted Cow, the establishment we're now drinking in (though 'establishment' might be too fancy a word, really—'divey pub' is far more accurate). 'If it makes any difference, I think this might be my last one. Ever.'

'Thank God for that.'

I roll my eyes. 'Well, I wanted a margarita…'

I can't help but join in with the laughter of the other two

at this. A margarita? In Moo? Not likely. Not unless it's the brand-name of a new kind of beer.

'Another one?' I stand up.

'Brilliant,' Sally says. 'And another packet of barbecue chips.'

'Titch?'

'Um, another lemon, lime and bitters, thanks.'

'Got it,' I say, and make for the bar.

I only get halfway there before I see her coming. I race back over to Titch and Sally. 'Oh, shit—oh, shit—oh, shit.'

'What?'

'What is it?'

I sink down into my seat. 'Incoming.' I wince. It's too late to say anything else, because, by now, Leaf's mother is standing over the three of us, hissing and spitting like an active volcano. Leaf hides behind her wide, brightly coloured peasant skirt and sturdy leather sandals.

'Which one of you is Sally?' The first white-hot blob of lava pops out.

'That would be me.' Sally raises a hand.

'Well, I'd like to know exactly what you think you're teaching my daughter. She's just come home to tell me she doesn't like having her period and that she wants to take the pills like the lady who smokes does. Would you care to explain that little gem to me?'

Sally nods. 'Sure…' she starts, before I kick her under the table. Now really is not the time to be too—well, *Sally* about this.

'Sally's just not used to spending a lot of time around children,' I say, trying to defuse some of Leaf's mother's anger. Frankly, I'm unsure if Sally's ever spent *any* time around children. After tonight's performance, I'm doubting it.

'That's obvious.'

Sally holds out the last few chips sitting in our plastic, doily-lined basket to Leaf. We bought them with our first round of drinks. Leaf reaches out for one with a smile. However, her mother smacks her hand away at the last minute.

'What are you doing? You know we don't eat things like that. It's all about making good choices for our bodies, remember? Those chips are full of preservatives and colours and are cooked in animal fat.'

Sally makes a 'yum, yum, my favourite' face, but I manage to kick her fast enough that the expression has disappeared before Leaf's mother looks back over.

'Sorry,' she says meekly, or as meek as Sally gets, anyway.

'Don't think I won't report this to Mrs Tuddle,' she keeps on.

'Ooohhh, Mum…' Leaf says from behind her. 'Don't do that. Mrs Tuddle's boring.'

Leaf's mother grabs her daughter by the arm. 'Mrs Tuddle is very good to run your group every week. You should be grateful.'

Leaf sighs a very Sally-sounding kind of sigh.

Oh, God.

'Right. That's it, young lady.' And, without saying goodbye, Leaf's mother hauls her daughter out of the pub and is gone.

I puff out my cheeks, exhaling loudly. 'I guess you're just lucky she didn't find out about the king-size Snickers bar. Or the $400. Or the "what's an orgasm?" speech.'

Sally snorts. 'She might have benefited from the orgasm one. Now, where's that drink you were talking about?'

We roll back to the house on a bit of a high (three *crème de menthe* and lemonades tend to do that to you, as well as clearing your sinuses beautifully). When we get there, we spend another hour or so chatting on the swing chair, clutching mugs of tea, before we head to bed.

Unfortunately, our newfound, *crème de menthe*-styled elation with life doesn't hold over till the morning after, and nine a.m. sees the three of us around the kitchen table being more than slightly hungover. Well, two of us anyway.

The mood doesn't really alter over the next few days, however much I try to drag my housemates out of it.

Sally glues her eyes to the TV once more, her leg aching. Titch has several more teary phone calls to Andrew and still refuses to talk to me about what she blurted out about our mother. Fergus finally gets kicked by a cow. And me—well, I pace the house trying to sort out what Titch was on about the other night, racking my brain as to what's going on with Sally and wondering guiltily whether I should give Andrew another call.

I just don't understand it. How can Titch be worried she'll be anything like our mother?

Our mother was a perfect example of what the older generation like to call a 'good for nothing'—a drug addict who caused my grandparents nothing but pain. A drug addict who used to turn up on my grandparents' doorstep eight and a half months pregnant, not knowing who the father of her baby was, and then leave three weeks after the fact, *sans* child (pity she didn't give away naming rights as well). In fact, Titch is so far removed from our mother that a drop of alcohol has never passed her lips. Can you believe that? Not a drop. She's always been frightened that our mother's addictive personality has been passed down to her, the first child, the first in line. Thus, no alcohol. Not one cigarette. She even used to refuse painkillers at the dentist.

So, no, I don't understand it, this thing about Titch being like our mother. I don't understand it at all. And Sally. I have no idea what's going on with her either. Those two incidents in the supermarket were more than strange, even for Sally. And then how she'd acted in the car. It was as if she was a different person. Someone I'd never met before.

To add to this, there's the other thing I can't help but think about as I keep on with my mooning. The JL thing. I promised myself just a few days ago that I would stop thinking about JL. That I had to let him go. Those words were easy to come out with and, I have to say, made sense. Complete sense. But the truth is I'm finding it hard to put those easy, sensible words into practice. Especially here, in Moo. I'd forgotten how slowly things move here. How your thoughts have time to catch up with you.

It's around this time, however, that a few things start to happen that take my mind off myself again.

The first one is something that happens with Bert. Sally is out reading a magazine under a tree and Titch is visiting one of Nan's friends when Bert knocks on the front door, making me jump in my chair at the kitchen table.

'Just me, love,' he says.

'Come in, come in,' I answer, and after a second or two he appears in the doorway. I'm struck, once again, by how strange it is seeing Bert inside. He always seems so out of place indoors. It sounds like an awful thing to say, but it's like he's a dog who knows he shouldn't be inside the house. Bert belongs outside.

'I, er...' He nods his head in the direction of the bathroom.

'Don't be silly. Of course.' I shake my head and smile as he retreats. He's a funny old stick, Bert.

I almost forget he's in the house until a few minutes later there's a figure hovering in the doorway. I look up from my book and cup of tea.

'I...'

'Oh, sorry.' I jump up. 'Can I get you a cup of tea or something?'

Bert shakes his head quickly. 'No, no. It's not that...'

Slowly I sit back down again. Bert continues to hover in the doorway. He looks up at the ceiling, down at the floor, then up at the ceiling again.

I follow his gaze up to the ceiling, wondering if there's something wrong with it. I can't see anything...

When he coughs, I jump a bit again.

'It's, er, I…'

I've never seen him look so agitated. 'What is it, Bert?' are the firm words that exit my mouth. Frankly, I'm tempted to strike the name 'Bert' and insert 'Lassie'. *What is it, Lassie? What is it, girl?* But of course I don't.

He composes himself at this. 'There're drugs. In the bathroom,' he blurts out. 'I don't mean to pry, but I was washing my hands…'

'Drugs?' I stand up again.

Bert nods. Hard. 'On the shelf. Injections.'

'Oh!' I exhale now and laugh, resting one arm on the table. 'It's OK. They're Titch's.' But when I look back over at Bert again he doesn't look any less worried than he was before. I stare at him, confused. Why is he asking about this?

And it's then that it dawns on me—the drugs. He thinks they're illegal drugs. I open my mouth then, ready to put him straight when I see again how worried he is. He's scared. Scared that one of us, either Titch or myself, is turning into a carbon copy of our mother. Our mother the town druggie.

I pick my jaw back up off the ground and form some kind of an explanation. 'They're prescription drugs, Bert. From her doctor.'

Bert's expression doesn't change.

'I…' I begin, but then I realise I'm not sure what to say. I thought Bert was worried that the drugs were illegal drugs, and I've told him they're prescription. And that they're Titch's. 'I…' I start again, but then stop once more. I'm not quite sure where to go from here. I can hardly tell Bert about Titch being on the IVF programme. I mean, that's private. She's hardly told anybody about it—only the people closest to her.

Bert and I continue to look at each other. Me knowing there's more to this than he's letting on, and Bert not knowing how to tell me what he's getting at.

'Right. Er, I'd best be off, then.' And with that he's gone. Quick as a flash.

As I watch him lope across the yard from the kitchen window my brain tells me that, whatever this was about, I haven't heard the end of it.

My brain is right.

About an hour later, there's a knock on the front door.

'Don't get up—don't get up,' a voice chimes out as I get up. (Yes, same spot, same book, different cup of tea…)

I only just reach the kitchen door as a figure waddles past me.

Mrs Tuddle.

'Can I help you?' I say, as she keeps going up the hallway.

She stops then, and turns around. 'Just passing by, dear. I thought I'd check up on that new cleaner. I couldn't bear it if your nan's house wasn't cleaned properly. I'll just spot-check the bathroom, shall I? That's usually the best place to catch them out.'

'But it's fine,' I call out as she keeps going. 'There's no problem with the new cleaner…'

I stand in the same spot until, a minute or so later, the figure returns to the hallway and starts to waddle back down again.

'Not too bad,' she says as she passes me by. 'Not too bad at all.' She stops in the doorway for a second and turns around. 'I see you've been down to the cemetery. Yellow chrysanthemums. Your grandmother's favourite.'

'Oh. I think Titch went. I haven't been yet. I'm planning on going though.'

'Nothing on Lisa's grave, I noticed.'

Did you just? I think to myself, but I don't say anything. If Sally doesn't want to go to the cemetery, I'm not going to make her. 'Right. I'll, er, see you later then.'

I realise Mrs Tuddle is already making her way down the front steps.

What was that about? And why isn't she at home, resting after her operation? I shrug once more—maybe the woman's as high on painkillers after her operation as Sally was after breaking her ankle. Frankly, if it was true, it would explain a lot.

A whole lot.

Sally slinks into the house fifteen minutes later. Fourteen minutes after she's sure Mrs Tuddle has really gone.

'What was all that about?' she asks.

I look up from my book. 'What was all that about with Bert? Or what was all that about with Mrs Tuddle?'

'Well, both of them. They were certainly hob-nobbing about something out there.'

Now I really look up. 'They were talking out there?'

'Oh, yeah. Something is *definitely* up. Do you know what's going on?'

I fill Sally in on the morning's events, finishing just as Titch returns from her walk.

'You can stop talking about me now,' she says.

'OK!' Sally replies, giving me a sly wink.

'Hmm.' Titch gives us both the once-over. 'Something tells me you're both up to no good.'

'Us? Never.' Sally shakes her head.

'I won't even ask.' Titch sighs. 'I'm thinking of going to the hairdresser. Either of you want to come?'

Deadly silence.

Outside, a cow moos.

'Here? In town? In Moo?' Sally says eventually.

Titch nods.

My face registers the same expression as Sally's. 'You're going to *The Cow's Tail?*'

Titch nods again.

Sally and I turn to look at each other and Titch tuts. 'Oh, come on. How bad can it be?'

Sally laughs then. 'Um—very bad! Has 1989 somehow been wiped from your memory?'

'1989?'

I shake my head at Sally. 'Titch never got a poodle perm like we did. Remember? Titch has perfect hair. Titch has always had perfect hair.'

'Oh, come on.' Titch runs a hand through her glossy black locks—which, of course, fall back perfectly into place, because, as I said, Titch has perfect hair. Timotei hair, I used to call it.

'See?' I say to Sally again.

'We'll just get a cut. They can't really mess up a cut.'

'Ha!' Sally laughs. '1989. 1990. 1991. Should I keep going?'

I reach up and feel my own hair. It really does need a cut. The roots I can live with until I hit civilisation again, but I can't wait too much longer for a cut or all I'll have left is split ends.

'Think we should brave it?' I ask Sally.

She sighs. 'Oh, God. Why not? Everyone around here's looking at us anyway. May as well give them something to look at.'

Not surprisingly, The Cow's Tail looks exactly the same as the last time I was in here, about ten years ago. Same chairs, same capes, same washing basins...

Same magazines.

The only thing that's different is one of the hairdressers. Business must be booming, because they've hired another one. A younger one. Jody, her name is, and she was in the year below Sally and myself at high school.

Titch, Sally and I sit side by side and discuss what we want from our respective hairdressers before they leave to set up their trolleys. Sally, who gets the younger, more in touch, not yet blue-rinsed Jody as her hairdresser, has suddenly become brave in the heat of a hairdryer moment and has decided to get her highlights redone.

The hairdressers gone, I poke her in the arm. 'Good luck!'

She shrugs. 'What have I got to lose?'

'Your hair?'

'Yeah, well, I wouldn't be so smug if I were you. Ten bucks says they don't wash your hair before they cut it.'

Titch leans forward to look at Sally. 'Surely they don't just spray it?'

I nod.

'Don't they just do that to kids?'

Sally shrugs again, looking from one of us to the other. 'Ten bucks.'

I shrug back. 'You're on.'

'You know I don't like to bet.' Titch bites her lip.

'Oh, for God's sake, Titch. Live a little.' Sally throws her a look.

As for me, I throw one back at Sally. It's not Titch's fault she's scared of all the vices. Growing up with our mother around has made her petrified of taking one wrong step in any direction.

'Um, well—OK, then.' Titch shrugs.

Ten minutes and a few quick squirts of water later, Sally is twenty dollars richer.

'I guess that'll cover part of your colour correction,' I whisper meanly, when Jody is out of earshot.

'Either that or I'll be able to afford two paper bags to put over your heads. No, wait—I think those dinky little rain bonnets would be more the go.'

'Sally!' I say sharply. Her voice is way too loud. When our eyes meet, I can tell she's thinking about the other night, and our little 'discussion' in the supermarket car park.

'Sorry,' she says meekly.

'Shh, you two…' Titch leans forward again as our respective hairdressers come back from gathering combs and scissors and mixing up colour.

Titch and I are finished off in no time, as we only want a general tidy-up, but Sally's colour seems to take for ever. Every five minutes Jody opens up a foil or two and peeks inside, then closes the foil up again and says, 'Just a bit longer!'

Titch and I flick through magazines (in some of them it's still OK to like Michael Jackson!) and eventually give up and head off down the road to the Moo Inn, to buy takeaway skinnycinos (yes, coffee machines finally came to Moo...).

When we come back, Jody and Sally are discussing what Jody calls the 'good old days' (at least someone thinks of them that way).

'Here you go.' I pass Sally her coffee. 'You're sure you don't want one?' I ask Jody one more time.

'Nah, I'm trying to cut back. Supposed to give you cellulite you know.'

So that's where it came from, I think to myself. I knew it wasn't those toaster croissants.

Jody leans over Sally's head to check another foil. 'You know, I've got this mental picture of you at school, sitting outside the principal's office. I can remember it like it was yesterday.'

Sally laughs. 'Why doesn't that surprise me? If it had been a proper subject I would have got an A for sure.'

'Oh, and I remember about your sister, of course. That was so sad.'

Snap. Titch's head and my head whip around to look at Sally. Our bodies freeze. In her chair, Sally is frozen too.

And then we all wait.

We wait for the words that always come after any mention of Lisa. How she was so beautiful. So talented. So popular. How everyone loved her. How she was a pleasure to be around. How awful it was that she was taken at such a young age.

Staring at Sally, staring at herself, now white-faced, in the mirror, we wait.

Jody continues, 'But you know what I remember the most about you at high school? That photography competition they held when you guys were seniors. That photograph of yours that won—it was brilliant. I couldn't believe that it was of nothing—you know, just grass. Something I would never have taken a picture of. But it was so beautiful. So green. And so clear. I'd never…looked at grass like that before.'

The two of us slowly move our gaze from Sally to Jody as she speaks.

'Yeah. It was really beautiful that picture. I hope you've still got it.'

We keep staring.

'Do you? Still have it, I mean?' Jody looks from Sally to Titch and myself like we're a tad strange now.

'My scalp!' Sally says suddenly. 'It's burning! I need to…' She gets up and makes her way to the basin, pulling foils off as she goes. 'Ugh, just get them off. Get them off me!'

'Shit! Sorry!' Jody races over to the basin and starts to spray a thick stream of water over Sally's head. 'Is that better?'

Sally doesn't say anything, but takes large gulps of air.

Lisa, I think to myself. I knew this would come up sooner or later. It always does in Moo.

After her wash, Sally bolts, not even staying for her cut.

As she exits the salon I'm amazed to see her highlights look great.

Sally won't talk to either Titch or myself about what happened at the hairdresser, shutting herself into her room all afternoon.

I have to say I'm not surprised. As a rule, Sally never talks about Lisa. Not even in passing—and to have it brought up like that, out of the blue…it was a bit much for her, I guess.

Titch retires to her room with a book as well. So, with nothing to do and no one else's feelings to bolster (even Fergus ambles off for a late afternoon kip), instead of letting my thoughts of JL go, like I'm supposed to be doing, I find myself sitting on the floor in the lounge room once more, with the photo albums, wallowing in my own misery.

This time it's the more recent photos I pore over. In particular, my wedding photos.

I sit resting the large album on top of my crossed legs, my

fingers lightly touching the top corners of both open pages, my eyes staring as they move from scene to crisp scene.

I'd almost forgotten what a beautiful day it was. Warm and sunny, with only a few high, fluffy white clouds in the sky being pushed to and fro by a light breeze.

There's the tiny wooden church, bursting to the seams with guests. And the outside reception with white linen-covered trestle tables and country catering. Roast and veg and the largest pavlova you've ever seen, simply dripping with passionfruit, for dessert.

People told me afterwards it was the happiest wedding they'd ever been to.

Each photo overflows with roses. Yellow roses. And that's what I remember most about that day—the first time I saw JL's smiling face that morning, and the roses. There were hundreds and hundreds of yellow roses. In my hand-tied bouquet, in JL's buttonhole, in swag-like garlands in the church, strewn over the reception tables that sat on the grass. JL always gave me yellow roses.

Now my head jerks up, my eyes lifting from the photo album, as I remember something I haven't thought of before—except for our last anniversary. That night at the restaurant.

There weren't any yellow roses then.

Without looking back down again, I do two things. I close the album with a thump and put it down beside me, out of sight. And then I bring my right hand over to my left and ever so slowly slip off my wedding ring, trying not to think about what I'm doing. Trying not to think about what this action means.

I don't know if JL's still wearing his or not. I haven't looked on purpose. All I know is I really have to stop this now. Right now. And if I'm going to have any hope of stopping myself thinking about JL, my wedding ring has to come off. When I've removed it from my finger, for the first time since our wedding day, I clasp it in my palm.

Don't think about it. I won't think about it.

Instead, I concentrate on my body. My eyes feel red and sore and my neck hurts. Slowly, carefully, I bend it from one side to the other, then around in a circle, trying to stretch out the kinks. What I need is a shower. I'm not particularly dirty, but the comforting, enveloping warmth of the shower is where I've felt most at peace these last few months. I've tried having a bath, but for me it's not the same. I can never relax in a bath. After I've spent a good fifteen minutes getting the temperature right, I'm always left staring at the ceiling, wondering if it's too soon to get out and annoyed with myself that I've added too much or too little bubble bath.

I pick myself up off the floor and head for the bathroom on autopilot. I don't turn on the light, or the fan, but strip and wait till the water is scalding hot before I step up over the bath and under the flow. Immediately I turn and let the water run down my neck and back, turning my skin red and heating my muscles, raising my pulse-rate until I'm almost breathless.

I stand there for what feels like for ever, until I can't bear the heat any more and have to turn the heat down. It's only then that I finally unclasp my tight, red fist and put my wedding ring down on the side of the bath with a 'clink'. I avoid looking at it and, taking my time, wash my hair, scrub my face and brush my nails. That done, I reach for the soap, but in the dish there's only a tiny, useless sliver left. I hate leaving those slivers to get stuck onto the bottom of the fresh soap, so I bend down and go to shove it through the plughole.

Except that when I get down there, still holding the sliver of soap, I feel the sudden urge to sit.

So I do. I sit under the water, which seems harder and faster down here, letting my hair become plastered to my face. And then, hardly believing it, I start to cry. I never cry. But now I do. I cry like I've never cried before. Hunched up, knees pulled to my chest, with a crusty piece of soap stuck in my hand.

I cry softly at first, a little 'I'm feeling sorry for myself' kind of cry, but this quickly turns to awful, shocking, body-racking sobs that sound like they come from someone else. Someone I hardly know.

The room fills with steam as the minutes pass. And I keep right on crying. I don't even know why. Because I've finally removed my ring? Because of what I've just seen—the happy pictures from the past? Or because of what I've just realised—that I've lost more than I ever bargained for this year. More than I thought was even possible. Or maybe it's just because this—sitting in a shower feeling miserable, isn't what I expected from life. It wasn't on the life path trajectory that I imagined for myself. Perhaps a combination of all of the above.

I don't know, but I keep crying anyway.

'That's it.' An arm thrusts through the shower curtain, startling me. I choke and lift my head to watch as it pushes through the water. 'Christ, that's hot!' It turns the taps off. Then, 'Here,' the voice says, and another arm offers me a towel. 'Stop being so bloody maudlin, dry yourself off, and meet me outside in exactly one minute.'

Sally.

I don't even have time to yell at her before she's gone.

There's a second or two where I consider reaching up and

turning the taps back on, but then there's a 'Forty-five seconds!' warning from beyond the closed bathroom door and
I heave myself up and get out of the bath.

At 'Thirty seconds!' I'm drying myself off, and 'Fifteen
seconds!' sees me donning my dressing gown.

I make it out to the lounge with five seconds to spare.
Titch is there, red-eyed and in her dressing gown as well. I
go to stand beside her.

'Looking at this, were you?' Sally holds the photo album
up at me.

I nod.

'Using this again, were you?' Sally holds up the phone
at Titch.

Titch nods.

Sally makes a tutting noise as she puts both items down
again. 'Well, I don't know about you—and, frankly, I'm at the
point where I don't care—but I'm sick of this pathetic carry-
on. From all three of us. We've got to pull ourselves together.
If you haven't noticed, there's no food in this house and
nothing for dinner. I'm sick of starving and I've decided
we're going out. Titch and I are going to have showers—if
there's any hot water left.' There's a pointed look at me as
Sally says this. 'And then we're going down to the pub, where
we'll be dining on Moo's finest pub fare. And, again, I don't
care what either of you are about to say. We're going and
that's final. We're having steak, egg and chips, dessert, and way
too much to drink—because I'm buggered if I'm having
toast for dinner again. So get yourselves together. You've got
half an hour before we walk out the door.'

'Should give you time to put your lipgloss on, then,' I mut-
ter sulkily beneath my breath.

Though, underneath my surly exterior, I think she's right.

We do need to pull ourselves together. I'm getting kind of sick of our misery merry-go-round, with each of us taking turns trying to make the others feel better.

'Sorry?' Sally says. 'I didn't quite catch that.'

'Nothing…'

So, once again, we find ourselves at the pub. Sally orders us three plates of steak, egg and chips and she and I embark on getting ourselves distinctly sloshed on *crème de menthe* and lemonade. (She seems to have suddenly gotten over her former reservations where this dodgy concoction is concerned.) Titch starts in on several lemon squashes.

We've finished a packet of barbecue chips, three steak dinners, four hideously coloured green drinks, six beers, three lemon squashes and three portions of tinned fruit and ice cream when the fun really starts.

'You know,' Sally slurs, her elbows resting on the table and one finger pointing first to me, then to Titch. 'You two are a riot to live with.'

'Well, I'm sorry, but we're not having the best time lately.' I'm grateful Titch answers for us as my words seem to keep getting funnily rearranged in my head before I can get them out my mouth.

'Mmm,' I agree, nodding. 'S'true. And what makes you think you're the best thing since sliced housemate?'

'Sliced housemate? You're drunk,' Sally replies.

'You're both drunk,' Titch looks from one of us to the other, her eyes resting on Sally. 'Those highlights are really good.'

'I know!' Sally sits up.

'Did you want to tell us what went on there today? What the problem was?' Titch asks nervously, not sure what Sally's reaction is going to be.

'No. Nothing happened. The bleach was just burning my head, that's all. There was no problem.'

Titch glances at me.

'Now, talking about problems—you're the ones with problems.' Sally leans forward.

'Us?' I say innocently.

'Pffft,' Sally replies, waving a hand across the table and almost knocking all three glasses over.

'Pffft, what?' I say. Hang on. That made sense, didn't it?

'You both think you're got these unsolvable problems. But you know what? Your problems aren't so way out there. You're just ditherers. What you two need is a plan. An action plan.'

Titch sits back in her seat, surprised at Sally's words.

'S'that right?' I roll my eyes.

'And I suppose you have one in mind?' My sister sighs. 'An "action plan"?'

'Too right!' Sally pushes herself up. 'Want to hear it?'

'Can't wait.' I polish off my drink. God knows, I'll need it.

Sally's eyes move to Titch, who shrugs and looks away. She doesn't look impressed.

This is all the go-ahead Sally needs. She claps her hands together and gets this over-earnest look on her face, suddenly not so drunk anymore. 'OK. Look. The way I see it, you've both just forgotten what you really want. You both started out with a goal, right? You were on this certain path and you had your destination in mind? But along the way things have become—well, hard. You've tried to take shortcuts and you've become a bit lost, I guess.'

I raise an eyebrow at Titch, envisioning plaited, gingham-clad versions of us both skipping down the Yellow Brick Road.

'Well, is it true, or not?' Sally waits for a response.

'S'pose,' I say.

Titch inclines her head.

'Anyway, now you're both flopping around on the grassy verge, like goldfish chucked out of a fishbowl.'

'Hey!' That was uncalled for. It might be an accurate description of my life at the moment, but it was still uncalled for.

Titch just sighs. 'Now we're goldfish?'

'Oh, shut up.' Sally waves a hand at both of us. 'OK, so you're not goldfish. But you know what I mean. I suppose what I'm getting at is that the final destination—it's still there. You've just got to get up, brush yourselves off and step back on the path. You've got to remember what you wanted when you set out. When you took that first step.'

I look over at Titch who, beside me, has uncrossed her arms and is biting her lip. She thinks it's true, what Sally's saying. I can see it written all over her face. But for her it's so obvious. What she wanted when she set out seemed so simple—a family. A baby.

But what did I want?

I didn't really have any goals like that. I didn't start out *Moo to You* wanting a hugely successful business that made millions of dollars. I only wanted to make some pyjamas for my family for Christmas. And when Harry came along I was pushed into making decisions I didn't want to make. Then there was JL. Marrying JL was an easy decision for me. He asked, and everything inside me screamed 'Yes!'

And, sitting here now, listening to Sally drone on about 'paths', this is what I simply don't understand. I struggled so long and fought so hard for my business—something that I'd never planned to have in the first place—so how could I have been so willing to give up on my marriage—something I'd wanted so desperately? Because I didn't see a path winding before us to follow after we got married? Because I thought we'd reached the end of the path? That after the rings were on our fingers it was all said and done?

Of course I've heard people talk about how you have to 'work' at your marriage. How it isn't all 'easy sailing'. But, foolishly, I thought those comments were meant for other people. For people who weren't as in love as JL and I were.

I suppose, looking back, our problems really started at the same time as my problems at work. The thing that was so unbearable was that JL was just so bloody *kind*. It sounds strange, but it was bad enough having to go through my problems myself without having to come home and relive it every night—talking and talking and talking about it non-stop. I know he just wanted to help, to support me, but as the weeks passed I pushed him further and further away. No one else understood what was happening to me. Why should he?

I became more and more selfish. More and more self-involved. And then, before I knew it, he stopped asking, and both of us were seeking solace in the company of others. People who could make us forget what was going on at home.

I glance over at Titch, who looks right back at me. What Sally's saying—we both know it's true.

'OK. If you've got all the answers, what do we do now?' I ask her.

'That's my girls!' Sally says loudly, suddenly pushing herself up.

Just like the other day, every other patron in the pub turns to look at us. But Sally doesn't care now she's on an 'I mixed my drinks with my pain medication' roll. She seems to forget she has a broken ankle, and, despite our protests, somehow manages to haul herself up onto her chair.

'You!' She points at Titch, who jumps. 'Get back on that programme and demand your husband's seed, goddammit!'

'I…um…' Titch stutters.

'And you!' Sally points at me this time. 'Pull yourself together and steal your husband back from that sickly sweet "I shouldn't have had a second helping" French tart!'

My mouth hangs open, but I can't get anything out of it.

And then, in true Scarlett O'Hara style, she lifts her head and yells, 'By God, I'll never let you be husbandless or baby-less again!'

After we're asked to leave, Sally almost breaks her other ankle getting down off her chair—even with my help. Seeing this, Titch confiscates my car keys and tells me she'll bring the car around to the front.

It's chilly as Sally and I wait outside for our ride home, despite our high *crème de menthe* intake. I rub my arms up and down briskly. Fergus leans up against me for warmth.

'Hey, Dicey!' a voice calls out, and I strain my eyes in the dim light to see who it is.

It's Sorrel, one of the hippie-parented Moos, eating dinner with her family at the Moo Inn next door. I flipped through her wish book as I was putting them away last week. The thing is practically a work of art, with detailed magazine clippings and notes to herself about what her life is going to be like.

I wave back.

When I turn around again, I feel very, very sober.

'Where's Titch got to?' Sally asks.

'Hmm? Oh, getting the car.'

'What's up with you?' She gives me a poke in the arm.

'Nothing.'

'Come on…'

'Oh, it's just Sorrel over there. And all of the Moos, I guess. Things seem so simple for them. So uncomplicated.'

Sally snorts. 'Things are. Their average age is seven. They survive on two dollars pocket money a week and a Saturday packet of red frogs. Do you really want to go back there?'

I give her a look.

'Sorry—continue,' she says.

'It's just that they all seem to know what they want out of life. And look at me. How long has it been since I knew what I wanted? Months. Years, even.'

Sally snorts again.

'What?'

She simply shakes her head at me.

'What?'

'Oh, for fuck's sake, Dicey. Quit fooling yourself! It's obvious what you want. You want JL back.'

Raff! Fergus perks up at the mention of his favourite person's name.

I look down at him, and then over at Sally, uncertainly. Do I? My heart's started racing even thinking about it. God, maybe I do. It beats faster and faster.

'But—' I start.

'But what?'

'But we're separated.'

'So?'

I pause. 'Well, no one who's separated ever really gets back together, do they? I thought it was just what you did before things were, well…final.'

Sally looks at me like I'm crazy. 'Yeah, that's the rule. What are you talking about? You can do whatever you want. If you want him back, take him back.'

Sure—like it's that easy. I look away.

But Sally grabs my arm and makes me turn back. 'If you want him back, Dicey, take him back. But listen to me when I say this—you don't have much time. He's not going to wait around for you for ever.'

'But the FC…'

Sally snorts a third time. 'Her? Forget about *her!* Do what you want to do, babe. He's *your* bloody husband. You've got a little more claim over him than she does, I should think.'

I look into my oldest friend's eyes and realise, for the second time tonight, that she's right. And, despite the large amount of alcohol I've contaminated my gut with over the last few hours, it's telling me she's right too. How about that? I don't think I've listened to my gut for a long time. Usually I just feed it antacid until it shuts up.

'Oh,' Sally continues, 'and for God's sake put this back on.' She makes a rude gesture at me with one finger.

'Hey! Oh...' I see it then—my ring.

'The bloody melodrama.' She shakes her head as she removes the item and passes it over to me. 'You wouldn't believe it...'

Silently, I take the piece of platinum from her and slip it back onto my own finger. My ring finger. And it's warm. As if I'd never taken it off.

Titch drives up with the car then. As I get in I ask her if we can make a short stop on the way home—at the community centre hall.

And then I go home to write in my wish book until dawn.

By seven the next morning my wish book is over half full. All night long I kept at it—scratching away at the pages. I simply couldn't stop writing. Thoughts about what I wanted for the future tumbled out. Amazingly, a few weeks ago—a few days ago, even—I didn't think I had one. I saw the world and everything and everyone around me on a day-to-day basis—each new set of twenty-four hours something only to be 'got through', to be 'dealt with'. But now… Now things seem a little brighter. Like there'll be a next week, a next month, maybe even a next year. And perhaps, if I'm lucky, things to look forward to.

Before Titch and Sally wake up, I slide into bed and fall fast asleep, only waking again at around one p.m. because Sally stomps into the room and heaves herself onto Titch's bed.

'Ugh! What's the matter?' I open one eye.

'She's at it again. Out there.' Sally jerks her head in the direction of the lounge room.

I sit up a bit. 'What do you mean "at it again"? On the phone?'

'To Andrew. It's not pretty. I thought I'd better disappear for a bit.'

I glance out in the direction of the lounge. 'Is she…?'

'Crying? Yes.'

I lie back down again. 'I just don't know what to do for her. What to say. She was trying to tell me something the other night, but I don't know what exactly. Something about her being like our mother. But the next day she wouldn't explain. I can't seem to get anything out of her.'

'Tell me about it. I've tried too. What are you talking about though? About your mother, I mean?'

I shrug and turn my head to look at Sally. 'I've got no idea what she was going on about. It just doesn't make any sense. After all, how could she think she'll be anything like our mother?'

'I know. They're kind of…different people.'

'Just a tad different.'

'But, whatever it was, she meant it. She was kind of *frantic* when she said it, like it had really been bothering her.'

'Weird.'

'Mmm. I know.'

Silence.

'You're sleeping in late,' Sally finally says.

'I didn't get to bed till early this morning. I was, um, writing in my wish book.'

Now it's Sally who sits up. 'Really? About…?'

'Well, um, lots of things.'

'Anything about a certain someone whose pants you might like to get into?'

'Sally!'

She lets out an over-the-top huff. 'You know, it's OK to want to get into your husband's pants. In this day and age it's practically applaudable. You should be on *Oprah*.'

For something to do, I cross my arms and stick them behind my head, not really wanting to think about what happened between the two of us at the beach.

'I don't want to get into his pants, I want to… Oh, I don't know.'

'You *so* want to get into his pants.'

I shake my head at her. 'Sally, I—'

'Ooohhh! Hang on…'

I turn my head away quickly, but it's too late. Sally's already animated and has squirmed her way right to the edge of Titch's bed, as close to me as she can get.

'You've had it off! Recently too!'

'Sally…'

'No, there's no denying it. I can tell.'

I look at her now. 'It isn't what you think. It just…happened.'

'Irresistible, hey? I knew it. I knew he'd have to be good. I mean, he's French, after all.'

'Ugh!' I give up trying to explain myself. 'And he's *half*-French. How many times do I have to tell you?'

'Will you quit it with the "half-French" bit? Don't you get it? All the good things are handed down, even if you're only half-French. Looks, accent, dress sense, food and wine knowledge, shagability. It comes free with your birth certificate.'

'Shagability? That's sooo French, Sal. Really refined.'

'That's what I mean! Now, if *I* was half-French I never would have said that. But being full-blooded Australian, you see, it's all I can come up with.'

I shake my head at her again. 'You know, you really do speak some complete *merde* at times.'

'Thanks!'

'It wasn't a compliment.'

Sally shrugs. 'Still, I guess this all bodes well for getting back together.'

'How's that?'

'Well, most people tend to break up when the sexual attraction stores have completely dried up. At least you're OK in that department.'

I pause, not quite sure what to think about this.

'So, er, do you think she's finished yet?' Sally points at the door.

'Hmm? Oh, sure. I'm convinced they'll have sorted out all the problems revolving around their infertility by now. It must have been five minutes, after all.'

'Very funny. It's just that we need to go and get some groceries before we starve to death.'

Ah, yes—that. In my *crème de menthe* wish book crazed haze, I'd forgotten about the groceries we didn't pick up last night. 'You're telling me to get up and get showered, right?'

'Well, I can't drive anywhere. And I don't think Titch is in any state to be watching the road.'

'OK, OK,' I groan as I push myself up and swing my legs over the side of the bed.

'Don't make such a fuss. You've run out of pistachios anyway.'

Now there, I think, is something half worth getting out of bed for.

By the time I'm up and about, showered and dressed, Titch is off the phone and sitting on the lounge room couch beside a worried-looking Fergus, her knees pulled in to her chest. I go and stand behind her and she looks up at me.

'Want to talk about it?' I ask. But there's a quick shake of her head. No. 'Come on, then,' I continue. 'We're going to get some groceries. And don't say you don't want to come, because I'm not leaving you here by yourself.'

Perhaps Titch doesn't have the strength to argue, because she gets up obligingly and another five minutes sees us all piled in the car and heading down the driveway.

This trip to the store, we really stock up. Again, I clear out the pistachio supply, Sally concentrates on selecting a wide and varied chocolate biscuit rainbow, while Titch scouts out the tea aisle. The main food groups covered, we then move on to the basics—fruit, veg, dog food, washing powder, etc. And everything seems—well, normal. Normal for Moo, anyway.

At least it seems normal until we go to make our way home. We decide to pick a few things up from the bakery, so ask Maria, checkout chick extraordinaire, to keep an eye on our trolley for fifteen minutes or so. Then we make our way outside and start down the footpath, our mouths watering in anticipation of pizza bread topped with salami and bacon and fruit loaf stuffed with dried apricots. Oh. And maybe a few passionfruit iced cupcakes for Fergus.

With such important matters on our minds, we barely glance inside the pub as we pass it. That is, until a voice booms out at us, stopping us in our tracks. 'Yeah, I heard you three were in town,' it says.

Three heads turn and look at the figure standing inside the pub, arms resting on the window ledge, scowling at the world going by.

It's Mal.

Mal Eames.

Our heads turn back towards each other then, and we start shooting each other looks. We know Mal Eames all too well. Everyone in town does. He's a nasty drunk from a long line of nasty drunks.

Sensing something untoward is going on, Fergus steps forward, closer to the pub, and growls a proper growl, making us all glance down at him in surprise. Fergus never growls properly.

'Drop dead, Mal,' Sally pipes up.

Sally has a long history with Mal Eames I won't go into. Then she grabs our arms, tosses her hair back haughtily and stalks off as proudly as she can with a broken ankle.

Mal only sniggers drunkenly, barely even taking the words

in. I guess people tell him to drop dead every half-hour
or so.

'Little voices tell you to come back, did they? The little
voices in your head?' he continues.

'Shut up, Mal,' I hear someone else inside the pub call out.

'Little voices, little voices…' he sing-songs. I'm not sure
why, but his words disturb me. And Mal Eames has never disturbed me before. I slow down and turn back to look at him
uncertainly as Sally keeps tugging on my arm. Fergus moves
in close beside me, his body lying between myself and Mal.
Another low growl escapes his throat.

'Yeah, you know what I'm talking about, don't you, dar-
lin'? Maybe you've got them too. Maybe you've heard the little voices yerself.' He eyes me in a way I really, really don't
like.

'Mal!' The voice inside the pub warns him once more. I
still can't see who it is, but I recognise it. I think it might be
Dave Thompson's father.

'Little voices, little voices…'

'Right, that's it, mate.' It *is* Ed Thompson, I see, as he
comes over and drags Mal off his perch. 'Sorry, ladies.' He
nods his head at us. 'He's had a bit too much to drink.'

'As per usual,' Sally snorts, and pulls both Titch and I away
with a final tug.

We continue along to the bakery, but when we reach the
doors the crisp, buttery scent has lost its former appeal. I stop
outside the sliding door, making Titch and Sally stop with
me. Strangely, for once Fergus doesn't beg to go inside, but
looks up at us, waiting to see what we're going to do.

'What was that about?' I say, still confused at what's just
gone on.

'Beer. And lots of it.' Sally sighs.

I pause. 'No. No, there was more to it than that.'

'Yeah. Probably a litre or so more than you think. We're talking about Mal Eames here, Dicey.'

'No,' I continue, shaking my head this time. 'I mean it. He was trying to get at us. He was having a go at us about something.'

Sally looks doubtful, but Titch nods. 'That's what I thought too. Did you see the way everyone looked at him?'

I nod back. 'No one ever looks *at* Mal Eames. They look *away*. And Dave's dad getting involved. That's not like him,' I point out.

'True…' Sally says slowly.

We stand and look at each other for a few more moments until I shrug. 'Well, I've got no idea. I'm sure we'll find out, though. This is Moo, after all…'

We're back at the house, putting away our groceries, when we hear Bert's ute pull up outside. There's a split second where we freeze, turn and each raise an eyebrow. Something *is* going on. But before we can run outside to meet him Bert's run inside to us, puffing away madly.

'Oi! You three OK?'

He must be worried, I think to myself, because the normally overly polite and shy Bert has run straight into the open house and down the hallway to the kitchen without knocking or taking his work boots off.

When he spots us, he gives each one of us a quick, fatherly once-over. 'I heard there was some kind of a fuss down the pub with Mal Eames. He didn't touch you did he? I'll bloody—'

Wow. Swearing. From Bert! I decide to put him out of his misery. 'It's OK, Bert. It was nothing. I think Mal was just

drunk. Drunker than usual. Though it was kind of weird—
he kept going on about something. Something about "little
voices".'

I try to make my voice sound breezy, but I watch Bert
carefully out of the corner of my eye. Sure enough, recognition comes over his face and he looks away quickly to the
floor.

'You don't know what he was talking about, do you?'

'Er, voices? Dunno.'

'Not voices. "Little voices",' I say again.

Bert shakes his head. 'No idea. You know Mal. Bit of a
drongo, that one. Sheep short in the top paddock.'

I look over at Titch and Sally for a second before I decide to corner him. 'Come on, Bert. You're the worst liar I've
ever seen.'

Now he looks up from the floor to meet each pair of eyes
in turn. His expression looks rather like a startled rabbit's. 'Ah,
don't ask me, girls,' he starts beseechingly. 'Your grandparents
wouldn't have liked it.'

This stops me in my tracks. My grandparents? What have
they got to do with this? And Bert's face is beetroot-red now.
I've never seen him look so embarrassed.

'Bert, what do you mean?' Titch says.

His eyes move from Titch's to mine, imploring us not to
ask. But it's too late. Bert knows we're not going to stop
hounding him until we find out. His mouth purses and he
shakes his head again. 'No. I can't tell you. I couldn't do it to
your grandmother. Meself, I'd let sleeping dogs lie. But it's
up to you. If you want to know more, you can talk to Mrs
Tuddle about it.'

'Mrs Tuddle?' I say. 'What's she got to do with anything?
Is this about the Moos?'

Bert shakes his head once more. 'No, no. I mean in a nursing capacity, like.'

In a nursing capacity? But Mrs Tuddle hasn't been a community nurse for—well, years now. A good ten years at least.

It's Titch who cottons on first. 'Is this…is this about our mother?' she asks uncertainly.

But by this stage Bert has turned and is walking back down the hallway, and the only answer we get is a flip of his hand as he makes his way out of sight.

'How did you work that out?'

'Work what out?' Titch's pace becomes even faster and I begin to half-jog down the bitumen road in order to keep up with her long legs.

'That Bert was talking about our mother? That that was what Mal Eames was going on about?'

Titch glances over at me for a second. 'There isn't much else our grandparents ever kept from us. In fact, I can't think of anything else at all. It has to be about our mother.'

She's right, I realise. Why hadn't I thought of that? I ask my next question. 'Do you think Mrs Tuddle will be home?'

'Funnily enough, that's just what I asked Sally a few minutes ago. You know what she told me?'

'What?'

'She said, "I would be if I'd just had my uterus removed".'

I laugh. 'I guess she's right. Still, it didn't stop her coming around here the other day.'

Titch gives me a look. 'You didn't tell me she'd been here.'

I pause. She's right. I didn't. 'Sorry, I forgot.' I quickly fill Titch in on Bert's strange visit to the bathroom and then Mrs Tuddle's. When I'm done, Titch can't make head nor tail of it either.

We walk in silence for a while after this, my face swiftly moving back into worry mode as my thoughts take over.

'Are you OK there, Dice?' Titch slows down for a step or two and turns to face me.

I pause. Healthwise I feel fine, but emotionally...Mal Eames disturbed me back there. And then the thing with Bert... Why is it anything to do with my mother makes me come over all 'little sister'? Usually it'd be me asking Titch if she's OK.

'I don't know,' I say. 'It's just—you know. Mother stuff...'

Titch puts an arm around my shoulder and we set off again. 'I know. It'll be OK. Whatever it is, it's all in the past anyway.'

I nod again. 'I suppose you're right.' But I lean in against my sister anyway as we continue walking up and over the hill to Mrs Tuddle's.

As we go I think about what she's just said—that anything to do with our mother is all in the past. But is it? It doesn't seem that way around here, in Moo, where everyone can look at us and know what the two of us are the product of—a mother who loved nothing better than to shoot up, sleep around, drop the unwanted side effects on her parents and skip town for another round of fun and frolic.

Because around here that's what we are—what we've always been—the product of Helen Dye. Helen Dye—drug addict, thief and general town joke.

And I know they sound like harsh things to say, especially about your own mother, but they're true. Or were true. She *was* a drug addict (this was her main occupation in Sydney, between trips to Moo). She *was* a thief (she stole from my grandparents, she stole from the neighbours, and once she even stole from Titch's piggybank). And she *was* the town joke (naturally most of this was kept from my ears, but the sniggering and whispers were all too obvious).

I would have loved nothing more than to have had a relationship with my mother, but I didn't. I *couldn't*. She was never there to have one with. I didn't even have an address to send a postcard to if I felt so inclined. And, for the ninety-nine per cent of the time that she wasn't around, life for Titch and me was good and normal. My grandparents fed us, clothed us, schooled us, loved us. I didn't need my mother just as she didn't need me, Titch or my grandparents. She didn't need anyone, it seemed.

Of course they had to tell us when she died.

I mean when she killed herself.

No one ever told us that to our faces, but even though Titch and I were only nine and six respectively, we were still old enough and smart enough to eventually figure out what had happened—an overdose.

Only Titch has one good memory of our mother. Of a summer when she came home and stayed for a number of months. Not with my grandparents, but at the community hospital. The one Mrs Tuddle was Sister at. I was obviously too young to remember, but Titch says that our mother used to come over for dinner most nights, and that for a while everyone seemed happy, like things were on the up. Almost like we were a normal family. On the weekend there were trips to the lake, or to the beach, and our mother would go against Nan's wishes and sneak us double-scoop ice creams that we couldn't finish but wanted anyway.

I wish I remembered that as well, but I don't.

As we reach the top of the hill Titch and I both pause for a moment as we see Mrs Tuddle's green cottage down below. And then, at exactly the same moment, without speaking, we both put one foot forward and make our way down to hear whatever she has to tell us.

'Coming! I'm coming!' Mrs Tuddle's voice tinkles from inside. The doorbell Titch has just pressed is still ring-a-dinging away some silly tune or other. 'Coming!'

I can see her massive form moving from one side to the other behind the mottled yellow glass side-panels framing the door. Inside, the floorboards groan. There's some fiddling with the lock, a peek around and then the door opens wide.

'Well, hello, girls! This is a surprise!'

'Sorry, Mrs Tuddle, we should have rung first, but it's a bit urgent.' Titch nods.

'We brought you some fudge.' I hold up the small box— a local produce grocery store find.

'Ooohhh. Lovely! Now, where's that gorgeous Fergus?'

'He's at home, with Sally.'

'Oh. That's a shame, great big fellow that he is. It must be almost like having a man around the house. Oops, that was the wrong thing to say, wasn't it?'

Mrs Tuddle covers her mouth as she looks at me and I realise she's talking about the fact that JL and I have separated. God, everyone really *does* know everything around here.

'Well, are you coming in?' Mrs Tuddle continues. 'I was just putting the kettle on…'

'Thanks,' I say, and move forward first, into the hallway.

'That would be nice.' Titch follows close behind.

Mrs Tuddle closes the door behind us and motions us down the hallway.

'Um, how are you feeling, Mrs Tuddle?' I ask hesitantly as we go, passing by the chintzy living room with its red velvet couches and white lacy antimacassar headrests.

I shake my head as I look around. Amazing. I bet there's not a toilet roll in this place without a crocheted dolly cover to hide itself under.

'Are you, um, over the worst of it?' I ask hesitantly, not because I don't want to know, or don't care, but because Mrs Tuddle, being a retired nurse, has a tendency to tell you just that little bit too much information about her health. When I received a vivid blow-by-blow account of her knee reconstruction a number of years ago, complete with pictures, I almost fainted.

'Good! Good! Better than expected, in fact.' She pulls out two chairs for us at her old wooden kitchen table before lumbering over to fill up the kettle. 'But enough chitchat. I suppose this is all about that fuss down at the pub with Mal Eames?'

Titch and I eyeball each other. How did she find out about that so fast? She's supposed to be laid up in bed, taking it easy, not out on the town gossiping.

'Well, um...' I start.

'A nasty piece of work, that man. Mark my words,' Mrs Tuddle nods. 'You're best off not putting too much store in anything he says.'

I look over at Titch. 'Normally we wouldn't,' she says. 'But today was a bit different. There were some things he said, about "little voices". It was like he was trying to make a point.'

'And then we spoke to Bert…' I add.

'Ah, yes. I've just got off the phone with Bert.'

I shoot another look at Titch. Don't people in this town have anything better to talk about? Actually, forget I asked that. They don't.

'He was a little bit worried about what I might tell you—for your grandparents' sake, you know.'

Titch and I both nod. 'We know.'

Mrs Tuddle abandons her tea-making and turns around. All of a sudden she seems different. Taller and more important, like she has her Sister's uniform and cap back on, even though she's really wearing a dressing gown.

'I told him things are different now. Society is different.' She waggles a finger at us. 'There's no shame in talking about mental illness these days, and a good thing that is too.'

'Mental illness?' Titch says.

'Yes. Now, you girls open up that lovely fudge. Here's the tea.' She turns around, pours hot water in and flips the lid on the pot closed before moving over to place it on a trivet that's lying on the table. 'Cinnamon, dear, you fetch us some cups and saucers from the cabinet there, and, Lavender, you take the sultana scones out of the oven while I find the butter.'

The two of us do as we're told, quick smart, barely even noticing the use of our real names. In under thirty seconds the three of us are sitting down at the table again. Mrs Tuddle is pouring. She pauses when she gets to my cup and looks up, first at me, then at Titch.

'You shouldn't be cross at your grandparents, mind. For not telling you, I mean. Like I said, things are different now. But back in their day—well, those kinds of things weren't spoken of.'

'What kinds of things?' I pipe up, and get a look that sends me wriggling into the back of my chair. I certainly won't rush her again.

'Now, Lavender, you have a good fill-up on those scones, dear. You're too thin.'

'Yes, Mrs Tuddle,' Titch says meekly, and reaches for the scones.

'And plenty of butter on them too.'

'Yes, Mrs Tuddle.' She takes the butter as well.

'Good girl.' With a nod, she finishes pouring. 'Now, what was I saying? Oh, that's right. About your mother—may she rest in peace. Well, this may come as a bit of shock, girls…' Mrs Tuddle puts her cup down now, a worried furrow crossing her brow '…but she had schizophrenia.'

Titch has a sultana scone halfway to her mouth when the word 'schizophrenia' leaves Mrs Tuddle's lips. She promptly drops it onto her plate noisily, butter side down.

'Oh. Oh. I'm sorry,' she flusters.

'Don't you worry about that, dear.' Mrs Tuddle waves a hand. 'It'll taste just the same.'

'Schizophrenia?' I stare at the scone. 'Our mother had schizophrenia?' I only realise I'm speaking the words because they come out too loud and reverberate around the kitchen.

There's a pause. In the silence, I try to lift my head up, but I can't stop looking at the scone for some reason.

Finally, Mrs Tuddle speaks. 'It was a terrible shame. A terrible, terrible shame. None of us saw it coming. She was such a lovely little girlie. Full of life. And those curls! A regular little Shirley Temple, she was. I could have cried when she cut off all her hair that first time she went to Sydney.'

My mouth dry and my brain numb, I look up.

'And I'll tell you something. Mal Eames isn't going to be popular around here for telling you like he did. It was a very sad thing to see her the way she was, and anyone in their right mind knew that. I nursed her all the way through it myself, and the suffering that poor girl went through—well, nobody really knew. Not even your grandparents, I think.'

I stare back down then, at my plate, unable to meet either Titch's or Mrs Tuddle's eyes. I can't believe it. I simply can't believe what I'm hearing. But in the long silence that follows my mind starts to speed up. To remember.

Scenes and snippets of conversation come back to me. Things I've overheard about my mother. Things people have said. Things that just didn't make sense. Like the time she insisted on being served in the pub with no clothes on and the police had to take her away. Or the time she tried to convince everyone in town that my grandparents were slowly poisoning her.

Even at the age of seven I wondered why she liked drugs so much if they made her do and think things like that. I mean, it didn't exactly look like fun. But now...now these things start to make more sense. Faster and faster my mind starts to flit backwards and forward through my childhood, pulling out bits and pieces I haven't thought about for years. Things I hoped I'd never think about again. And as the silence continues I come to a horrible realisation...

All those awful, awful things my mother said and did in her life, all those awful things I hated her for, thought her embarrassing for, blamed her drug-taking for—she couldn't help it.

She couldn't help it.

Titch coughs, startling me. 'Wasn't there any kind of, um, treatment back then?' she asks.

'Oh, of course. When your mother was first diagnosed there were already several drugs on the market. But what you've got to remember is that those drugs, they're—well, they're not very nice drugs to take. Not that she didn't try. She tried everything. And your grandparents were always on the phone to doctors, calling around, driving her to the city, trying to find other treatments. But nothing was ever very successful. Sometimes it just isn't. Even with the advances we've had since then. You see, it's very hard to make someone take medication they don't want to take, and your poor mother, she went through hell with some of those drugs— tremors, drowsiness. One of them was so bad she could barely stay awake for more than a few hours a day.'

'But why did she leave?' Titch continues, looking confused. 'Why the coming and going from Moo? Wouldn't she have been better off here? With Nan and Pop?'

'Ah. That was the hard thing for her, poor lamb. She knew people talked about her behind her back. Some of it she imagined, I think, but others did talk, true enough. It wasn't that your grandparents were embarrassed—no, far from it. I've always said they did the right thing by their Helen. They were good people, your grandparents. The best kind of people. That was part of the problem, I'd say. Helen could bear to have people talking about *her,* but not about *them.*

'What you've got to understand is there was a lot of stigma attached to an illness like schizophrenia then. People thought that maybe they could catch it from her. Or that she was dangerous and she might hurt them or their children. They thought your grandparents should send her away. Where to, I have no idea. Anyway, I think it was easier for her when things got hard to simply run away. To leave Moo behind. Granted, she made her mistakes, and when things got harder she came home again. And the drugs she took—the illegal ones, I mean—well, they didn't help much either. But I've never passed judgement on her for that. No, not me.

'She was desperate, your poor mother. Desperate like only some young people get when they're sick. When they're dying. They know, you see, and they tend to grasp at anything. Anything that makes it all easier. Ah, now, Cinnamon, dear, don't cry. She wouldn't have wanted tears, that's for sure…'

I look up slowly. I'm crying? I *am* crying, I realise, as another big fat tear plops down onto my unbuttered sultana scone. I shake my head at Mrs Tuddle. 'What I don't understand is why no one told us?'

She sighs in return. 'I know, sweetheart, I know. I did try to convince your grandparents to tell you, but they thought you were too young. Then, when you were older, I think they just didn't want to bring it up again. They thought you'd forgotten. That the town had forgotten. And they wanted to forget themselves, I suppose…'

The three of us sit in silence, looking at each other, until Mrs Tuddle thumps a paw down on the table decisively, making both Titch and I jump. 'Now, what we're going to do is drink lots of tea and eat all these scones and try at least one piece of the fudge each. That's more like what your mother would have wanted. She loved a good sultana scone, that's for sure. So, do you think you can do that?'

Titch and I nod.

'And then, when you've got more questions, maybe in a day or two, you can come back for some more tea and we'll have a good old natter. Just the three of us. And I'll show you some old pictures, of when your mother was a girl…'

So that's what we do. Titch eats three heavily buttered sultana scones, I eat two, and we both have a piece of fudge
and three cups of tea to wash it all down with. Most of this
is done in stunned silence.

I'm thinking about whether a third scone is a good idea
or not when, for some reason, I start to put two and two together. 'Mrs Tuddle? The bathroom. The other day. With
Bert. What was that about?' I blurt out.

'Ah…' Mrs Tuddle looks slightly caught out.

Titch glances from one of us to the other.

'I wasn't meaning to pry, you understand. It was just
that Bert…'

'Yes?' Titch persuades her to go on.

'Hmm. How can I put it? Bert sent me over after he saw
your drugs, dear, in the bathroom. He was concerned…'

'Oh!' Titch sits up straight. 'Oh, no.'

'He was worried that they were for something like your mother had.'

I almost snort scone out through my nose. My mother had *no* trouble in the conceiving department. But then I remember my sister's feelings. 'Sorry, Titch.'

She gives me a wry smile, and I can tell she's thinking the same thing I am.

'He thought you might be having some problems…' Mrs Tuddle continues.

Titch sighs sadly. 'I *am* having some problems. Just not the kind he's thinking of.'

Across the table, Mrs Tuddle looks at her for a moment or two. And then she reaches her hand out to cover Titch's. 'Don't you worry, love. It'll all work itself out. I know it will.'

I watch her hand, her fingers curled over Titch's, and have a sudden sense of *déjà vu*. There's something about her hand. And the way she says the words too, that make something click together in my mind. I keep watching, staring, trying to remember what, but I can't for the life of me. Finally I shrug to myself and put it down to something that must have happened when I was a child.

After I have that third scone, and Titch has yet another cup of tea, we're more than ready to roll our way home. We get up and say our thank-yous and goodbyes, and I make a last-minute decision that a trip to the bathroom might be wise.

Leaving Titch and Mrs Tuddle talking near the kitchen door, I nip down the hallway and enter the land of crochet (crocheted toilet mat, crocheted toilet seat cover, crocheted handtowel, crocheted doll-like toilet roll cover, crocheted toilet brush handle!). In fact, everything's so crocheted I bet the cat never stands still, just in case.

On my way back up the hallway I pass Mrs Tuddle's spare room. The door on my left is wide open, and as I go something purple catches my eye. Something purple and…spangly. I stop dead and look closer. In the mirror facing me I can see the reflection of several items hanging behind the spare room door. Several items that include a turban. And a veil. A spangly purple turban and veil.

I make a noise as I stare, and suddenly Mrs Tuddle is hovering beside me.

'I…I only just remembered. I was coming down. To close the door.'

I look over at her. 'You?'

Mrs Tuddle looks worried. Really worried.

'You were the tarot card reader? In Byron Bay? You?' And it's now that I remember and quickly look down at her hand. The hand that had covered Titch's only half an hour ago. No wonder it jogged my memory—it was the same hand that grabbed mine that day during the reading. When I tune back in with a shake of my head Mrs Tuddle is speaking.

'I… You won't tell anyone, will you? It's… You see… You probably don't know, but my mother and my grandmother…they were a little bit psychic, you see. And there's…well, there's a bit of it in me. I don't talk about it. Not around here…' She laughs a small laugh then. 'I suppose there's a lot of things we don't talk about around here, aren't there? We're a bit backward in many ways.'

I stare at her, my mouth hanging slightly open.

'I used to read for your grandmother, you know. We'd talk a lot about your mother.'

Now I really stare. 'You contacted my mother?'

Mrs Tuddle shakes her head quickly. 'No, dear. No. Nothing like that. I got a few feelings from time to time, that was all. That she was happier. Things like that.'

'Oh.'

'I don't think your grandfather knew, though. I don't think he would have approved.'

'Oh,' I say again. It's all I think I can say right about now.

'Yes…' Mrs Tuddle reaches out to touch my arm. 'Please. Don't tell Lavender. Or Sally.' She looks anxious. Worried.

I wake up to myself. 'No. It's OK. I won't. Not if you don't want me to.'

There's a small pause as we look at each other. For the first time, I think, woman to woman.

'And you know, dear, everything I told you that day. I did mean it. Like I told Lavender, things will turn out for the best. For both of you. And in all kinds of ways you'll never expect.'

Titch is waiting for me outside, walking around Mrs Tuddle's front yard and sniffing a few of her prize-winning roses. 'Are you all right? You took a long time.'

'Sorry.' I shake my head, still trying to get my thoughts together. 'I was just, um, saying thanks to Mrs Tuddle. For talking to us.'

'Oh. That's nice.'

'Hmm? Yes, well…' I remember Mrs Tuddle's words then, and repeat them absent-mindedly. 'There's a lot of things we don't talk about around here, aren't there?'

Titch gives me a strange look, but then nods slowly. 'A lot of things.'

We start the short walk home, and as we go Titch begins to piece the past together bit by bit. 'I remember something about her shaking, you know. About the tremors, like Mrs Tuddle said. And the sleeping. I remember us going to visit her in the community hospital and Pop calling her "sleeping beauty" and telling her all she needed was a kiss from a prince to get better. She thought that was funny.'

Silence.

'Dicey, say something. Please.'

I look over at my sister's worried face. 'Sorry. It's just…'

'I know. It's a shock. Finding out, I mean.'

I nod. 'You're lucky, you know. Remembering things like that. All I seem to remember is people talking *about* her, later on. About the…bad times. I can't remember her being— well, being a mother. My mother. I've racked my brain, but all I can come up with is these vague, unfamiliar pictures of her, like I'm seeing the past through someone else's glasses. I don't even think they're real memories. More like things I've seen in the photo albums that I *think* I'm remembering.'

'Well, you were so young, after all. What were you? Almost six when she died?'

'I'd just turned six.' I nod and concentrate on kicking a small pebble that's just in front of my foot. It goes skidding out onto the road. Titch and I watch it travel away from us.

'What's wrong?' She touches my arm.

I shrug. 'I don't know. I just feel…awful. It's just that I've thought such terrible things about her. That she was pathetic and weak and basically an all-round terrible person. I thought she hated us, that she didn't care. That she didn't care about anything. She always made me feel that we were boring and stupid and the wrong colour. That we were an embarrassment and that she'd rather be anywhere than with us. That drugs were more interesting than we were. I guess…I guess I never saw her as a person. With her own problems. It was all about me.'

Titch smiles at this.

'What?'

'You were six, Dicey. It's only natural that it was all about you. That's how six-year-olds think.'

'I know. I know. I just wish someone had told us sooner.' Slowly, I shake my head.

God, it's so stupid. Why *didn't* anyone tell us? Maybe not when we were so young, but when we got older, at least—when we could understand what had gone on. I mean, how could they let us go on thinking she behaved like she did out of *choice?* And how could our grandparents have really believed that we'd forgotten? You don't just forget about something like that!

I stalk the final few steps up to the top of the hill, stop and put my hands on my hips. 'Ugh. I feel so…' I pause.

'So…?'

'Frustrated!' I exhale loudly as Titch comes to a standstill beside me.

'Mmm. Me too.'

I glance over at my sister's serene face. 'Yes, you're really showing it—as per usual.'

'Well, I am!' she insists.

I exhale again. 'OK. I believe you.' The pair of us survey the rolling green countryside around us. Suddenly, it feels wrong. On a day like today, with news like this, we should be surrounded by jutting, jagged mountains and brown dirt—not lush pastures dotted with fat, contented cows. 'Don't you just want to scream?' I turn to her.

'Um, sure.'

Another glance. Obviously the thought hasn't even crossed her mind.

'It's all wrong. So unfair.'

'It *is* unfair. So, why don't you, then?'

'Why don't I what?'

'Scream,' Titch says matter-of-factly.

I turn to meet her eyes. 'Want to join me?'

She smiles. 'OK. Why not?'

'Right, then. One, two, three…'

And on the count of three we both scream. As loud and as hard as our lungs will let us. The noise seems to bounce off the hills around us. After we've expended all the air in our lungs, we look at each other and laugh.

'I wonder what she would have said about this?'

'What do you mean?' Titch asks.

'About us standing on top of a hill. Screaming.'

Titch shrugs. 'She probably would have liked to scream along with us. I think she had plenty of frustration of her own to get rid of.'

She's right, I think, and smile. 'Once more?' I say. 'For, um, Mum?'

Titch returns my smile with a nod. 'For Mum.'

We spend the rest of the afternoon on the swing chair, with mugs of tea, plates of biscuits and memories of our childhood.

'It's strange that I never really heard anything about it,' Sally says at one point.

But I don't think it's so strange at all. Like our grandparents always said, 'little pitchers have big ears'. In a small town, people know enough not to gossip in front of their kids. And then, of course, Sally moved away from Moo soon after she finished high school. The town's never really forgiven Sally's family for their move to a fancy new estate on the Gold Coast, or for their half a million dollar lottery win. Pretty funny, really, considering everyone around here enters the lottery once a week like it's a religion.

So, my grandparents thought it was all over and done with. Forgotten. Maybe they thought Titch and I would never find out what really happened to Mum. Or maybe, like

Mrs Tuddle said, they simply couldn't bring themselves to talk about it to us. To anyone. Maybe it was just too painful.

After dinner, the three of us go our own separate ways to think. Sally reads a novel, Titch stays out on the verandah, and I go for a walk with Fergus. When I come back, Titch is still sitting on the swing chair, her legs folded under her and her wish book, of all things, on her lap. Even in the half-light I can see that her eyes are red, and I go over to take a seat beside her.

'We're a bit like that today, aren't we?' I say with a sigh, as Fergus lies down on the floor with a large thump.

Titch searches for a tissue in her pocket and blows her nose quietly.

'Have you been writing all this time?' I nod at her wish book.

'Dicey?' She turns to me, not giving me an answer. 'The other night? The thing I said about Mum?'

'About if you were like her?' I ask.

'Yes. That's… I think that's what's been bothering me. What's been holding me back.'

I pull my legs up and hug them. 'What do you mean?'

Titch pauses for a moment before she speaks again. 'I guess after the first two rounds of IVF failed I started to think—well, that maybe it was fate. That there was some-thing in it.'

I glance over at Titch, my forehead wrinkled.

'That I wasn't meant to have any children. That—you know—perhaps the universe was telling me something. That I'd be a failure as a mother. Like our mother.'

'Oh, Titch.' I drop my legs and turn around fully. 'You can't be serious.'

She wipes at her eyes with the tissue. 'I know it sounds

stupid, and silly, but after things go wrong again and again and again, you start to wonder if you're doing the right thing.'

'But of course you are!' I reach out and grab my sister's hand. 'Titch, if I know one person who'd be a great mum, it's you. You're so patient! And kind! I mean, look at me. I'd be a disaster. But you—you'll have lots of kids. I just know it. I've always known it. And I can *see* it too. You'll have to buy one of those awful people-mover vans.'

Titch laughs a watery laugh at this. 'I'll tell Andrew you said that. He'll be distraught. He's always fancied himself in a green MG.'

'Well, maybe you can get a green people-mover, then. Think of it as a compromise.'

I manage to squeeze a second laugh out of my sister with this. But when she stops laughing I see it instantly. The thing she hasn't told me. The thing she's holding back. Slowly, her eyes slide to meet mine.

'Titch…' I say.

She looks away quickly.

'Titch…'

'No, I can't.'

'Yes, you can,' I tell her. 'You have to. You have to tell me.'

'I can't. I haven't even told Andrew. I haven't told anyone.'

I squeeze her hand. The hand that I'm still holding. 'Well, you have to start. Telling, I mean. You can't just hold everything in, Titch. It's bad for you.'

Slowly, slowly, slowly, her eyes move again to meet mine. 'The last time. When things…didn't work. I…I bought a big box of painkillers.' She practically whispers the last word.

What? *What?*

'I locked myself in the bathroom and…' She shrugs.

Suddenly I'm all action. I jump off the chair so I'm in front of her and I grab both her arms. Hard. 'Titch!'

'I know, I know,' she says.

I shake my head. No. She doesn't know. At all. If Titch ever…*ever* did anything to herself. God, I don't know what I'd do. My eyes fill to the brim just thinking about it.

'Don't, Dicey. Don't cry. Please don't cry. I shouldn't have told you. I know I shouldn't have told you.'

I grab on even tighter. 'You should have told me before you went out and bought anything. You should have *told* me!'

'I know,' she says sadly.

We look at each other for a long time. Around us, everything is quiet. No cars. No TV. Nothing. Just the sweet chirping of a few cicadas.

'I couldn't take them,' she says eventually. 'The painkillers.'

I keep looking at her. At my sister. 'Why? You decided you didn't want to…to die?'

Suddenly the silence is broken. Titch's laugh slices through the quiet like a knife. 'No! Because…' She laughs harder now. 'Because…'

'Because what?' Why is she laughing, for God's sake?

'Because they gave me pills by mistake. Instead of gel capsules.' She's crying now. But only because she's laughing so hard. 'And you know I choke on pills.'

I want to laugh too. But I can't. Because the wiring's all wrong. What Titch has just told me and laughing. I simply can't combine the two.

'Oh, Dicey, I'm sorry. I shouldn't be laughing.' Titch gulps, trying to calm herself down. 'It was just that it *was* funny. I was sitting there in that bathroom with this huge box of painkillers that I wouldn't be able to swallow.'

I stare at her.

'Oh, Dicey. Come on. It is just a *little* bit funny.'

I keep staring.

Titch takes a deep breath. 'I ended up sitting on the floor of the bathroom laughing till I cried. And then…well, I just cried. For all the times things didn't go our way. And for being so…so damn hopeful all the time. And for the baby that didn't get its chance.'

Now I stop staring. 'Oh, Titch.' I've always known that she thinks about the baby she wasn't able to carry to term as real, but until now I don't think I knew just how real.

'Anyway, I sat there and I cried about all that, and then to top it all off I had a cry about how I was going to have to stop IVF as well.'

'What?' I butt in. 'Stop? Why?'

'Because…' Titch says slowly, looking me right in the eye. 'Because of what I tried to do there. In the bathroom. Because sitting there, with my pills, wanting to die, to have everything over with, made me just like Mum. And if I was anything, *anything* like her at all, I knew I couldn't have children. That I didn't deserve to. That it was probably all meant to be. Like I said—fate.'

I shake my head now. Side to side. Harder and harder. 'No, Titch. No. That's not true. You know that. You know you don't have Mum's problems.'

She exhales slowly. 'I know that *now*. I know that now.'

We sit, together on the verandah, our arms around each other, for a long, long time.

'You know what?' Titch turns her head to look at me.

'What?'

'I hate you so much.' She gives me an extra hard squeeze.

'Well, I hate you more.' I squeeze back just as hard.

When I finally pull back, I take a good look at her. At the woman sitting beside me.

'With all that behind you, it must be such a relief for you to find out. About Mum, I mean. That there was a reason she was the way she was.'

Titch sighs. 'It is, but I feel so sorry for her. She could have had such a happy life, but it was just eaten away. Like you said before, it's just so unfair.'

'I know.'

'Anyway—' Titch places her hands down firmly on either side of her '—I've decided.'

'Hmm?' I say, still half thinking about Mum.

'I'm going to try again. With the IVF. I'm going to try for a third time.'

'What?' I quit dreaming. 'Titch! That's fantastic!'

I don't think I've ever had such good news before. Ever.

'I'm going to give up work for a year and really give it a go. Eating properly. No stress. Just really concentrate on it. Andrew was offered a job last month. Close to home. We decided he shouldn't take it because of the pay cut, but I think maybe we made the wrong decision.'

'It'll be worth the pay cut. To be together.'

Titch nods. 'I know. Anyway, I'm going to give it a shot. My best shot. Because...' she smiles shyly now '...I really want to be a mother. And I think...I think I could be a good one.'

I grab her and give her another hug. 'You *think?* I don't *think* you will be. I *know* you will be. Now, have you spoken to Andrew yet? About any of this?'

Titch shakes her head. 'I will though. Tonight.'

I clap my hands together and hope that my face doesn't crack from smiling so hard. 'He'll be so happy.'

Titch smiles again. 'I know.'

'Right.' I jump up from my seat. 'I'm going to go have a shower and let you get on with it.'

And that's what I do.

An hour later, when I peek outside to check up on her, Titch is still writing, her tongue sticking slightly out to the side. It always has done that when she concentrates really, really hard. Ever since I can remember.

Honestly, over the next couple of days it's like my sister has turned into a different person. She sleeps less and moves around like a whirlwind, cleaning up the house and starting on the baking again (except this time she eats most of it). Sally and I don't complain about any of this, but sit back, watch in awe, and stuff our faces full of sweet, vanilla-laced, home-cooked goodness. Fergus particularly takes to her custard slice.

It's during all my sitting back and watching Titch get on with her life that I build the courage to do what I have to do. That is, confront JL.

'You've just got to do it.' Sally whacks the verandah railing with her cast in order to make her point. 'Ow! That hurt.'

'But what would I say?' I groan, and lean back on the swing seat till I'm looking at the roof above me. 'It's too embarrassing…'

'Embarrassing? What's embarrassing about it?'

I groan again. Louder this time. 'Oh, I don't know. Maybe it has something to do with the fact that we're *separated*.'

'Separated, schmeparated.' Sally waves a hand.

I sit up. 'What's that supposed to mean?'

'Beats me. And it doesn't matter. What matters is, if you say that word one more time I'm going to have to kill you. Look, kiddo, it doesn't matter if you're separated. You've just got to *tell* him.'

I want to scream. 'But tell him *what?*'

Sally sighs. 'Geez, Dicey. Sometimes I wonder if there's anything going on in that head of yours at all. I don't know—maybe you should tell him that you can't stop thinking about him? That you still love him? That you want to get back together? It seems pretty straightforward to me. Do you want me to write it down on the back of your hand for you in case you forget?'

'Ha-ha. It's all very easy for you to hang about spouting wisdom.'

There's another sigh. 'I know it's going to be difficult, but what are you going to do otherwise? Pine away for ever? It's worth a bit of embarrassment, isn't it? *He's* worth a bit of embarrassment?'

Reluctantly, I nod.

'You've seen Titch reach out for what she wants. So how about you?'

'I know. I know. I've got to do it.'

'That's right.' Sally eyes me. 'But you could be a bit more enthusiastic about it. How about once again—with feeling?'

'I've got to do it.'

'Oh, come on.'

'I've got to do it!'

'That's a bit better. And again?' Sally punches the air.

I stand up. 'I'VE GOT TO DO IT!' I yell at the grass in front of me. At the cows.

'That's the girl!' Sally comes over and gives me a whack on the back.

I cough. 'Ow! What was that for?'

'Ah, you know—just a bit of "yay, team!" And maybe I'm still mad I didn't get to join in your screaming session after Mrs Tuddle's. Titch told me about it.'

'Maybe some other time?' I laugh.

'Whenever you feel you can pencil me in, babe.'

So, full of courage and an extra round of yelling (I could get used to this yelling thing...), I bite the bullet, beg Sally to watch Fergus, jump in the car and drive the long drive to the city.

It's almost dark by the time I get to JL's house. I pull up on the opposite side of the street, half hidden by a large, purple-flowering jacaranda tree, and go through my speech one more time in my head. I've had plenty of time to prepare it—the whole one and a half-hour drive, in fact. And I've got to admit that as I've honed the piece, adding and subtracting bits, working out exactly what I want to say, it's got to the point where it isn't half bad at all.

Smug, but still scared out of my wits at what JL's going to say back, I reach for the door handle.

Which is right when her car pulls up in his driveway. The FC's car, that is.

Oh, fantastic. What's she doing here?

She gets out of her sickeningly spotless oh-so-tasteful navy blue baby Peugeot, clicks the central locking shut with a snap, and swings her long blonde hair from side to curvy side all the way up to JL's front door. I notice with disgust that she doesn't even do anything sadly self-conscious like I'd do in such a situation—check her teeth for spinach in the rear-vision mirror (even if I hadn't eaten the stuff for weeks), touch up her lipstick, smooth her outfit down, fix her hair, or even do the 'oh, I just saw something really interesting behind me that attracted my attention' thing when JL opens up.

People like that shouldn't be allowed to live.

I watch as they do the Continental kissy-kissy thing on each cheek (Um, hello? You're Canadian! I want to yell out) before JL says something and then ducks back inside for a second. For his jacket, I see in a moment. And then he switches off the light behind them and they head back down the front steps.

This time I don't look at the FC at all. My eyes are transfixed by JL.

He looks really, really good.

He's wearing a black Saba turtleneck I picked out for him about a year ago, and a pair of Tsubi jeans I bought for him last Christmas that are now faded just the right amount. There's a touch of stubble, but not too much, and he has his old suede jacket slung over his arm.

I gulp. I bet he smells really good too.

The FC clicks open the central locking again, and they get into her car and leave.

It's only when they reach the end of the street that I get the idea. I should follow them. Why? I don't know. The idea just leaps out and grabs me by the throat. For some reason I suddenly need to know where they're going. What they're doing together.

Quickly I start up my own car and speed off down the road, scared that I've already lost them. But I haven't. I manage to spot them again, turning right at a roundabout up ahead, and from then on I follow at just the right distance. Not too close to be seen or noticed, and not too far behind so I lose them, either. Just like I've seen them do on all the cop shows. Sometimes I even get tricky and let a few cars slide in between us.

As it turns out, they don't drive very far at all. Only over to the local café strip—a *faux*-French-looking place that JL and I used to stroll by on our power walks and laugh at. It's a place for people with too much money and time to come and drink coffee and vie for the best spot to park and show off their Mercedes. What is he doing here? I scrunch up my nose. One guess—the FC's choice.

But if JL doesn't like it, he certainly doesn't say anything about it. In fact he looks as happy as a pig in mud when he gets out the car and takes the FC's arm before they cross the street. When they reach the other side he points to something—a red Ferrari—and they both stop for a second and laugh. It's that laugh, that one synchronised action between them, that makes my heart plummet to the bottom of my chest.

Oh, God. What am I doing here? That's *our* joke they're sharing. My joke with JL. And, to make things even worse, they look more like a couple than JL and I ever did. There was never any denying it—as human beings go, he's a better-looking one than I am. And now he's traded up to a superior model. The Ferrari itself. Except that this time the laugh's on me.

I want to turn the car back around again and leave, but I find that I can't. I don't have the energy. Instead, working my way through the packet of pistachios in my bag, I sit and watch. I watch JL and the FC choose their table. I watch them read the menu and enjoy a cocktail. I watch them eat dinner, drink, talk and laugh.

And, sitting there, I don't cry. I don't feel anything at all, really. Except frozen. To me, their date is like a car crash on the side of the road—you know you shouldn't look, and you know you probably won't like what you see, but you look anyway. You can't help but look.

It isn't my finest moment.

The minutes tick by without me even noticing. My eyes are staring, glued to the scene in front of me. It's a good two hours before they get up and leave, and the Peugeot glides off back in the direction of JL's house. I'm still sitting in the car, watching dumbly, and the thought comes to me that I could follow them back. I could follow them back and see what happens next—check to see if she stays the night at JL's or simply goes home.

I only consider this for a second. Because the frozen part of me doesn't want to know. Doesn't care anymore. So I keep sitting. Maybe even for another hour. And then I turn the key in the ignition, pull the car out once more and head for Moo.

The next morning I sleep in till I can't pretend I'm asleep a minute longer.

'Are you getting up today?' Sally pokes me for what feels like the millionth time this morning.

'Umph,' I say, face down, into my pillow. Translated, that means a multitude of things, but mainly 'please bugger off and leave me alone'.

The problem in getting up is that I don't want to be with myself today. Some time very late last night I stopped feeling sorry for Dicey and turned just plain angry. So angry my legs tensed up, cramping, and I needed to get out of bed and stretch them. Now I'm in a foul mood. A black mood. And, frankly, it's a mood I don't want to rise and face. So, I stay in bed and keep dozing, hoping the feeling goes away.

It doesn't go away.

At one p.m., Sally stomps into the room, pulls the sheets

off me and continues her nagging. I know it's one p.m. because that's the first thing she tells me.

'It's one o'clock, for Christ's sake, Dicey. Now, get up and tell me all about it.'

'No,' I say into my pillow. 'Go away.'

'I'm not going away. Tell. I'm taking it it didn't go well?'

'Go *away!*'

Sally humpfs a loud, harassed humpf. 'Sometimes, Dicey, you are just so bloody frustrating!'

People in glass houses…I think into my pillow.

'Well, if you don't want to talk to me, then maybe you'll talk to someone else. He's been looking for you.' Sally leaves the room.

Someone's been looking for me? A he? I almost sit up. But then I hear the movement across the floorboards and the stinky breath hits me like a tidal wave.

Fergus.

'Oh, Fergus, you go away too,' I moan.

Of course he doesn't. And between lying in bed being covered in dog slobber and getting up and facing my revolting mood, I'll take the revolting mood any day. Within five minutes, I'm up and stalking out to the bathroom. After a shower, I'm still not feeling any better, so I stalk out to the kitchen.

On my way I pass Titch, who takes one look at me, says, 'There's tea on the kitchen table,' then bolts for her life, going for a walk and taking Fergus with her.

I fetch the tea and then keep stalking all the way out to the swing chair.

Sally gives me approximately five minutes' grace before she's out and badgering me again. 'So?' She leans up against the verandah railing in exactly the same position she used during yesterday's pep talk.

I groan one more time. 'Can't you just leave it?'

'Hell, no.'

'Ugh!' I sit back in the seat, splashing some tea onto the floorboards below me. 'If you must know, I didn't even get to speak to him.'

'What?' Sally pushes herself upright. *'What?'*

'I. Didn't. Even. Get. To. Speak. To. Him.'

'Yes, I heard you the first time.' She gives me an evil look. 'You mean you chickened out?'

'No. I was all set to go in, and then the FC beat me to the gate by about three seconds. They went out on a date.'

'Oh. The FC again. I should have known.'

I pause. Is that right?

'Don't look at me like that,' she says. 'So what if she was there?'

I can't believe what I'm hearing. 'Well, what was I supposed to do? Run out and push her to one side? Beat her to the door?'

'Yes.'

I shake my head in disgust. 'Oh, Sally, just shut up, will you?'

Sally looks like she's about to leave, but then she pauses for a second. 'No. I won't.'

'What's that supposed to mean?'

'It means I'm not going to stand by and watch while you ditz this up.'

'Ditz this up? Ditz *what* up? There's nothing *to* ditz up. Don't you get that? I went there last night and he was on a date, Sally. A date! And they had a great time. He was happy.'

'And are you happy?'

I put my tea down and stand up. 'No. No, I'm not bloody happy. But I stuffed up my chance, didn't I? I blew it.'

'But how do you know that? Like you said, you didn't even speak to him.'

'I didn't have to!'

'Right. So that's it, then? That's the end of it?'

'Yes.'

'Well, that's a pretty bloody sad attempt, I have to tell you.' Sally reaches into the waistband of her shorts and pulls something out which she begins to wave in the air. 'And what about all of this then? You're telling me you're going to throw all of this away, everything you want, just because some stupid blonde chick with long legs and an accent took your husband out on a date?'

It's my wish book.

'Hey, give that back!' I lunge forward, making a grab for it.

But Sally's too quick for me, and tucks it quickly back into her waistband again. 'No! Give me an answer!'

'Yes!' I yell. 'Yes! I'm going to throw it all away. Now, give it to me!'

Silence.

But my words seem to reverberate around the verandah. I'm going to throw it all away. All of it. Everything.

Sally stops dead as soon as the words pass my lips and hands the book over slowly. 'If that's the case, if you're really going to throw it all away, then you're not who I thought you were, Cinnamon Dye.'

Well, that makes two of us. I've got no idea who I am any more. I'm not surprised no one else does either. I look at Sally coldly. 'You made me go there. You talked me into it.'

'I didn't talk you into doing anything you didn't want to do.'

'It doesn't feel that way to me. Maybe…' I pause, my eyes narrowing.

'Maybe what?'

'Maybe you just want me to fail. God knows, I fail at everything. Maybe this was just a little extra something to make you feel better about yourself. Like the brides you talk about. The brides who make their bridesmaids wear ugly dresses.'

Sally shakes her head and almost laughs. 'Yeah, that's it, Dicey. That's it. Oh, and before I forget, I've got a lolly-pink dress laid out on the bed for you. It's got lovely puffy sleeves and a big pink bow right where your arse should be.'

I want to scream. 'Why is everything such a big fucking joke to you? Do you think this is funny? *Do you?*'

'No, I don't, actually. I don't think this is funny at all.'

I look down at my wish book and want to rip it in two. But I stop myself at the last second. Instead, I run. I run down the front steps with it, right to the end of the front yard. Then I hurl it. I hurl it as far as I can and it flies. It ends up hurtling through the air and dropping right down into the holding paddock below, where it hits a cow on the backside.

The cow moos loudly, startled. 'Yeah? Right back at you!' I yell at it, and it gives me a strange look before it runs off.

Behind me, Sally laughs. Laughs long and hard. And another day, another time watching myself yell at an innocent cow, I might laugh too. But not today. I point my finger at her all the long way back.

'See? It's just like I told you. Like we spoke about. Yelled about. In the car park. I don't see why I should forgive you for anything. This whole trip *has* just been one big joke to you.'

Sally looks away when I say this.

'Oh, I'm sorry I'm boring you. That we're all boring you. Titch, me, Moo. Maybe you should go and liven things up, like you usually do. You know—burn something down, shoot a cow…?'

'What?' She looks back now. She looks at me as if I've lost my mind.

'Well, that's what you usually do here, isn't it? Piss everyone off.'

Sally pauses. 'Is that what I do?'

I don't even think about what I'm saying any more, I'm so over the edge. 'Yes, that's what you do,' I yell at her. 'You go so loopy when you're here that Titch and I didn't want to bring you with us. You're embarrassing. An embarrassment. To us. To Moo. I don't even know why you wanted to come. You don't belong here.'

Silence.

And then something I thought I'd never, ever see—not in my lifetime, not in the next—happens. Sally with her suddenly white face (as white as it was the other day at the hairdresser), bursts into a flood of tears.

Holy shit.

For a minute or two I'm so gobsmacked I can't do anything but watch my friend cry. Because Sally doesn't cry. Sally doesn't cry at the movies. Sally doesn't cry when she breaks her ankle, Sally doesn't cry when her heart gets broken. Sally doesn't cry full-stop.

Finally she gulps a noisy gulp and I wake up to myself and take a step forward. 'Sal—Sal, I didn't mean it. I'm sorry. I…' I take another step.

And then she looks up. Right at me. Through my eyes to somewhere deeper. And I know, instantly, that I've gone too far. Way too far.

'Just go away,' she says, emotionless.

'Sal, I—'

Just go away!

And I am so freaked out that's exactly what I do.

★ ★ ★

But I hang around. That's for sure. I watch Sally good and hard from inside the house. Mainly because I'm afraid she really has gone mad. At first she cries a bit more. Then, after a while, she starts walking around the yard, then stalking around the yard, then yelling at the sky and the trees and the grass. I'm guessing there's not going to be any beautiful grass pictures taken today, somehow…

I watch from the kitchen window, my mouth hanging open in shock. The Sally out there—it doesn't look anything like the Sally I know. It's just like that night we had to dash to the supermarket with Leaf, when Sally went off the wall and later apologised. Once more she seems—smaller. Brittle. And I wonder and wonder and wonder just what it is I've said.

I mean, I know I shouldn't have told her Titch and I didn't want to bring her down to Moo with us, and I *really* shouldn't have called her an embarrassment. But the reaction I'm seeing out there on the lawn—it's not…it's not right. It's not…

Well, Sally.

The walking/stalking/yelling goes on for about an hour. And then, just as suddenly as it started, it stops. Sally flings herself under the huge Moreton Bay fig tree in the corner of the yard and stays there.

I watch her for another ten minutes or so before I become brave enough to tiptoe out onto the verandah. I watch for another ten minutes from the verandah before I become brave enough to tiptoe down the steps. Just as I'm about to try and summon up the bravery to start tiptoeing over the grass, Sally turns around and bellows.

'Oh, for God's sake. Stop messing around and just get your arse down here.'

Ah. OK. I don't waste any more time tiptoeing.

'Um, I'm really sorry about before. About what I said,' I tell Sally when I reach her. She doesn't look at me, but pokes the stick she has in her hand into the soft ground underneath the tree. 'I didn't mean it and…'

She looks up now, her eyes and face red. 'Of course you meant it.'

'Sal…'

'Don't you think I know?'

I pause. 'Know what?'

'Know what a big *embarrassment* I am. To everyone here. To you. To Titch. To my parents. To Bert. To Mrs Tuddle. To *Moo*.'

'I…'

Sally laughs, but there's no joy to be heard in it. 'I always have been, haven't I? It would have been so much better if *I'd* been the one who died, wouldn't it?'

What?

'Oh, come on.' Sally's eyes bore into mine. 'Don't think you haven't seen it in everyone's eyes. Perfect, perfect Lisa. Pretty Lisa, popular Lisa, perfect, perfect Lisa. Smarter, nicer, just all-round better human being Lisa. Why was Lisa the one to get leukaemia when it could have been Sally?'

Oh, my God. Slowly I sit down on the grass beside my oldest friend. 'Sally, no one thinks that.'

'Don't they? Sometimes I wonder if even my parents think that.'

I know Sally's parents, and I can guarantee, however hard things have been for them, and however much they love and miss Lisa, they haven't thought this.

'Sal, that's not true.'

'Isn't it? The funny thing is, I don't really think I was like this at all until Lisa died. When I realised I couldn't fill her shoes I think I went the opposite way.' Sally looks over at me again. 'It's hard, you know, trying to fill the shoes of a saint. Eventually you give up. Causing a fuss—it was the only way to get any attention at all. Mum and Dad…they just shut down. If they weren't being hauled up to the principal's office they might have forgotten I existed. At first it was like playing some kind of role. But somehow, over time, the lines blurred between that and who I really was, I think.'

'Oh, Sal…'

I don't know what to say. Being a teenager, I didn't think about it like that. I never wondered *why* Sally was always in trouble. She just *was*. At the time it seemed exciting. But now…

'I thought coming back here, after all this time, things would be different. But they're not. Everyone who looks at me just sees a less lovely version of my sister.'

Something comes zinging back to me then. 'Do you really think so? The other day—at the hairdresser's—Jody remembered you mainly for your photography. Not just for Lisa. Or only for how you behaved in high school.'

Sally shrugs.

'Well, it's true. And why shouldn't she? There were plenty of things you were far better at than Lisa—don't you forget that.'

'Not much.'

'Oh, come on.'

I pause now, wondering whether I should say what I've never been brave enough to say.

'What?'

Sally must see what's going on in my head. She stops poking her stick into the ground and throws it a few feet away.

I take a deep breath. 'Don't hit me or anything, but Lisa…she was always a bit too good to be true.'

Sally looks at me for a moment, not saying anything, and I wonder if I've said the wrong thing completely. Just as I'm contemplating making a break for it before she throttles me, she laughs out loud.

'Finally! Someone gets up the guts! Lisa could be a complete bitch when she wanted to be, believe me.'

I snort. 'I think anyone with a sister would believe that.'

'Well, except you. Yours really is close to perfect.'

I make a face. 'I know. Believe me, I know.' In the silence that follows I swivel around to face Sally better. 'I am sorry, though. About what I said. About…everything.'

Sally smiles a half-smile. 'Yeah, I know. Me too. Hassling you—it's just me trying to…' She pauses and takes a deep breath, and in this moment, I can see her pushing back the tears that are filling her eyes. 'Trying to be a better sister than I sometimes was to my own.'

Late that afternoon I take Fergus for another walk, in the hope of clearing my head. Frankly, the poor thing looks exhausted. With all the thinking going on around here, I don't think he's been walked so much in his life.

Raff.

Fergus keeps looking back hopefully in the direction of the house. I tell him he can go back if he wants. But, suddenly loyal, he doesn't, and he sticks by me as we walk up and down the hills of Moo.

It's around four, when I'm hiking up to the top of yet another hill, that I see the house on the opposite rise. The old King farm. Dave's house. I pause for a second before I decide. And then I walk the short distance back into town, pick up a box of chocolates and a mini Wagon Wheel for Fergus (which he gulps down immediately, along with three bowls of water) and start the walk back again.

A blue heeler greets us noisily at the farm gate. Fergus, almost three times his size, cowers behind me from the first bark.

'Dicey!'

I hear the voice soon enough. It's Dave, walking around from the back of the large, sprawling house.

'And is that Fergus behind you?' He laughs as he gets closer.

I roll my eyes. 'He's not really a coward. He's just guarding me from a surprise attack that might come from behind.'

'Of course.'

'Fluffy! Shut up!' Dave yells at the barking dog, and it shuts up immediately.

'Fluffy?' I look down at the dog, then back up at Dave, who opens the gate for me. 'That's an, um, interesting name…'

'Yeah, well, we bought him as a working dog, but I think he's some kind of a poodle in disguise. Now he's just the kids' pet.'

I laugh at this. 'Come on.' I reach back and grab Fergus's collar and drag him out from behind me. 'I don't think Fluffy's going to bite. Much.'

Fergus gives me a look, to see if I'm having him on, before he decides to trust me and runs through the open gate over to Fluffy. They spend a moment or two sniffing each other before running away to play.

'A regular love-in.' I shake my head as I walk through the gate myself and Dave closes it behind me.

'That's Fluffy for you. He loves to entertain. He'll have his tea set out next, you watch.'

I can't help but laugh again. I'd almost forgotten about Dave's weird sense of humour. 'Come on up,' he says, nodding his head in the direction of the house, and we start walking. 'I think Mandy's got to go pick the kids up from karate soon, but we can have a cup of tea. Or do you only drink coffee now you live in the big city?'

I give my old boyfriend—my first 'real' boyfriend—a look. 'Tea's fine, you big dag. I brought some chocolates.'

'So I see. I thought they were for Fluffy.'

'Into chocolates, is he?'

'Oh, yeah. Flowers too. If he doesn't get a heart-shaped box of chocolates and a long-stemmed bunch of red roses on Valentine's Day he can be a real handful to have around the rest of the year.'

We walk up the front steps and on to the wide verandah. It's a gorgeous house and truly gigantic, as only the really old houses around here are, with a red tin roof and beautiful iron lace on the front. It even has the original little red tin awnings over each of the windows along the sides, I notice.

'Mandy?' Dave calls out as we walk into the hallway.

Again, it's like stepping back in time. There's a beautiful feeling of spaciousness—something you just don't get in new houses these days. Directly in front of me, at the other end of the house, the back door is open, and it lets the breeze travel straight through the hall and out the front door.

'In here,' a voice calls out, and the two of us follow it through to the kitchen.

'Mandy, Dicey's here,' Dave says as we step into the room.

Mandy looks up from where she's standing at the oven, pulling a tray out. 'Dicey, hi! Nice to see you.'

'You too.' I smile.

'You know, the kids have been raving about having you three as Big Moo these past weeks.'

'Thanks. It's been fun doing it.'

Mandy looks over at her husband. 'Speaking of which, I've got to go pick them up. Can you just pop that second tray of biscuits out of the oven when the timer rings?'

'Sure.' Dave nods.

Mandy takes her apron off and throws it onto the kitchen table as she moves out of the room. 'I'll be back in a tick, Dicey, and we'll finally get to have a chat, hey?'

'That'd be great,' I say. 'See you soon.'

'Oh, and help yourself to the jam drops,' she says, as she runs down the hallway.

'Mmmfff,' Dave says, already onto his fifth one.

'You're terrible.' I shake my head. 'I'm sure those are for your children.'

'Well, I'm just helping to keep their arteries healthy, you know?'

'No, I don't know. Now, put the kettle on, you slacker. I need that cup of tea.'

Dave and I sit on the verandah and watch the cows go by as we sip our tea. It's amazingly peaceful up here, the highest point in Moo. Minutes pass before either of us speaks.

I finally look over at Dave, deadly serious. 'You're so lucky.'

He stares at me, seeing that, for once, I'm not having him on. 'Yeah. Yeah, I am. But look at you—glory, fame…'

I snort. 'Mmm. That really worked out for me.'

'Dicey…' Dave starts, but then he pauses.

And it's funny how I knew this was coming. That the moment I spoke to my old boyfriend for more than a few minutes he'd go all deep and meaningful. With anyone else I could have discussed the lighter things in life. The biscuits. His kids. How the farm was going. But not with Dave. He always had a miraculous way of cutting through the crap.

With everyone and anyone. I think that's why I've been avoiding him.

Now, in his pause, I sigh. I think back to the house. To Titch and Sally, who both seem to have faced their demons in the last couple of days while mine have joined some kind of a house of horrors union in order to gang up on me.

'Sometimes I wish I'd stayed here, you know? That I'd stayed and just—well, got on with things.'

Dave laughs. 'What things? Like waiting to die?'

'That's not true. You're hardly "waiting to die", as you put it. You've got a lovely wife, two great kids, the perfect farm and a gorgeous house…'

'Not to mention a pansy dog,' Dave cuts in.

'Yes, not to mention a pansy dog.' I have to laugh despite myself.

Dave shakes his head. 'But, Dicey, that's me. Not you. I was meant to stay, and you—well, you were born for bigger things. Staying would have killed your spirit. You know it would have.'

'I feel like having left's killed my spirit lately.'

Dave turns around in his seat properly, to face me. 'But that's just how you feel now. It'll pass. I knew it'd be like this…'

'Like what?'

'Whenever you've lost your way before it's been because you've stopped listening to what you really want and started listening to what everyone else wants. Remember the trail-riding thing?'

'Oh, God.'

The 'trail-riding thing' *was* a disaster. I was waitressing at the Moo Inn when the opportunity came up to lead a bunch of kids on a five-day horse-riding trek. I hated horses (and kids, at the time) and all my instincts told me not to do it,

but the money was great and Dave, my friends and my grandparents talked me into going ahead with leading the group.

One lost horse and one child with a broken finger later,
I wished I'd listened to those instincts.

'And what about the time—?'

I hold up my hand. 'Please—point noted. Let's just leave
it at the trail-riding.'

Dave laughs. 'Sorry. I guess what I'm trying to say is I think
that what happened to you happened for a reason.'

I give him the eye.

'No. I mean it. You might think it all sounds like a lot of
hooey, but I like to think that's the way things work. Staying would have been too easy. Maybe you had to leave to
learn something. To make you a better person. And I know
it hurts now, but think of yourself as a snake—'

'A snake?' I butt in.

'Just listen. It's a good thing, really…'

'I can't wait to hear *this*.'

Dave laughs before he continues. 'Like I was saying, it hurts
now, because your skin's thin. You've shed the outer layers
and exposed what's underneath. But the skin will grow back
and you'll toughen up. You'll see.'

I'm ready to laugh his words away, but when he comes
out with them my smile fades. I have to stop and think for
a moment, because what he's just said—about my skin being
thin, about me 'shedding layers'—that's exactly how I *have*
been feeling lately.

It's as if everything's been hurting just that little bit more
lately. Raw pain that makes me wince. But maybe there *is*
hope, like Dave's suggesting. Maybe my skin *will* build up
again with time. Come to think of it, since I've been in Moo
the process may have already started. Cell by single cell.

I turn to look at Dave, and I'm suddenly thankful for the basic wisdom this simple town has offered me since I've been back here. I wish I'd sought it out before. That I'd thought to come back and remember who I used to be. Who I still am, somewhere deep down inside.

I hope.

'You know what I think?' Dave continues. 'I think, Dicey, maybe it had to be this way. That there wasn't any choice. That it was—is—just your destiny.'

The next evening we hold the last of our scheduled Moos meetings. This time there's no last-minute screaming at Sally to hurry up with her lipgloss. Five minutes before we're due at the community centre hall to begin setting up, Sally is dressed, glossed and ready, waiting serenely on the verandah, like this is what usually happens.

I laugh out loud.

'Come on, Fergus,' I yell, and I pass Sally and head for the car, where Titch is already getting in the passenger side door.

Fergus gallops up from underneath the house, already nice and dirty even though he had a bath earlier this morning. 'In you go.' I fold down the driver's side seat and shoo him over to the far side.

Sally finally makes it over, sees the state of him and sighs. 'Just my luck.'

We make our way down to the community centre hall

and quickly set up the tables and chairs we'll need for this evening. It's a special night tonight—we're having a game or two outside, making organic, meatless sausage rolls and organic, sugar-free cordial, and then the parents are coming early so the kids can read to us all from their now completed wish books.

Funnily enough, Titch, Sally and I seem to have conveniently 'forgotten' ours.

Everything goes as planned. The kids have their tear around in the front yard with an over-excited Fergus, and when they're sufficiently but not too worn out we herd them inside, wash their hands and start in on the feast.

Like I thought they might be, the organic, meatless sausage rolls are rather tasteless, stuffed with their nut filling, but with a dousing from a contraband bottle of revolting special kids' edition green-coloured tomato sauce they manage to reach edible status (the kids get strangely excited about this, so much so I can't tell whether they're truly excited about green-coloured tomato sauce or whether it's the preservatives kicking in). The cordial passes for cordial. I guess it's difficult even for hippies to screw up a watered-down orange drink.

Finally, the parents begin to arrive, the tomato sauce is quickly hidden away, and the show begins.

And it is a bit of a show. Just like I noticed on the evening of our first Moos meeting, the eclectic mix of parents sitting in the community centre hall is obvious once again. Rachel is out there, sitting next to Camilla's infamous 'my dad', who eyes her warily, as if his fat wallet and tiny mobile phone might go missing at any time. And there's Dave and Mandy, chatting to Leaf's mother, who's waving her hands around animatedly. Probably telling them all about our little trip to the shops.

'Right, then.' I turn around to look back into the kitchen. 'Everyone out there's got a drink. So, are we almost ready for some food?'

Titch nods as she helps a couple of the kids place sausage rolls on trays so they can pass them around. 'Just about.'

I go over and heap a pile of napkins on each tray, and then Titch and I shoo the kids off to let their parents taste exactly what organic, meatless sausage rolls are like without contraband tomato sauce. Basically—*blech*. When we've tidied up a bit, we head out there as well, for a quick chat before we get started.

Naturally, when we're ready to roll and Sally has reappeared from sneaking a cigarette behind the toilet block, Rainbow volunteers to go first. She stands up at the front of the room and clears her throat before she begins, a smile plastered to her face like she's auditioning for a beauty pageant and has just found out about the Vaseline-on-the-teeth trick.

'My wish book, by Rainbow Sorenson.' She pauses and looks up at her mother, who nods encouragingly. 'What do I wish for in my life? I wish that I could fly like a care-free kite…'

Sally kicks me on the ankle with her cast. 'Oh, my God,' she leans over and whispers. 'Her mother may want her to be a tree-hugger, but that kid has a long and illustrious career in bullshitting ahead of her. Oops. I mean PR.'

'Shhh.' Titch gives Sally a look.

Still, it's true, and I have to try hard not to vomit as Rainbow continues for another two pages of poem. How is it that some kids learn to lie so early, or at least learn the benefits of sugar-coating the truth? She can't truly want to be a 'care-free kite', can she?

Hamish, my little friend, goes next, and pulls on everyone's heartstrings with a few of his comments.

'I wish that it was my birthday every day and that we could have my favourite ice cream with the cookie-dough in it that my mum says is disgusting. I wish that my tooth would fall out, but I know it won't because I only play with it and I'm too scared to tie it to the door handle, like Dad says I should, but I wish that it would fall out anyway. I wish for a yellow Labrador puppy that Mum says I might get for Christmas if I'm good. And I wish I could have my old dog, Scooter, back. Because sometimes I yelled at him and that was bad, but most of the time I hugged him, but even when I yelled at him he always wagged his tail at me so that later I wished I hadn't yelled at him in the first place.'

Hamish gets a loud round of applause. And as I check out his parents I know exactly what he's getting for Christmas. So does he, by the look on his face. Little scammer. I laugh to myself.

Madeleine and Leaf take their turns after Hamish, followed by Sorrel. It's funny how a lot of what they're saying, despite their different backgrounds and ages, is the same. I expected the kids' wish books to be full of wants for the latest Nikes, the coolest clothes and expensive toys, but what they're asking for—it's mostly the simple things in life. They want to be happy, to have fun with their friends, for their parents to be less busy, to pay them more attention and to have more time for them.

It's Camilla, however, who makes everyone stop and listen up. She leaves her seat beside her father reluctantly, but he pushes her up and waves her on all the way to the front of the room, while her mother watches on, expressionless (botox?). Her wish book, I notice, isn't as intricately decorated as the other ones we've seen, but she opens it up anyway and begins speaking quickly, as if she wants to get this over and done with.

'I wish that we didn't have the big house any more. When we had the old house, once Mum put picnic food in a basket and we ate it right in the living room. Like a pretend picnic. That was fun. But we can't do that in the new house because of the carpet. I wish that dinner took ages and ages to get ready. That's when I'm in the kitchen with Mum and I get to sit on the bench and talk about school. I wish that Dad didn't go to work. Dad just goes to work and sleeps. And on the weekend he mows the lawn and looks after the pool. I hate the pool. I wish we could still go to the public one, but Dad won't let us because he says…'

And on and on it goes, only getting marginally better as the wishes continue.

Ouch.

By the end of Camilla's speech no one really knows where to look, so it's a relief when Tom and Jo get up and read from their books together, alternating with their wishes.

When the kids are finished, the parents file outside and leave us with their offspring for a few moments to say our goodbyes. I'm glad to say they all seem to have had a good time with us for the last few weeks, and they leave at least semi-reluctantly. Hamish even tries to steal Fergus, but his parents kind of notice him attempting to stuff the twice-his-size dirty animal in the back of their car and give him back to me.

When the last child has been waved off, Sally heads for the kitchen to clean up and Titch and I are left standing in the doorway.

'You OK?' I glance over at her.

She nods. 'That poor child.' She shakes her head.

It's obvious she's talking about Camilla.

'Well, here's hoping her parents heard her tonight.' I look back outside.

Titch nods again.

I sigh. 'I don't know about you, but I've had it.'

'Go and take a seat outside for five minutes. Fergus is in the kitchen, busy polishing off all the leftovers, so there's not that much left to clean up anyway.' She touches my arm before she turns and heads for the kitchen.

'Thanks,' I say, and walk down the few steps in front of me to stand on the grass. After a minute or two I take a seat on one of the large rocks bordering the flagpole.

'Hey,' a voice says from behind me. It's Sally. Lost in my thoughts, I didn't hear her thump over.

'Hey,' I say back. 'Take a seat.' I hold an arm up so Sally has something to grab onto as she sits down.

She gets halfway before she hits the rock with a whump. 'Ow. I'm starting to feel like an old person. I can't get up or down from anything these days.'

I glance over at her. 'I have to say I'm, um, still kind of freaked out about yesterday.' We hadn't had much of a chance to speak about it again last night, as Titch stayed up quite late. 'I really am sorry about everything I said.'

Sally waves a hand. 'Don't mention it. I had it coming to me. Ever since we've been back I've been trying to block it out. Anything to do with Lisa. To not think about it. I'm guessing that was a mistake, because it seems to have blown out of proportion. I know some of it's true—people do remember Lisa when they look at me. But that's OK, you know? She was my sister, after all. I've just spent too much time reading how *I* feel about it all into what *they're* thinking.'

'How *do* you feel about it all?' I ask hesitantly.

Sally shrugs. 'I think I have to stop feeling guilty. Lisa getting leukaemia—it wasn't fair on any of us. She was robbed; my parents were robbed. And the money…' She trails off.

'Winning the lotto?'

Sally nods. 'It was less than six months after she died. My parents still talk about that. What they could have done with it all—better doctors, better hospitals, better treatment. They would have spent every cent. All of it.'

Silence.

'You know, there's someone you forgot. You were robbed too.'

Sally looks back over at me. 'Yeah, I know,' she sighs.

'Coming back here must be really hard.'

'It is. Moving away made it easier. I was glad when Mum and Dad decided to move away. But coming back—the guilt comes back too. It's a reminder of what you're trying to forget.'

'But it's OK to forget. You're not forgetting about Lisa. You're forgetting about the bad times.'

'Except the good times were here too. That's the problem. You'd understand that better than anyone.'

I nod. In all kinds of ways. Not just my grandparents, but my mother, my childhood with Titch, my wedding…

'Anyway, enough about me.' Sally waves a hand. 'I said plenty myself yesterday that I should be apologising for.'

I snort. 'Well, yes. Except everything you said was *true*. I know you're just worried about me. Trying to make me do the right thing. I know that. I knew it yesterday, I think. It's just easier not to hear the truth, that's all.'

Sally pauses. 'I *am* worried about you.'

I turn around and look at her properly now.

'I know you've decided you want JL back, and that you're too scared to do anything about it in case he doesn't feel the same way—but, Dicey, you've got to do it. And really soon. I think it'll all work out if you just go for it. I'm not trying to set you up to fail…'

I groan and cover my face with my hands. 'I can't believe I said that. About the bridesmaid's dress.'

Sally laughs. 'Me either! What a riot! I'd never pick lolly-pink anyway. From what I've seen around the traps, lime-green's always the worst. Or yellow. For that jaundiced look.'

'Gee, thanks. That makes me feel a whole lot better.'

Silence again.

My thoughts wander back to Lisa for some reason. 'You know,' I say eventually, 'maybe we should both go down to the cemetery before we leave. Together. We can take some flowers.'

Sally looks over at me. 'Yeah. Yeah—OK. That would be nice.'

Behind us, there's a howl from Fergus. Sally laughs.

'He always hates it when the kids leave,' I say, explaining.

'I guess that's it for the Moos, then, hey?'

I nod. 'I can't believe how amazing that was tonight. How in touch all those kids are with what they want out of life.'

'I'll say. Especially that Camilla. *Bang*. There it is. As a parent, that stuff's got to rip right through you.'

'I just wish I had that kind of a grasp on what I want out of life. I feel like I used to, but when I wasn't looking it just slipped away.'

Sally sighs. 'Maybe that was the problem—you were looking in the wrong direction.'

'Something like that. Frankly, I'm tired of everything

screwing with my head. I can't remember what normal feels like. What it used to feel like not to be a failure…'

'God, for the last time—you're not a failure!'

'Well, to be seen by everyone as a failure, then. It's all semantics.' I wave one hand dismissively.

Sally shakes her head at me. 'What am I going to do with you? It's not semantics. It's that you truly *believe* you're a failure that makes me so furious. You've shut yourself inside for the last few months, watched all the news programmes and read all the papers, and now you actually believe all that bullshit the media's been putting out there. You've got to let it go, Dicey. It doesn't matter what they say, or what anyone else thinks, for that matter. But what's going on in your head *does* matter. If you start believing you're a failure, you're done for.'

Too late, I think, and give a small shrug. Beside me, Sally groans.

'If I could get up and give you a good shaking, I would. You've got to put it all behind you and move forward. Like, right now. The same as you need to do something about JL. It's a package deal. You've got a chance to take that first step onwards and start putting things right, and you've got to take it while you still can. It's like a window in time, you know? It won't last long, and if you don't make the first move now…'

'I know. I know. I won't stand any kind of a chance at all.'

Sally reaches over and squeezes my hand. 'Tomorrow, hey?'

I look at her and nod slowly. 'Tomorrow.'

I toss and turn all night, not able to get to sleep again as my thoughts whirl around inside my head. My covers go off and on, I get up and drink a glass of water, I go back to bed, get up and bead a bag for an hour, watch half an hour of TV, drink a glass of milk and go back to bed. Nothing works. At about four-fifteen a.m., I get up again and decide to go for a walk.

Being careful not to wake Titch or Fergus, both sleeping beside me, I throw on a pair of tracksuit pants, a long-sleeved T-shirt and a baseball cap, grab the torch out of the dresser drawer in the hall and head out.

It's chilly as I creep down the stairs, and when I'm far enough away from the house not to be heard I walk faster and faster down the driveway and out onto the road, warming up as I go. I think I half knew where I was headed even before I started out, and now I turn towards the place instinctively.

It doesn't take me long to get there. I'd know exactly

where to go even if it was pitch-black outside—despite the fact that my feet rarely trace the path I'm taking. Soon enough I'm sitting on the cold concrete of my mother's grave.

I haven't been here for years, not since soon after my grandparents' funerals. I'm not a great believer in visiting graves. I tried it a few times, leaving flowers for Nan and Pop, but I quickly realised they weren't there. That is, I couldn't connect with them here, in this rather ugly part of Moo, complete with a stunning view of the power lines. So I stopped coming.

Someone hasn't, however. All three graves are weeded and have bouquets of flowers on them. Plastic flowers, but non-faded, non-dirty plastic flowers nonetheless. Bert. I'm sure of it. For a moment I feel bad, coming here without flowers—and, even more importantly, without Sally, as we discussed coming together. But I know she won't mind. I'll come back with her and our flowers, like we agreed, before we head back to the city.

I sit in the quiet, trying not to think about very much, just wanting to be still and by myself for a while. And I must sit for quite some time, because the shapes around me become clearer and more defined as the sun slowly starts to rise. When I begin to be able to read the names on the headstones from some way away, I turn around to face my mother's headstone, crossing my legs.

I always thought it was wrong that my grandparents buried her here, in Moo—the place she could never get away from fast enough. I always believed she should have been cremated and her ashes spread. Not anywhere in particular, but so they could be taken away by the breeze. Now, though, I see why they knew it would give her comfort. How it wasn't for them at all.

As the sun continues to rise, I read aloud from the head-stone in front of me.

Helen Dye
Beloved daughter of Merle and John Dye
Loving mother of Lavender and Cinnamon Dye
Long may she rest in peace

I take my time in reading, thinking about the words as I go. When I'm done, I decide they're simple, but to the point—just like my grandparents. Anything fancy, too over-worded, or anything that carried too much information would have been just plain wrong. Of course up until now I always thought those words farcical—'beloved daughter', 'loving mother'. But now… I shake my head. I wish my grandparents had told us. I wish they'd tried to explain. Even if not when we were children, when we grew up.

"'Beloved daughter",' "'loving mother".'

I say the words out loud once again.

"'Beloved daughter".'

Twenty-eight years old. I shake my head again at this. Twenty-eight years. Four years younger than I am now. I thought, as a child, that twenty-eight was an old age to be. An ancient, grown-up age. Now, twenty-eight sounds scarily young. And, to add to this, she battled her illness for ten of those years—having been diagnosed, as Mrs Tuddle told Titch and myself, at the age of eighteen. That was a year before she had Titch, and years after she left home.

My eyes turn to my grandparents' graves. It must have devastated them to have had such a happy child and then have everything, suddenly and without warning, go wrong. To get past the childhood illnesses and accidents and then watch everything about your child change…her whole personality. And not have a diagnosis for so long. I can't imagine it. I can't imagine how distressing and life-altering it must have been for them. And how frightening it must have been for her.

I sit for a long time, thinking about all of this, and, as I think, a great wave of shame washes over me. Look at the opportunities my grandparents gave me, and, with my health never in question, here I am sitting on my mother's grave feeling sorry for myself at the grand old age of thirty-two. Four more years than she ever had.

I wish, now, that I didn't feel the need to be so 'strong' when my little empire crumbled. I wish I had the sense to reach out and let JL help me. But at the time I didn't feel I could let anybody in, for fear of looking feeble. I was painted as the star of a one-woman show—someone who'd made it on her own in the male-dominated world of business. Well, the truth is, I might have ensured my pyjamas remained quality controlled and double-stitched no matter what, but it's a shame I didn't pay the same attention to the seams of my life.

In one short stint of time I managed to lose almost everything that was important to me—my business, my balanced existence, my self-esteem. And then, even more idiotically, I threw away the most important thing of all— the one thing that could have kept my head above water— my husband.

Since then I guess I've basically been walking around in a circular daze—not knowing what to do with myself or how to start doing it. During my tossing and turning earlier this morning I was thinking long and hard about what Dave said the other day—that maybe this was my destiny. Was it? Is it? I'd prefer not to have had to learn things the hard way, but maybe he's right. Maybe I am a better person for what I know now?

In some ways, I suppose I am.

And it's here, on my mother's grave, that I force myself to look back, blinkers taken off, and see things for how they really were. Not how Harry thought they were. Not how the media saw things. But how they were for *me*.

It was during the downhill slide, after one particularly long and wearying bout of Harry yelling at me, that I knew for sure that things had to change. I left the office building and didn't go back. And after that day I didn't talk to Harry any more. Not directly, anyway. I started talking to him through lawyers. I thought I was being smart the day I hired two of my own. But Harry was smarter. He already had a team of lawyers, two accountants and a publicist. In hindsight, I should have traded in my two lawyers and Simon, my half-arsed media advisor, for one decent publicist. Because that's when things got nasty.

Suddenly I was all over the media. My lovely little fairy-tale had turned into a long-taloned, eye-gouging Jilly Cooper novel. And, unfortunately, I wasn't the heroine, but the wicked bitch. The media made out like I'd seen poor old Harry coming from a mile away. That I'd done a song and dance with my pretty little youthful frame, clopped him one over the head with my designer handbag and made off with his money.

After all, it couldn't possibly be *his* fault things had gone wrong. He was a cute little wrinkled old man. He'd always used a cane, but now all too quickly, Harry needed a wheelchair. And oxygen. Not to mention long daily strolls, pushed along by a nurse, which strangely gave ample opportunity for his picture to be taken and a few breathless words uttered.

I really could have clopped him over the head with a designer handbag when I saw that.

The media crucified me.

And there was no way out. Nowhere to go. I couldn't afford to buy Harry out myself and I couldn't raise the money to do so now my name was mud. There was no point him buying me out either. I was the face of the outfit.

Within months, it was all over.

It was the hardest decision I've ever had to make, throwing in the towel on my own company. Still, I made it. And, despite what the media's been saying about me lately, I believe it was the right thing to do. It's just that it's hard not to listen to the things they say about you. It's hard not to start believing them. Or perhaps it's easier to believe the bad things you hear about yourself than the good things. To concentrate on the negative rather than the positive. It's funny how I didn't take in half of the lovely things journalists said about me years ago, but now they've turned on me I gobble up every word.

I glance back over at my mother's grave. Maybe that's what things were like for her too? Like Mrs Tuddle said, plenty of people said bad things about her and my grandparents. Of course, my problems were nothing compared to my mum's. Her destiny was one she couldn't control, even if she'd wanted to—her brain was working against her and she chose to throw away the small amount of control she had left and move onto anything she could get her hands on—illegal drugs, alcohol, cigarettes. Anything to make her feel better. Then there was the long spiral downward before she made a final decision, just like I had to—but hers was to kill herself.

In some small way I think I know part of what she felt.

How sometimes it's easier to let go and just fall. How after you've held on so long and so hard there's a point where you've had enough and falling seems like the better, quicker option. When I made up my mind to let my company go, that's what it felt like. A release.

I run both my hands along the concrete edge I'm sitting on. Perhaps that's what death was like for Helen Dye. A release. A safe place to go when she couldn't bear the cycle any longer. The sun on my back, I look up at the headstone again and smile. Something tells me that if she were here now, she'd tell me that this time I shouldn't let go. That this time I should hold on tight. And something else tells me that she'd give me the same advice Sally did last night. Don't wait around till tomorrow. Reach out for what you want. Ask for it.

I know they're both right. If JL says no—well, it's my loss, and I'll have to deal with it accordingly. But not knowing. Isn't that a worse sentence? A lifetime of what-could-have-beens.

It doesn't sound like much fun.

A few hours later, at a more human-friendly time of day, I take a few deep breaths for courage and pick up the phone. Again, of course, I have prepared a speech that has been practised over and over. But as soon as JL picks up and says hello, all my fine words disappear.

All I can say is a croaky, 'I need you.'

He gets it. JL always gets it.

Unlike some other people I could mention… (That would be me).

He doesn't say much, but he tells me he'll come down to Moo tomorrow. To talk.

When I hang up the phone again, I look down and see that my hands are shaking.

Frankly, I don't think I've ever been so scared in my life.

The day passes by slowly. Ever so slowly. It's as if each tick-tock of the clock in the kitchen suddenly begins reverberating around the whole house, each movement of the second hand clicking over in my brain. To escape the sound, I take my fifteenth cup of tea out onto the verandah and sit back in the swing chair. It's another gorgeous day today—blue skies and a gentle breeze—and the occasional 'moo' can be heard from the paddocks below.

After a while, Sally comes out to join me, her wish book in her hand. 'How's it going?' she asks, settling in beside me.

'Slowly,' I say with a sigh. 'Really, really slowly.'

'Well, he'll be here in no time. You'll see.'

I nod. 'Have you been writing?'

Sally gives me a mysterious look. 'Maybe. Maybe not.' There's a long pause as she sips her tea. A too-long pause.

'What is it?' I don't take my eyes off her.

'Um…'

'Come on,' I try.

'It's just that I don't want to butt in again.'

'Like you're going to be able to help yourself!'

'Mmm. That's true.' Sally perks up when she hears this, thinking it's an invitation. 'Having been there myself and all, I thought you might like some, er, advice on the getting back together thing.'

'That's if we get back together.'

Sally tuts. 'Oh, don't be such a Negative Nelly.'

'You're starting to sound like Pop.'

There's another tut. 'Well, he was a smart guy. Now, do you want to hear this or not?'

'Um…' I pause, thinking. But then I laugh. 'Probably not. But feel free to go on.'

When Sally does go on, however, her face is serious. 'I just wanted to remind you that things—well, they won't be like they were before. If there's something I know a thing or two about it's relationships on the rocks, and there's no point in denying it: getting back after being separated—it's really difficult. You can't go back to where you were before, and you don't know how to start over. But you'll work it out—you really will. If you want it enough, that is.'

Looking at Sally, I suddenly feel very serious myself. 'I do. Want it, that is.'

'I know you do.' She pats my hand, which is resting on the seat. 'Looking back, the one time I tried I don't think I really did want it enough. But you do. I can see that. Everyone can see that. And I'm betting JL will too.'

'I hope so.'

'Just think of it like a plate that's been dropped and has smashed clean in two. You can glue it back together pretty successfully—you may even be able to hide the crack. But you've got to let the glue harden. If you keep testing it to see how strong it is, picking at the weak spot, you'll always have this plate that's really made of two pieces. I know that sounds stupid...' Sally's eyes seem worried.

But I shake my head. 'No,' I say, thinking about what she's said. 'No, that doesn't sound so stupid to me at all.'

'Really?'

I smile at her. 'Really. Thanks.' I take a sip of my tea. 'Sal?'

'Mmm?' She looks over.

'Are you...are you happy?'

'Yep.' She doesn't even pause for a second.

'So, what you were saying back when we first got here—about being the queen of failure—you don't care about that? About all your, um, marriages ending?'

Sally gives me the eye. 'Well, I'd prefer that they hadn't, but that's just the way it is, isn't it?'

'Um, I guess,' I say quickly. 'I'm not having a go at you or anything, it's just that…'

'I'm so well adjusted? So youthful to be thrice divorced?' She flips her hair back.

'Sure. That's what I meant to say.'

Sally laughs now, and thumps her bad leg on the floor-boards. 'All I want is to get my leg out of this stupid cast. Then I'll be truly happy.' But then she must spot the confusion on my face, see that I'm looking for a different answer here, because she continues, 'Look, I'm not the kind of person who makes big plans. Or who thinks too hard. I have a hard time working out what I'm going to have for dinner each night. Just go a bit slower this time, hey? You'll work it out. You'll work it out no worries.'

Beside her, I take a deep breath in and then exhale. 'I hope so,' I say. 'I really hope so.'

The package, addressed to me and redirected from my post office box, arrives by courier late in the afternoon.

I sign on the courier's dotted line, then carry the large box up onto the verandah, where I take a seat on the swing chair and slowly open it. Inside, packed neatly, are folded pieces of newspapers and magazines, videotapes and other such things. Media clippings, I realise.

Oh, God. I've forgotten to cancel my clipping service.

Of all the things to forget to do…

Quickly, I pick out the first piece of paper I find. When I unfold it, I see it's a large, two-page spread from a week-end paper. Again quickly, greedily, my eyes start to scan the page, soaking up the words. Until, that is, they get to about the third paragraph…

And then they stop.

Because, as I keep reading the same tired old phrases that I've seen a million times before, I realise I'm not feeling anything here. I realise I don't care. I really don't care what this person, this newspaper thinks about me. I *have* heard it all before, and it wasn't true then either.

Slowly, my fingers refold the piece of paper and put it back in the box, which I close and dump on the verandah, finally kicking it back under the swing seat. Then I pull my feet up, stretch out, and wait for sunset.

And when the beautiful pinks, purples and oranges fill the sky, I make a silent cold tea toast. To my mother and to new beginnings. Or, to be more exact, to the new beginning I've decided I'm going to have for the both of us.

JL's car pulls into the yard just after eleven, making me jump. I've spent the morning alternately pacing the verandah and making endless cups of tea that only get half drunk before they go cold, waiting for him to turn up. But now that he's here it all seems a bit real, and my hands start shaking again as I put away the last few plates I've just dried. When I'm done, I wipe my hands on a handtowel and head on out of the kitchen to meet him. Sally and Titch are both standing in the hallway, eyes wide, and Sally gives me the thumbs-up as I go.

With half my innards crawling up my throat, I run down the front the steps and over to the car, where JL's just getting out. 'Hi,' I say hesitantly, when I get there, with a small wave.

'Hello.' He doesn't smile at me, and diverts his attention to Fergus, who's just run up and has now practically bowled him over. The next five minutes are spent giving Fergus the good ear-ruffling and belly-scratching he deserves, and I almost feel like I've been let off the hook until JL stands upright again. 'We should talk,' he says, his expression still not giving anything away.

I nod and look back up at the house, where I can see Titch and Sally peeking out of one of the front windows. I turn back again to see JL wave at them, but then the curtains quickly drop. 'Let's go somewhere,' I suggest, not wanting my future spied upon.

'It is up to you.' JL shrugs.

We end up driving a good twenty minutes away to a National Park. It's a beautiful spot that I haven't been to in years, and the two of us, along with Fergus, are soon walking through the dense trees and then clambering up the hot and sticky sand dunes.

It's worth the effort, however, when we reach the top of the hill. The breeze hits our faces as soon as we step out of the shaded dunes, and suddenly there's water everywhere, as far as the eye can see. To our left and right pristine beaches stretch on for ever, while out in front a large, rocky outcrop provides a soundtrack of waves bashing against each other, turning the rocks into strange-looking black rectangular formations over the years. Up above, the seagulls squawk noisily, sending Fergus into a mad dash from one side of the hill to the other, in the hope that he'll catch one. (He'd better not, as he's not really supposed to be in the Park in the first place.)

On a fine day I know you can often spot pods of dolphins in the water. But today I don't look.

As Fergus runs around letting off steam, JL and I go over and take a seat on the grass. There's almost an arm's length distance between us, I notice. He sits with his legs outstretched. Mine are crossed. The body language experts would have a field-day with us, I think to myself. Neither of us says anything for quite a while, but eventually the silence gets to me.

'I, er…'

'I…' JL starts speaking at exactly the same time.

'You go,' I say quickly, looking away.

JL doesn't argue. 'You want us to get back together? That is what this is about?'

Thinking I'm going to be sick any minute now, I nod.

JL shakes his head and looks away. I guess he's going to tell me to get lost, and I don't blame him. But then, just as quickly, he turns back again and meets my eyes. He's obviously angry. Very angry. Angry in a kind of way I haven't seen in JL before, and it scares me. I've got to say something. And now.

'I'm, um, sorry about…about Simon,' I stammer.

A noise comes from within his throat and he jumps up. 'You think that is why I am angry? Because of Simon?'

I look up at him. 'I…'

'Simon is nothing but a fool.' He gestures any thought of him away. 'He has nothing to do with this. Nothing. This is not about other people.'

'I…'

'Tell me. Tell me now what this is about, Dicey, or I am leaving.' JL turns to go.

'No…' I swivel around, still sitting down. 'No!' I say a bit louder, and he stops in his tracks.

I stop breathing. I have to tell him what he wants to hear. Now. Right now. Because this is it. My last chance. And suddenly, looking up at JL, I'm scared. I'm scared that I don't know the right answer, the right thing to say. I think back to the night I drove to the city, preparing my perfect little speech to win JL back along the way. But now I realise everything I wanted to say that evening was rubbish. It was all honeyed words. All…bullshit. So, instead, I do what I have to do. I do what I should have done months ago…

I tell the truth.

I reach down, right down into the bottom of my heart, drag it out and dust it off. 'It's— I… That I let you go,' I blurt out, falling over my words. 'That I shut you out. When we needed each other most.'

There's a long pause and JL eyes me unblinkingly, then he bends down quickly and grabs both my arms. 'How could you do that, Dicey?' he yells. 'How could you?'

I sit back a bit in fright.

When he sees this, his expression changes instantly. He looks shocked. 'Sorry. Sorry. I did not mean to hurt you…'

He lets go and sits back down beside me once more. When he looks at me again, he seems defeated. Tired. As defeated and tired as I've felt myself these past few months. And I realise, with a stabbing pain in my chest, that he's been feeling the same things I have—just from some distance away. I shake my head. It's not Simon that's the fool. It's me. All me. We could have gone through this together, JL and I. It would have been better. And so much easier. Why couldn't I have let it happen that way?

I start to cry now—not nice daytime TV tears that trickle elegantly down my face, but sobs that choke me, making me cough. 'I'm sorry. I'm so sorry…'

JL doesn't say anything, and finally I pull myself together. I take a deep breath, then exhale.

'I want to try and explain,' I say then. 'About the last couple of months. About the business…'

'Ah, the business.' JL sighs. 'I was wondering when that

would come up. Why not let *me* explain? The past few months as I see them?'

'Sure.' I nod, more than happy for someone else to speak. 'Go ahead.'

'I know it was hard,' JL starts. 'Very hard for you. As you say, you were "royally screwed". I think that is the expression?'

I nod.

'Yes. You were "royally screwed". Harry knew about business. You did not. You trusted him. There was no reason not to. And you deciding to leave when things did not feel right—well, that was the bravest action I have ever seen anyone take. I thought, after this decision, that everything would be OK. But it was not, was it? You could not let it go. You started doubting what you had done. And with all the attention it got worse. You started to believe that things could have been different.'

'I…'

'No. Let me finish. It was like an ulcer in your mouth, I think. You could not help yourself. You could not leave it alone. It became larger and larger. Sorer and sorer. You believed you had lost everything. That you were a failure. A failure as a person. As a human being. So then you listen to no one. No one who really knows you and loves you. Not me, not Titch, not Sally. No one. Instead you take advice from fools like Simon—people who know nothing about you. Nothing! You are like Midas, but not with gold. With failure. And it is all in your head. You think anything you touch will fail. And it will, because you believe this to be true. You are a failure at one thing, so you are a failure at everything. Your business, your relationships. It is as if you cannot believe in this one thing any more so you refuse to believe in anything. And so you throw everything away. You feel sorry for yourself. It made me sick to see you do this, Dicey. Sick. I could not help you, however I tried. Could not do anything…'

Oh, God. Now I think I really am going to be sick. I want to die. I want to wither away and die. Right here. Right now. I open my mouth to say something, but JL stops me again.

'No. I am not finished. So I thought about this very hard. And after a long time I realised there was only one thing I could do to help you. To help both of us. I had to step away. I was not prepared to let you push me away like that, so I had to step away and let you make your mess. And then I had to hope that, when you were done, there would be something left for us.'

Wait. What? I don't understand.

'What do you mean?' I butt in.

JL sighs. 'I mean that when you asked me if I was having an affair…?'

I nod.

Beside me, he shrugs. 'I lied. There was no affair.'

My hands instinctively clench into fists when I hear this. There was no affair? He lied? But that means…

'You lied?' I blurt out, reaching over to grab his arm. 'You *lied?*'

JL nods.

'But…' I start, a look of horror taking over my whole face, my whole body, as I realise just what this means. It can't be true. It can't be.

'Yes?'

'No.' I shake my head. 'No.'

'Dicey, what is it?'

I take a deep breath. The deepest one I think I've ever

taken. And with it I try to work out just how I'm going to
say what I have to say.

'I've got something to tell you.'

'Yes?' JL leans forward. 'This I can see.'

One more deep breath for good measure. 'I, um, lied too.
About having an affair, I mean. With, um, Simon…' The
words tumble out with a whoosh as I exhale.

There's a pause.

A long, long pause in which we stare at each other, neither of us knowing what to say.

'I…ah…I did not know that.' JL eventually speaks first.

'No,' I reply, for something to say.

God, what a mess.

In the silence, I look out at the rocks in front of us, trying to get my head around everything. JL lied about having
an affair. Lied so that I'd stop hurting him, so that I'd stop
lashing out. And I lied in the hope of tying things up. To
put an end to the awfulness that was happening at home. The
too-long silences. The absences. The awkwardness. And—
worse—that means all this time, these past few months, JL's
been quietly, patiently waiting in the background of my life
for me to…well, to come to my senses.

Ugh. There's that sick feeling again. I'm just an evil person. An evil person who doesn't deserve anything. I've behaved like a child. Like a petulant two-year-old. And I hate
myself for it.

I look over at him. 'But Aimee…' I start.

'What about Aimee?'

'I thought… You and her…'

'Yes?'

'I saw you. One night. At a restaurant having dinner. You
looked so happy together.'

'You were spying on me?'

Oops. 'Not spying. I was just…out.'

'Ah. Well, Aimee is just a friend.'

I give JL a look and he shrugs. 'I admit that, yes, I do like her. It is only natural. And the possibility was there. That is part of why I said yes to your question at dinner. It could have happened, but it did not. And it did not happen because I wanted to give us another chance. In the end I decided that I would wait. Until the end of the year. That is what I told Aimee, and she understands.'

I do the calculations at high speed in my head. It's mid-November. So Sally was right. Time *was* running out after all. And quickly.

'But what about that night?' I can't help but ask the question

'Which night?'

'I mean the day you came down here. When you had to race off. You said you had an appointment. I thought she was here. That you had to get back to the hotel.'

JL shakes his head. 'Then you were mistaken. Aimee was not here. I could not stay because it was too hard. Too much…'

'Oh,' I say, and feel my face get hot as I remember the day in vivid detail.

'That day. At the beach…' JL continues.

'Yes?'

'We should not have. It was…it was all wrong.'

So he'd felt it too. 'I know.' I bite my lip.

'I was angry. I wanted to hurt you.'

'I know,' I say again. 'It's OK. It was…both our faults.'

JL nods, agreeing with me, and then there's silence again.

I shake my head slightly as I look out at the ocean. I guess

Mrs Tuddle was right after all. JL and I *were* hiding things from each other. And, *boy*, did we need to talk.

'Er, Dicey?'

I look over at JL and see that the expression on his face has changed completely. A broad smile is now sweeping across it.

'I have something to tell you. Some good news.'

'Really?'

'The day you left for Moo—the papers you saw in the kitchen…'

'Mmm?' I hope he's forgotten my little comment about them being divorce papers.

'My novella is going to be published.'

My mouth falls open and I end up clapping a hand over the top of it—to stop the flies getting in, as Bert would say.

'You're joking.' I finally manage to get a few words out. 'But that's amazing!'

JL waves his hands. 'It is only a small publisher. Hardly any money at all. But they will publish it in both French and English—which is, as you know, what I want.'

'That's incredible!' I still can't believe the news.

'What you saw that day—those were the contracts.'

I remember what he's just said about the money involved. 'So you'll have to keep working at the café? You won't be able to write full-time?'

JL laughs. 'Like I said, it is hardly any money at all. But I like working at the café, so it is not a problem.'

I shake my head, still in shock. This is JL's dream. It has been for years. My face splits into a wide, wide smile for him. 'I'm so happy for you, JL. Really.' Involuntarily, I reach out and touch his arm.

'Thank you.'

Noticing what I've just done, I pull my hand back towards me a little too suddenly and our eyes meet. We keep looking at each other, and I can see we're both thinking the same thing: now what? Where do we go from here? How do we get to square two? Is there a square two? And, please God, let there be a square three…

'It has been good for you? Being here?' JL breaks the silence.

I nod.

'I thought so. I was happy when you said you were coming here.'

'I feel like…like I'm finally able to let a few things go.' I want to tell him about Mum, but somehow don't feel now's the time. Instead, I look back out at the waves crashing in front of us.

'That is good.' JL nods. 'You know…' He pauses. 'It was just business. Nothing, really. In five years no one will remember.'

'Well, that makes me feel better about it all,' I say with a weak smile.

But JL simply shakes his head. 'No. It is a good thing. What? Did you think that one day everyone in the world would wear your pyjamas?'

I snort at this and reach down to pluck a blade of grass. 'That's kind of the way Harry presented it to me.'

JL laughs. 'Harry tried to put glitter in your eyes. Dicey, all things end. The pyjamas—they could not last. It was a silly trend—people looking like cows.'

I must look offended at this, because JL waves his hands.

'No, no. I do not mean the idea was silly. It was a fine idea. And you made the most of it. What I mean is, when you die, that is not what you want people to remember about you. That you once made pyjamas that many people bought. Is that right?'

This makes me pause. I've never thought about it like that before.

'You are much more than black-and-white pyjamas with tails, Dicey. Much more. If that was all you could have given to the world, it would have been a waste of your life. There are many things, after all, that are far more important. Eating, sleeping, loving. Pyjamas—they do not come into it. There are many things more important than pyjamas.'

Like us, I think. And my eyes well up again. A mental picture jumps into my head of that night I spent going through the old photo albums, the happy pictures of our wedding. I'd give anything to go back in time now and change things if I could. Anything. The tears start to brim over. Over the past year I've forgotten everything that was important to me on that day. I've thrown it all away like yesterday's rubbish.

'What is the matter?' JL asks.

'I do want more than black-and-white pyjamas with tails,' I sob, feeling like an idiot.

JL smiles. 'I know you do.' And then he reaches over and wipes my tears away with his thumb.

I sit there and cry for what must be ages, realising, as I do, that the things I want in my life now are such simple things that six months ago I would have been ashamed of myself for even thinking about them.

I want to paint Nan and Pop's house. I want to wake up to the sound of cows mooing in the morning. I want the green grass and the blue sky. I want Titch's peanut biscuits and five-hundred cups of rainwater tea a day on the verandah. I want roast dinner with three veg with Bert on Sundays.

I realise that this is the end of thinking about *Moo to You*. I don't care if I never make another pair of pyjamas again. I never really cared about my business like I cared about those other things—Moo, my grandparents, Titch, Sally, JL. The business was my dream, for a while, but then it got out of control. That was the reason I gave it away. I didn't like what

I was doing. In my confusion I knew that, on some level, but I've forgotten to feel good about the choices I made.

Now, I turn to JL who wipes the last tear away from my eyes. 'How did you know all of this?'

'Ah, remember I am six years older than you. I went through my pyjama empire failure a long while ago. Before I even met you.'

I laugh at this and JL smiles. 'Let me ask you something.'

'What?' I locate a ragged old tissue in my pocket and blow my nose.

'If I had asked you, at the start of your business, "What is the worst that could happen?", what would you have answered?'

'At the very start?'

JL nods. 'Before I knew you. When you were making little bags and selling them at the markets.'

I think for a second. 'Well, that no one would buy them, I guess. That I'd make a loss on the material and the time I'd put into sewing everything.'

JL gives me a look. 'So you did well, then, yes?'

This puts me in my place. 'Um, well, yes. Yes, I suppose so.'

'And what have you learnt?'

This question I think about for a long time before I answer. 'I…I think I would have been happier if I'd kept things smaller. I didn't want to head up some multimillion-dollar company. It just made me feel like a fish out of water.'

'And when were you happiest?'

I think hard again. I've got to get the answer right. 'When *Moo to You* was a proper small business and we were selling pyjamas at the markets and at boutiques. When I was employing about six people. And when the product was around me, like all over the house, and not out at some nameless manufacturer. It was better that way. I liked it when it was a cult product and not something anyone could just go out and buy at any old department store.'

JL nods, smiling slightly, and I feel pleased with what I've said. 'So what will you do now?'

I shrug and look away, checking on Fergus, who's still running around on the other side of the hill with the seagulls. 'I don't know,' I say as I turn back.

'Is that so?' JL replies, with mock surprise.

'What's that supposed to mean?'

'Well, I have heard some things, you see. About some bags.'

'Bags?' I frown, then I realise what he's talking about. He means the little bags I've been sewing and beading. 'That's just for fun. To keep me busy.'

'Titch and Sally say they are very beautiful.'

My eyes narrow. 'When were you talking to Titch and Sally?'

JL shrugs.

Those pair of… Oh, well, what can I do about it? I made my own sneaky calls to Andrew, after all.

'Perhaps you could make these beautiful bags? Perhaps make *them* a cult product?'

'No.' I shake my head hard. 'No, I couldn't.'

JL nods back, equally hard. 'You could. It is quite possible.'

And that's when it comes to me. I guess he's right… I guess it *is* possible. I could make those 'beautiful bags', as JL calls them. I really could. People would probably talk about what I was doing at first—but so what? They'd probably talk just as much if I sat around and did nothing. And I suppose I can't spend the rest of my days like a dog on a choker chain, with fear of failure pulling me back every time I try to lunge forward and do something with my life.

Speaking of lunging, JL pushes himself up now, to stand in front of me. He silently offers me a hand, which I take equally silently, rising to find myself on a slight mound, so I'm the same height as he is—looking straight into his eyes.

We keep looking at each other without saying anything, and after a while I feel like asking about us: what's going to happen to us? About that square two and, hopefully, square three that I was thinking about before. But I don't. There's been enough talking already. Instead, I lean into him and we stand there, remaining silent, for a long, long time, listening to the waves and Fergus yelping at seagulls.

We'll talk later.

Right now, this is enough.

When I get back to the house, after I see JL off, I'm surprised when I go inside to find that Titch and Sally are packing a few things up.

'What are you doing?' I pause in the doorway to Titch's and my room.

'We have to go home tomorrow. Or at least I do. Andrew's home soon, and I have to be back at work soon.'

'Oh,' I say, realising she's right. I haven't been thinking in days, so to speak, for what feels like a long time now. The end of our stay has snuck up on me.

Titch stops moving around the room and looks at me carefully. 'Aren't you going home?'

The question takes me by surprise, because no answer jumps into my head. I've just assumed I'll be going back to the city, but the word 'home' makes me pause now.

'I…' I start. 'Well, I have to go back.' This is true. There are things I have to take care of—packing up the townhouse, giving back the car—but something tells me I don't need to pack everything I've brought down here with me. Something tells me I'm coming back here. To Moo. For good.

'I knew it! Didn't I tell you I knew it?' The voice booms out from behind me, making me jump.

Titch looks over my shoulder at Sally. 'Yes. You told me you knew it. Six times already.'

'But I did know it! Both things. I told you she'd work it out with JL. *And* I told you she was getting the itch to move back here.'

'The itch?' I give Sally a look. 'There's no itch.'

She gives me a wicked grin in return. 'You've got the cow-pox. You've got the cowpox!' she sing-songs, returning to childhood.

'I do not have the cowpox…'

'Do so!'

'Do not!'

Titch just shakes her head with a sad smile and goes back to her packing.

'So it went pretty well with JL, did it?' Sally gives me a punch on the arm.

'Hey! Cut it out!'

'Well, answer me!'

I can't help but smile. 'Well, yes. It did, actually.'

I get another punch on the arm for this.

'Ow! Will you stop that already?'

'You two,' Titch says sharply, and we both stop fooling around instantly. Titch never speaks sharply. Then she laughs as she sees our faces. 'Don't leave everything till the last minute.'

'But that's what I always do…' Sally says.

'Me too,' I add.

Titch groans. 'I know. Believe me, I know.'

With this, Sally returns to her room to keep packing, and I head out into the lounge to survey the damage. I have a nasty little habit of leaving things lying around everywhere, and the only way to even start packing is to move everything into one room first.

I take one look at the buffet cabinet and see I'm going to have my work cut out for me. Lying on top are four unfinished bags and hundreds of miniature piles of beads and sequins. I had no idea I'd accumulated so many bag-making materials in so little time. But before I start tidying I think of JL's words, and I stand back for a second to take in what I've already accomplished without even realising it.

It's funny, I think to myself as I stand there, but this is just how I started making my pyjamas all those years ago. Maybe JL's on to something after all? Maybe this is my second chance. My chance to get things right. In all kinds of ways.

'Oh!' I say as a head pokes around the door, making me jump and lose my train of thought.

'Shh!' Titch puts a finger over her lips, and then I watch as she tiptoes over, carrying something in her hand.

'What is it?' I whisper.

She's trying her very best not to laugh. 'Look what I found. In the kitchen.'

I take a good look. It's an undecorated exercise book. One of the wish books.

'Sally's?' I ask.

Titch nods. 'Have you noticed her scribbling away in it?'

I think back. 'Only once. She was carrying it around with her.'

'Well, I noticed her a few times. Anyway, the point is, I thought it was mine and opened it accidentally. Take a look.'

I pause. 'Really? But isn't that a bit…?'

Titch shakes her head. 'No, it's OK.'

Reluctantly, I open the book, expecting to see pages filled with frenetic handwriting—the wishes of Sally. What I find, however, is rather different.

Each and every page is filled with a line of teeny, tiny ants. Ant-sized ants. Drawn in an ant-marching line, starting on page one, they walk their way through the book, taking little detours on the way. They form circles on one page, love-hearts on another, and on some they just march straight across.

Titch stifles her laughter again and again as I flip slowly through the book to the last page. The final ant has his face turned towards me, a big cheesy ant grin plastered all over it. Finally, dumbfounded, I close the book and hand it back to Titch.

And then we look at each other and laugh out loud.

Soon enough, thump, thump, thump can be heard coming up the hallway.

'What's so funny?' Sally stops in the doorway, hands on her hips.

'We were just, um…' Titch falters.

'We were laughing at your joke. At the, um, cowpox thing!' I lie at the last second.

Sally nods. 'Took you long enough.'

'Well, you know—your humour—it's highly sophisticated.'

I get an assessing look for this one.

'Right. Whatever you say. But do try and keep it down. Some of us are *packing*.' She stomps off again, triumphant that for once she is doing the right thing while other people aren't.

Titch and I glance at each other and start laughing again.

'Cowpox!' Titch giggles.

'Oh, God, that reminds me.' I stop laughing at the thought.

'What?'

'There's something I've got to do.'

And before Titch can ask any more questions, I've run out through the front door to the end of the yard and am searching, eagle-eyed down below. Fergus joins me—though I don't think he knows what we're scanning the grass for.

'Looking for this?' A voice booms out from the toolshed on my right.

'Bert?'

'None other.' He steps out from the dark, putting his trusty old hat on as the sun hits him. He walks over to hand me what I'm looking for. 'Thought you might have dropped it—by "accident", like.'

How embarrassing. 'That day? You were watching?'

'No, no. You know my sight's terrible. And my hearing—well, love, that's even worse.'

I give him a look. There's absolutely nothing wrong with Bert's eyesight, or his hearing, for that matter. In fact, they're probably both in better condition than mine. I look down at my wish book. It's obviously landed in a great pile of mud—or, worse, a fresh cow pat—but it has been cleaned up lovingly by someone who cares.

'Thanks,' I say. 'Really.'

'My pleasure.'

'You didn't happen to, um…?'

'No. You know me. Can't read to save myself. Now, I've got to get back to my tool-sharpening before it gets too dark.'

Hmm. Another look. Bert loves reading—anything from

Reader's Digest to Dickens. He even has the whole hardback Harry Potter collection.

'Well, thanks again.' I hold the book up.

'Yep. No worries.' With a wave, he heads back to the tool-shed.

I'm halfway to the house when his voice booms out once more. 'Oh, love—I forgot to ask. Did he say yes?'

I turn around. 'Bert!'

But there's only a chuckle left where he should be.

Great. It'll be all over Moo by tomorrow.

Oh, who am I kidding? With Bert's connections, it'll be all over Moo in half an hour.

But you know what? I don't care. So maybe I *have* got the cowpox after all. Fergus certainly seems to have caught a dose, I think, as a bee buzzes in close to us and he goes mad, chasing it across the yard, bumping into things as he goes.

With a short laugh, I turn around once more and make my way back to the house. I've got to finish packing before Titch sees I haven't even started yet and does it all for me. That's older sisters for you. But of course I get waylaid again.

Walking up the front steps, I feel my wish book, warm and mud-encrusted in my hand, and I swivel on the top step and sit down. Then I pull out the pen that's clipped into the middle of the book and write my final entry.

This is what it says...

It's a beautiful day. There's not a cloud in the brilliant blue sky. The house has been repainted a bright, bright white, and the cows, all with red satin bows around their necks, are peering over the fence to see what's going on in the backyard.

There's a marquee and people milling around with champagne flutes in their hands. It's a reception. JL and I have just renewed our vows and I'm there, on the lawn, with a very nice bag indeed, and I've never been happier. I'm even happier than I was on our wedding day, because this time around I truly know what I have and what I could lose.

Sally's there. I can't believe it. She's with that cute guy from the supermarket—George's housemate. And there's Titch. She's huge. The ultrasound says twin girls. Andrew is beaming. Next to him, Bert is looking decidedly uncomfortable in his 'I've just given the bride away' suit. Fergus is walking around with his nose in the air, knowing he's special because he's the best man and that later, for dessert, a whole bag of mini Wagon Wheels will come out of the fridge just for him.

Everything is perfect. Just as it should be.

It's like a dream.

And I'm hoping I never wake up.

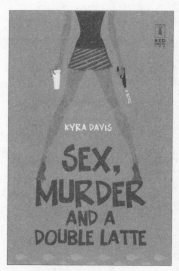

Also by Allison Rushby

It's Not You It's Me

A novel about exit lines—
and Ex Appeal...

Charlie is off on the adventure of a lifetime,
and is pleasantly surprised when on the plane
she bumps into international celebrity and rock-star
sex god Jasper Ash—who also happens to be her
former best friend, flatmate and...almost-lover!
But "what could have been" ended with the classic
excuse, "It's not you, it's me." This will be a
European tour you don't want to miss.

RED DRESS INK
™